Y0-DAE-097

Edging Past Reality

A collection of short stories

by
David Fingerman

Copyright © 2008 by David Fingerman. All rights reserved.

Two Harbors Press
212 3rd Avenue North, Suite 570
Minneapolis, MN 55401
612.455.2293
www.TwoHarborsPress.com

The Meadow was previously published in *The Midnight Gallery: 1998*
Grandpa's Watch was previously published in the Anthology *The Darker Side of Outer Darkness: 1997*
Mosquito Tim was previously published *The Vampire's Crypt: 1999*
The Witness was previously published in *Kracked Mirror Mysteries: 1996*
Nothing But Air was previously published in *69 Flavors of Paranoia: 1998*
A Mistake was previously published in *Just Write Magazine: 1994*

All rights reserved. No part of this publication may be reproduced, stored in a retrieval system, or transmitted, in any form or by any means, electronic, mechanical, photocopying, recording, or otherwise, without the written prior permission of the author.

ISBN - 978-1-935097-07-5
ISBN - 1-935097-07-5
LCCN - 2008909722

Book sales for North America and international:
Itasca Books, 3501 Highway 100 South, Suite 220
Minneapolis, MN 55416
Phone: 952.345.4488 (toll free 1.800.901.3480)
Fax: 952.920.0541; email to orders@itascabooks.com

Cover Design by Brent Meyers
Typeset by Peggy LeTrent

Printed in the United States of America

Edging Past Reality

Reality

A collection of short stories

For
Beth
Thank you for your love and
support while I chase my dream.

Acknowledgements

I would like to thank my family and friends for the continual support and encouragement to press forward. The Minneapolis Writers' Workshop and The Southside Writers' Group. John-Ivan Palmer for his invaluable insights and critique. And Maria Murad, a teacher whose knowledge of the English language surpasses everyone I know.

This book is a work of fiction. All names and characters are either from this author's imagination, or are used fictitiously. Any resemblance to persons living or dead is purely coincidental.

Table of Contents

Forward

Welcome to David Fingerman's death farm of terminal terror.

Don't even try to imagine what leads an author to such a deranged imagination. But as a professional hypnotist, I have to warn you. Suggestion can be dangerous. The shaman points the hexed bone at someone's face and they drop dead. Could it happen to you? Is your mind strong enough to resist the possibilities these stories suggest? Do you really think you can to repel the Fingerman strain of voodoo? Famous last words: "He'll never get me!" Right.

In this collection be ready to walk through a world of unhinged assumptions. Expect to kiss your sanity good-by. The most common and familiar elements of life—a lovely forest, a welcome hotel, freshly fallen snow, your job—will explode into a circus of horror. Once the sinister Fingerman points to where it leads, you might think twice about casual temptation. Or pulling a fast one. Or simply minding your own business. Can you hear the faint, distant music of madness already? Can you feel the biting breeze of pain up ahead?

This is your last chance. Get out while you can.

John-Ivan Palmer
Minneapolis, Minnesota
July 22, 2008

TOO YOUNG

TO KNOW ANY

BETTER

MARTY'S TOY

Past the rows of superheroes, super villains, games of violence, death, and destruction that are fun for the whole family, hung MEGA-GLOP. The green-skinned, orange-eyed monster with pointed white teeth, complete with two large fangs and a removable brain, stared at Ellen Donahue. Red paint, supposedly signifying blood, streaked down the side of its mouth. Plastic ripples coursed down its chest; bulging muscles in a steroid body looked as if it were trying to break through the plastic wrapping. Its hands were half-clenched, about to grab. At the ends of its fingers, long black talons stood ready to tear its prey apart. The only one of its kind left, it hung suspended from the hook. All the other dolls, even monster dolls, seemed to shy away from it.

"Marty will love you." Ellen picked it from the rack and threw it into her cart. She had to hurry if she was going to get home before her kids.

Sara walked in the door ten minutes after her mom. Ellen cursed under her breath that the day flew by so quickly. She hadn't even started dinner yet.

1

"How was school, sweetie?" Ellen bent down and gave her eight-year-old a hug.

Sara started talking with enthusiasm. "We were taking a spelling test and Miss Stokes wouldn't let Jimmy Poole go potty and Billy Ferguson jumped up and yelled 'Jimmy Poole just peed his pants!' and everybody laughed and Jimmy Poole started crying and ran out of the room. Miss Stokes had to call the janitor to mop up around Jimmy's desk."

Ellen sighed, knowing that the boy had been branded for life. "You be nice to Jimmy Poole, okay? I don't want to hear about you joining in when other kids pick on him. Now go wash up and you can help me with dinner."

Marty walked in as Sara ran up the stairs.

"Happy birthday, champ." Ellen kissed him on the top of his head. "How does it feel to be ten? And how was school?"

Marty shrugged his shoulders. "S'all right, I guess." He threw his backpack on the kitchen chair. "Jimmy Poole wet his pants. I gotta do a science project for next week."

Ellen wondered how many seconds it took for the entire elementary school to hear about Jimmy Poole. "What kind of project?"

"I dunno. I have to think one up."

"Well, you'd better not wait until the last minute again. Remember what almost happened last year."

"I know," Marty said. The thought of summer school made him shudder.

A scream from Sara's room shattered the half-second of solitude. Ellen groaned before tearing up the steps.

"What is it?" Ellen couldn't keep the exasperation of too many of these episodes out of her voice.

"Roscoe got out of his cage!" Sara yelled.

The door to the wire cage flapped down. Inside, the cedar chips lay undisturbed. The water bottle and food dish were full.

"How many times have you been told to check the latch?" Ellen said.

Sara wavered on the verge of tears.

Ellen felt guilty about exploding at her daughter. She stuck her hand in the cage and touched the exercise wheel. "Still warm," she said. "He must be close."

Hope filled the little girl's eyes as she dropped to her knees, checked under the bed and slowly scanned the floor.

"Damn gerbil," Ellen muttered as she stomped back downstairs.

~ ~ ~

After the dinner dishes were cleared, Sara turned off the lights and her mom brought out the cake. They both sang "Happy Birthday," but Sara seemed more concerned with watching where everybody stepped.

"Happy birthday, sweetie," Ellen handed him a gift. "From me and Sara."

Marty tore off the wrapping and stared face-to-face with MEGA-GLOP. It had been too long since Ellen had seen him smile like that.

On the back of the package it showed how to take off the back of the doll's skull and scoop out the gray glop it had for a brain. Hours of fun, it promised, as you could squoosh it between your fingers or splat it against a wall – guaranteed not to leave a stain. Once back inside its head, the glop would reform to look like a brain again for next time.

Marty didn't bother to read the package. He just tore it apart to get to the toy. The MEGA-GLOP and Marty stared at each other, and Ellen could've sworn that the monster's evil smile grew.

Later that evening, another scream from Sara's room made Ellen shiver. She ran up the stairs thinking of squashed gerbil under her daughter's backpack, or something equally as gruesome. Sara stood next to her bed, the sheets turned down. Resting on her pillow a gray gelatinous brain jiggled. Ellen held her arms open and her daughter raced into them. In as stern a voice as she could manage, while trying to hide a smile, Ellen yelled. "Martin J. Donahue, get in here, NOW!"

~ ~ ~

Two nights later, Marty sat at his desk and cursed. It wasn't fair. It seemed as if every kid in school had a computer, except him. How could anyone expect him to do a halfway decent science report without access to the Internet? He cursed the blank piece of paper and the typewriter in front of him.

As he looked for distractions, something caught in his senses. It smelled a little bit like the week-old bologna sandwich that his sister had left in his room last summer. If Sara left food in his room again, this time he was going to make her eat it, no matter what it might be.

Crawling on hands and knees, he searched his room. Then he found it. Next to a gnawed-on lamp cord, lay Roscoe. Dried blood had seeped out of its tiny ears and mouth, staining its face. Marty picked it up by the tail. The thing was rigid. Its tail looked more like a stick shoved up its butt.

So many options. He could flush poor Roscoe down the toilet, call his mom (she would probably give it a funeral and bury it in the backyard), or he could hide it under Sara's pillow. That might be crossing the line, he thought. It would be fun, but not worth getting grounded for a month. Well, maybe it was.

Then he glanced at the paper and a brilliant idea popped into his head. He could do a real science project. He was willing to bet that no one in the fifth grade had dissected a gerbil before. That was something they did in middle school. This was great. He could label all the parts, take pictures and everything. *This could be my first A in science.*

Marty carefully laid Roscoe's body on the desk and went to get the needed supplies. He came back with his mother's camera, the rubber gloves she used just to wash dishes, and an exacto knife, all of which promptly dropped to the floor.

Roscoe hadn't moved, but in just a few short minutes, someone had come in and busted the gerbil's head open and hollowed it out. Marty's first thought was Sara, but it was fleeting. No way would Sara dare touch it after it died, let alone rip its head open. The thought of his mother doing it was equally absurd. He began to doubt his own sanity when he glanced, then stared. MEGA-GLOP.

The toy's bright orange eyes glowed and the bottom half of the white fangs looked brown. A minute tuft of fur was wedged between its small teeth. Marty jumped halfway across the room without taking his eyes off the doll. They stared at each other for some time before Marty inched closer.

Someone must have played one wicked joke. Somebody must have been hiding and done this. It couldn't have been Sara. Could it? No way!

Marty grabbed MEGA-GLOP and half-expected it to leap from his hand. The plastic felt warm, and its eyes no longer glowed.

He turned the doll around and pulled off the back of its head. The toy fumbled out of his hands. It bounced on the floor before coming to a rest by the leg of the chair. Marty watched, stunned, as the brain oozed out of its skull. The normal gray blob looked pink.

Marty crept up to it and poked the goop with his finger. He was ready to expect almost anything, and was slightly disappointed when it felt like the slime it always felt like. He scooped it into his hand and let it roll back into MEGA's head.

Late into the night, he lay awake staring at his birthday present. Normally he liked the quiet darkness, but tonight there was something comforting with the light on. Sometimes he thought he saw the doll's eyes blaze fire, but when he blinked and looked again, they were the same dull orange. The doll frightened the hell out of him. His wild thoughts took MEGA-GLOP to places he didn't want to venture into.

~ ~ ~

The alarm clock blared. Marty forced his eyes open and slammed his palm on the off button. The last thing he remembered was the sun peeking in the window. It took a few seconds before he realized that he'd fallen asleep. The first thing he did after sitting up was to look over to his desk. MEGA-GLOP sat still and smiling. Its fangs were white again, and no fur could be seen in its mouth. *Maybe it was all a bad dream.*

"Get up sleepy-stupid-head," Sara said from the doorway.

He could hear her laugh as she raced down the steps. It was the first morning that she hadn't asked if he'd seen Roscoe.

Marty struggled to his feet. His head ached, and he had to fight with his eyes to keep them open. If it had been a nightmare, it was a nasty one – one with a very uneasy sleep. The thought of a dream quickly vanished when he noticed Roscoe still on the desk. Marty slid him into the drawer just in case his sister came back. He didn't know how he could explain this one. She would no doubt think he killed her pet. She knew he wasn't too fond of the gerbil. The way it looked now, mom would believe it too.

Downstairs, his mother had the cereal and milk already out.

"I'm not feeling too good today, Mom. Can I stay home from school?"

Ellen walked over and put her hand on his forehead.

"You're not warm, but you don't look too good. What hurts?"

Her voice lacked concern and Marty knew she was running late for work.

"My head feels like it's going to explode," he said.

Ellen let out a long breath. "Why don't you take some aspirin and go back to bed for a little bit. I'll check up on you before I leave. It's too late to get a sitter. If you stay home, you'll have to be by yourself."

"That's okay." Marty tried to sound sicker than he really felt.

"He's faking it, mama," Sara jumped in.

"Am not, ya butt-head."

"Mom, he called me a butt-head."

"That's enough from both of you. Marty, go back to bed. Sara, finish your cereal."

Marty watched his mother go through the breakfast ritual. He knew she believed him because she wasn't yelling and lecturing.

The bed felt warm and Marty began to nod off. The downstairs door slammed and he woke up instantly. Alone at last. He peeked out his window and watched as his mother drove away. When she was out of sight, Marty threw on his clothes and dashed out of the house, grabbing MEGA-GLOP on the way.

Dew still sparkled off the grass as Marty came out of the garage dragging a shovel in one hand and holding his doll like it was stinking garbage in the other. He walked past the alley, cut through the Johnson's yard, and crossed the street to the farthest corner of a vacant lot. A chill echoed throughout his body as he dug. MEGA-GLOP stared up at him from the ground, its orange eyes bright in the morning sun.

Hard dirt and large stones made digging almost impossible, especially with an old, battered shovel. With blistered hands and a sore back, Marty finally gave up. The hole wasn't as deep as he'd hoped, but his muscles told him it was deep enough. He used the blade of the shovel to push the doll into the shallow grave; he didn't want to touch it. Then as best he could, Marty hard-packed the earth over his toy. On the way home he felt lighter, both mentally and physically. He tried to think up excuses that his mom would believe if she noticed his birthday present missing.

Ellen came home a little after noon. Marty heard the car pull up and had himself tucked into bed before the garage door closed. Her footsteps clicked up the steps. He closed his eyes and turned his face into the pillow before she entered the room. He could smell her perfume as she bent over and kissed him on top of his head. Her footsteps faded and when there was no more sound, Marty rolled over. A lump caught in his throat when he saw her standing in the doorway. She looked at him very calmly and said, "You're grounded." Without another word, she turned and walked away.

Marty sat up wondering what had gone wrong. He rolled out of bed and noticed muddy footprints leading to his bed. His pillow and sheets were covered with dirt. He swore under his breath. The way his luck was running, he figured she'd be back any minute and ask where MEGA-GLOP was.

Clouds rolled in as Marty sat at his window and watched the kids come home from school. He saw Sara dash down the sidewalk and wondered how far she'd get before tripping and skinning her knee. She probably had to hurry and tell mom who wet their pants in class today.

The screen door slammed and Marty stood at the top of the stairs, laughing at his sister as she tried to catch her breath. By the time he got to the kitchen, his mother was helping Sara off with her jacket.

"The O'Connell's dog got killed," Sara shouted. "Someone chopped his head off."

"Oh my goodness. Who would do such a thing?" Ellen said.

Marty remembered the black lab strutting around the neighborhood like he owned everything in it. He never bit anyone that he knew of, and was gentle around kids. No one ever complained that he wasn't on a leash. He liked that dog.

"They found him in the vacant lot right behind us," Sara said.

Goosebumps formed a blanket around Marty.

"Why would somebody do that, mama?" Sara asked.

"I don't know, sweetheart. Maybe it was an accident."

Marty could tell that she didn't feel like discussing senseless violence to an eight-year-old any further.

"Why don't you get washed up and you can help me with dinner?"

"That's not what I heard," Sara said as she ran out of the room. "Lopped his head right off."

Marty felt somewhat shocked at his sister's indifference as

he raced out the screen door. He ignored his mother's screams to get back inside. He ran to the spot where he had buried the doll, expecting to see the carcass of O'Connell's dog. The vacant lot was empty. Everything looked the same as earlier in the day, only shadows had repositioned themselves. Patches of weeds grew haphazardly between rocks and over hard ground. There was no dog. It occurred to him in a wave of relief that even if Mr. O'Connell's dog did die, maybe MEGA-GLOP had nothing to do with it.

He stared at the ground he'd previously dug up, and fought with his curiosity to see if the doll was still buried. A heap of trouble waited for him at home, so he was in no hurry to get back. Drawn like a magnet, Marty began to kick away loose gravel. He dropped to his knees and shoved his hands into the loose earth.

A trembling came up from the ground like lightening shooting into his fingertips, crackling up his arms. Marty stopped, scared to go further. The shallow grave broke apart; his monster doll sprang to the surface. Its eyes glowed crimson hate while it hissed like the sound of fingernails on blackboard. Blood, real blood, dripped off its fangs and oozed down its face. In the monster's clawed fist, a skull, its long snout pointed accusingly at Marty. Upside-down, it looked like a cannibal's ornamental bowl. Inside, a mush of gray and red filled the container. Outside, scraps of black fur, matted with blood and dirt, dangled from bone.

The gag reflex took over as Marty stumbled backwards. Crab-walking on all fours, his only thought was to get away. Jagged stones and old broken glass bit into his palms. He didn't notice the blood and pain. Twisting around onto his knees, Marty boosted himself up to his feet and ran. He didn't dare look around until he was safely behind the door of his house.

Thoughts of the creature close at his heels made Marty choke back a sob as he peeked out the window. He would've bet that MEGA-GLOP would be waiting at the door, its eyes burning into his soul. Instead, the only scene past the door was an empty back yard.

"What am I going to do with you?"

Marty jumped halfway to the ceiling as he spun around. His mother stood behind him, the wooden spoon in her hand.

"I've tried to be patient with you. I've tried to understand you, but you keep shutting me out. I just don't get you, Martin!"

Marty cringed. When she held the wooden spoon and called him Martin, there would be no reprieve.

"I thought you were getting too old for this." Ellen grabbed him by the ear. "I know I am."

He wanted to tell her. He really did. But she had warned him about his over-active-imagination enough times. As real as this was, he knew she'd never believe him.

She dragged him past the window, and Marty tried to stop and get one last peek, make sure the doll hadn't followed him home. His mother took the delay as resistance and twisted his ear even tighter. Marty winced trying to hold back tears, promising himself that he was too old to cry.

~ ~ ~

Marty stood by his bedroom window trying to survey the outside through the dusk. It still hurt too much to sit. When his mother noticed the blood dripping off his fingers, concern didn't eliminate the punishment like he had hoped, only doubled it. The pain from scrubbing off dirt and applying antiseptic hurt worse than the paddling.

Marty's bedroom stood right above the kitchen, but from the second floor he was able to see a small section of the vacant lot. Through the weeds, acting like a cloak, two blazing orange eyes stared back from a corner of the lot. Sparkling in the night, teeth shined like stars.

A scream caught in Marty's throat. He raced into bed, an ostrich hiding his head beneath the pillow. In eye-clenched darkness two globes of fire branded into Marty's mind. They stayed with him, floating in his nightmares until he awoke to his sister's voice.

"You look really sick," Sara said.

Past her shoulder, standing on the desk in a dirt shroud, MEGA-GLOP scowled. Eyes of molten steel said, "I'm home."

Marty threw up before he fainted.

~ ~ ~

Cool waves washed up on the beach splashing Marty and Sara as they made castles in the sand. Alone, they looked out over the ocean. A bubbling cauldron formed at the horizon and sped toward the shore. Neither one could move. The foaming water stopped just feet from land. Fire shot up from the ocean as a giant serpent raised its head above the surface. Orange eyes as bright as the sun glared at the children, sending beams of light into their bodies like a spit. It opened its mouth and let out a shriek that made the ground shake and wash the waves back out to sea. A red snake jetted out its mouth past a row of drooling fangs, wrapping itself around Sara's neck. She didn't scream, didn't even fight as the monster tongue brought her up to the creature's head. It bit down on her throat and with a snap of its mouth, separated her body, flinging it out to sea. The red snake smiled grotesquely as it came at him.

~ ~ ~

Marty screamed, his eyes snapping open. Lying on the pillow next to him, MEGA-GLOP smiled a serpent's smile. Marty screamed again and heaved the doll across the room. Sara, sitting beside his bed, playing the nursemaid, also began to scream, and ran.

The familiar clomping charged up the stairs. Ellen ran into her daughter at the bedroom door.

"He just started screaming, mama. I didn't do anything. I promise!"

Marty looked at his mother and saw her eyes widen. She quickly recovered and sat on the edge of the bed, gently wiping the sweat from his forehead.

"You okay? You had me scared half to death. Do you know that you've been asleep for almost a day? I was about to call the doctor back and give him holy hell if he told me not to bring you in. If you're hungry, I'm going to make macaroni and cheese for dinner. Listen to me, I'm babbling. How do you feel?"

The mention of food made his stomach rumble, and macaroni and cheese sounded good. Marty smiled. "A little bit better. I just had a bad dream. I'll be down in a couple of minutes."

"Take your time. It'll take about ten minutes." Ellen kissed him on the forehead and left the room.

"You were scary looking," Sara said.

"You're scarier looking," Marty said.

"You're an ugly poop head!" Sara yelled and ran out of the room.

Marty got up and went down the hall and into the bathroom. Walking back to his room, he heard Sara messing in his things again. He'd warned her enough times to stay out of his stuff; now he was going to teach her a lesson.

"Get out of my . . ." His words stopped.

His desk drawer was open. Clenched in its talon hands, MEGA-GLOP was tearing apart the remains of Roscoe. The gerbil's head was completely gone as the monster doll chomped its way down to the tail, bones and all. It looked up and smiled at Marty, who stood too terrified to move.

MEGA-GLOP stopped gnawing and ducked further back into the drawer. Its eyes lit up like a jack-o-lantern's, with a yellow tinge glowing in the center. Paralyzed, Marty could only watch as Sara entered the room.

"Well?" she said. "Are you going to apologize?"

Like a full moon, the monster slowly rose above the drawer, silently perching itself on the edge. Its face scrunched up in a deformed smile while its tongue flicked gerbil meat from between its teeth then licked its fangs. Painted blood along its mouth glittered like a newly formed scar. Marty tried to utter a warning, but the words choked in his throat.

"Goddammit!" could be heard from the kitchen. "We're out of milk." Ellen's voice traveled up the stairs. "I'm going to run to the store. I'll be back in a couple of minutes."

MEGA-GLOP sprang toward the girl, leaping high in the air.

"I wanna go with you, mama," Sara yelled as she dashed out of the room.

The monster's face went from devouring hunger to panic as it began its downward arc to the child that was no longer there. MEGA-GLOP's arms flailed, grasping for anything. It landed at Marty's feet, looked up, and hissed. Brown and yellow spit flew, hitting the leg of Marty's jeans. The denim sizzled and burned, rubbing against Marty's shin. The pain snapped him back.

"Marty, keep an eye on dinner. We'll be right back," Ellen yelled. The door slammed shut.

Marty looked down. MEGA-GLOP was examining his leg through the eaten material. It gently touched the wound, more curious than anything, then opened its mouth wide and sank its fangs into flesh.

A scream rattled the windows and made MEGA-GLOP grab its demon ears. Marty kicked and flailed his leg, but with the doll's teeth clamped to his shin, it rode his leg like a bucking bronco. Marty ran out of the room, yelling. He tried to grab the creature, but it clawed its talons down Marty's hand, tearing off the bandage.

At the top of the stairs, Marty grabbed MEGA-GLOP's leg and yanked. He finally pried the teeth loose, taking a chunk of skin and muscle with them.

Marty's leg buckled, and he rolled and bounced down the steps with the toy in his hand. They both hit the floor with a thud. The back of MEGA-GLOP's head snapped off. Inside, the brain pulsated. Worms, or veins, wove around and through it, glowing the same sick neon orange as its eyes.

The doll looked around for the back of its skull while Marty held his wounded leg and watched. The molded piece of plastic had skidded into the kitchen and lay rocking back-and-forth on the floor. Ignoring the pain as best he could, Marty got up and ran after the toy. As MEGA-GLOP bent over to pick up its piece

13

of head, Marty grabbed the monster by the waist and jerked it off the ground. At the same time, his knee locked and Marty lost his balance, skating along the linoleum floor.

The front door opened as Marty was waving his arms, trying to regain his balance.

"Can't we keep him, mama? Please?"

His feet slid from under him.

"I said no!"

On the way down, MEGA-GLOP's face connected with the edge of the table, disconnecting its brain and sending it flying into the air.

"But it'll die if I let it go."

Marty watched the brain sail up and start its descent.

"Fine. You can hold onto it just until we find the owners."

It was like watching in slow motion as it landed with a splash in the boiling pot of pasta.

"What if the owners never come?"

Steam shot up from the water as Marty scrambled to his feet and limped to the stove.

"Then we'll see."

He looked into the pot just in time to get a nose full of rot smell and see the brain fizzle down to nothing.

"Look what we found," Sara said. Cuddled in her arms was a white kitten that couldn't have been more than a couple months old. "I think I'll name him Snowball. Mom said I can keep him."

"I thought you were going to the grocery store, not the pet store," Marty said.

"I found him, silly. He was hiding under some bushes. We never got to the store."

Ellen walked into the kitchen and looked at horror at her son. "What did you do? Are you all right?"

Marty shrugged his shoulders. "I fell down the stairs."

"Sara, run upstairs and get the first-aid kit."

After his sister was out of the room, Marty said, "Mom, I

hate cats. They make me sneeze."

Ellen looked at his wound. "We won't have him long, I promise. Sara will want to get rid of him as soon as she finds Roscoe, if you know what I mean." She grabbed some paper towels and dabbed at his leg.

Marty cried out from the pain, but smiled like a conspirator. Ellen walked over, turned off the stove and carefully lifted the pot to carry it to the sink. Marty choked. They weren't actually going to eat that now, were they?

"Let me help you." Marty limped and skillfully slid into her hip, grabbing her arm.

"Be careful!" she screamed as the pot broke from her grasp. They both jumped back as scalding water and noodles sloshed across the floor soaking a lifeless MEGA-GLOP doll.

Marty stood over his birthday present, no longer afraid. Its eyes were dull, almost rust colored. Its teeth no longer resembled razor-sharp weapons but looked like little plastic chips painted white. Without a brain, the doll looked pitiful, weak. Marty looked inside its head and saw molded plastic. He was actually beginning to feel a little sorry for the monster that tried to kill him just minutes ago. For the first time since opening it up, Marty saw what appealed to him in the first place; just a harmless little monster that needed a friend. It made Marty think of himself. They had a lot in common.

Ellen groaned while massaging her forehead. "What am I going to do with you?" She went to the broom closet and grabbed a mop.

"Well, it's not any good without milk, anyway," Marty said.

"Not funny," Ellen responded. "Go get my purse. Maybe we can bounce a check and order pizza."

~ ~ ~

Sara stood in the doorway to Marty's room, tears streaming down her cheeks. "Have you seen Snowball? He's missing."

Half asleep, Marty grumbled, "No."

He'd been up most of the night, secretly working.

Tucked safely in his desk drawer, Marty's science project was done. All neat and properly labeled, a tiny heart, liver, kidneys, lung, and other animal parts were carefully glued inside a crude drawing of a cat. The only thing missing was the brain – that was another experiment.

As Marty fell back asleep, MEGA-GLOP snuggled next to him, softly purring.

THE MEADOW

Across the road from old Doc Kelly's small home, stood the most beautiful meadow Melanie had ever seen in her eleven years. The long grasses swayed with the gentle rhythm of the breeze. Waves of green and gold flowed across the field inviting her to enter its gentle palace.

The sun blazed down on the land, scorching flowers and plants, burning the surrounding grasses in its long, harsh drought. As shrubs withered and died around it, the meadow seemed to dare Mother Nature to turn up the heat and brighten the sun.

With the porch floorboards creaking under her weight, she heard the familiar scurrying behind the doctor's front door. Tobin was already clawing to get out before Melanie knocked.

The door opened only a crack, but the Airedale terrier squeezed through and jumped on the girl, trying to lick her face. Melanie pretended disgust, trying to hide her giggles, as the dog's stub tail gyrated back and forth.

"Tobin, get down!" the doctor said.

Allen Kelly limped toward the door, his wooden cane supporting his weight. Melanie thought he looked older than last week. His eyes had bigger circles, and the lines on his face

17

seemed deeper.

"How's Tobin today?" she asked as the dog swept between and around her legs.

Dr. Kelly gave Melanie the leash as Tobin jumped up, trying to catch the loop in his mouth.

"Don't take him too far today, he's a little slow getting up. I think it's just too hot for a long walk."

"Is it too hot for my little baby?" Melanie said in her baby-talk voice. "You're such a beautiful puppy." She knelt on the porch and let the dog slobber on her face.

~ ~ ~

As they walked, Tobin led Melanie to every tree along the path as the sun beat down. The dog panted heavily as sweat lined Melanie's face. "It's not the heat, it's the humidity," she explained as they walked down the road, back to the house.

A slight, dry, breeze carried the scent of clover to Melanie's senses. So fresh and clean, the aroma contradicted the brown grass and dried brush around them. Across the way, the meadow seemed to issue an invitation. Tobin stepped into the road, tugging Melanie to the long, cool grass.

"Tobin, come!" Dr. Kelly shouted from his front porch.

The dog yanked the leash free and ran to his master. Melanie quickly followed, wondering if there might be an emergency.

"Don't trust it," the Doctor said in answer to her question before she asked. "Somethin' ain't right in there, somethin' unnatural."

Melanie thought about it for a moment then nodded her head. Something certainly didn't make sense. There was no logical reason that a small patch of land, no more than an acre, remained untouched from the sun's aggression.

The thought passed, "See ya in a couple of days, Tobin?" Melanie asked.

"We'll call," Doc Kelly smiled. He turned around and let the dog back into the house.

As Melanie walked home past the meadow, despite Doc's words, she couldn't resist taking in the beauty and inhaling the meadow's fragrance.

~ ~ ~

More than a week had passed and Melanie became worried. Dr. Kelly hadn't called once to see if she could walk Tobin. It could be the heat; it hadn't let up at all. If anything, it became worse. But, she thought, he would have at least called, wouldn't he? Maybe he fell, got hurt, and couldn't get to the phone.

She called and with each ring Melanie's nerves heightened. After receiving no answer on the phone, her distress finally convinced her to walk the mile-and-a-half to his house to see if he was all right.

In a cloudless sky, the sun pounded to keep pulse in Melanie's head as she walked down the road. The tar seemed to soften with every step, its fumes scratching her nostrils, making her stomach queasy. The closer she got to the doctor's house, the more it felt as if the heat were using her skull as a drum. If she hadn't already been more than halfway, Melanie would have turned back home. But he was a doctor – what better place to go?

Waves of heat danced from the ground and Doc Kelly's house looked to have a life of its own. It seemed to breathe through the waves, but that's not what caught Melanie's attention. The meadow swayed in its own flow, greens and golds complimenting each other. But what made her stare was the size. She could have sworn the meadow had grown. Melanie couldn't remember how big it had been, but she was sure it hadn't stretched past the Doctor's house so far. Could it?

There was an urgency as she pounded on the doctor's door. Each knock tightened the vice around her skull. If she could only to get out of the sun, lie down for just a bit, she was sure she'd feel better.

The familiar scratching that Melanie took for granted wasn't there, and neither was the customary tapping of the cane.

He can't be gone, she thought. *Where would they go? Where could they go?* In the blazing heat, a chill crept up her spine. She turned the knob. The door was unlocked.

Inside, the house was dark and warm, the air stale. An odor of urine and feces made her gag. As Melanie opened her mouth to call for the doctor, a low, vicious, growl caused her to shiver. Slowly, she turned to the direction of the threat. Under the coffee table was a Tobin that Melanie had barely recognized. The dog's sunken face exposed a pair of snarling fangs. His once fluffed, kinky, well-groomed coat hung from the bones, dirty and matted.

"My God! Tobin?"

Recognition flashed in the dog's eyes when he heard his name. The fangs slid back into hollow cheeks and his tail quivered on the floor. He crawled out from under the table as Melanie dropped to her knees.

"You poor baby, what happened? You look half starved." Melanie cradled the dog to her chest. "Let's get you somethin to eat, boy."

After the dog devoured a bowl of food, Tobin was Melanie's shadow as they did a room-to-room search. Melanie prayed that Doc Kelly wasn't there. If he were, there would only be one reason that he would have left Tobin in such shape, and Melanie didn't think she'd be able to handle that. She didn't find the doctor, but did see his cell phone sitting on his bedside table.

Tobin scratched at the front door begging to get out. Melanie had forgotten about her headache until she let the dog outside. The sun beat down compressing her head so hard she felt nauseous. As she stepped back into the house, Tobin raced across the road toward the meadow.

"Tobin! Come back here."

Tobin stopped, looked back and then ran again, galloping into the tall grass. With her head ready to explode, Melanie ran after the dog. As she entered the meadow, the green and gold rose above her head. It grew thick enough that Melanie lost sight of the dog, but she could still hear him up ahead.

As if by magic, the sky darkened almost to night as thick clouds from nowhere covered the bright sun that had raged every day for over a month. What should have been comforting and cool with the sun now hiding, felt anything but. A stench of rot and decay replaced the sweet smell of clover. Deeper into the meadow they went. Melanie heard a sickening crunch as she stepped down. Under her foot lay the carcass of a crow, half its flesh torn away. Melanie gagged as she lifted her foot from the goo.

"Tobin! Where are you?"

In the distance she heard the echo of a bark.

Melanie walked on. Thick black sap bubbled up from the ground smelling like tar. Her sense of direction vanished. All she could do was hope to follow the dog's bark that seemed to be fading farther and farther away.

Throughout the meadow, bodies of squirrels, mice, rats, birds and other animals she couldn't recognize from decomposition, littered the ground. Black puddles with a reddish tint that looked like blood mixed with black goo, reeking of sulfur, dotted the land. She stopped to close her eyes and massage her temples. The ache started to ease, and just as Melanie opened her eyes, a bolt of lightning lit the sky.

Her jaw dropped in a silent scream. For an instant, the time it takes a flash bulb to flash, Melanie wasn't in the meadow. As far as the eye could see, she was in a midnight field void of any life. A sea of black with tree trunks long dead and broken branches pierced the ground like daggers.

With the blink of an eye, it disappeared. The dried grass was back, slapping at Melanie's body like leather straps in the brisk wind. A boom of thunder set off another bomb in her head.

"Tobin! Where are you?" she screamed as tears burned her eyes.

Standing still, Melanie strained, trying to hear the Airedale. The wind blew harder and each blade of grass stung like a snapping whip as it slashed at her skin.

"Melanie," came a whisper.

I'm going crazy, Melanie thought. *The wind is calling my name.*

"Melanie. I'm over here," the faint voice called.

It wasn't the wind. "Dr. Kelly?" Melanie shouted. The wind seemed to carry her words away.

Tears of happiness replaced tears of fright as Tobin trotted into view. Before Melanie could grab and hug the dog, Tobin turned around and disappeared into the tall grass. Melanie raced after him.

Doc Kelly was lying on the ground with sludge oozing up to his chest, covering him like a blanket. In his hand he held a small pocketknife. Scattered on the ground were bones of birds. He looked up and saw the horror on Melanie's face. Her eyes answered all his questions as to how he looked. She wiped away the tears and dropped to her knees locking the old man in a bear hug.

"You have to get out of here," he whispered in a coarse voice. "This place is evil."

Melanie released her grip and looked into his face. Fear and frustration played in the gaunt, blue eyes; eyes that had lost all hope. But a stubborn determination that would not give up kept him alive. Thin blue lips stretched across his teeth in a dying man's smile.

"You're the one who told me to stay out," Melanie said. "What happened?"

Doc Kelly looked at her and shook his head. "I was stupid. Tobin didn't come when I called. I saw him earlier sniffing around the meadow, and just assumed he went in." He looked at his body, half-covered in muck and let out a long sigh. "I forgot I already put him in the house. Stupid, huh? I swear I couldn't have walked in more than twenty feet before I got lost. I must be getting senile in my old age."

"You're not senile, and now all three of us will get out. We'll get you to a hospital."

Melanie pulled out her cell phone and got no signal. A sudden clap of thunder sent the phone fumbling from her hand.

As she reached down to pick it up, Dr. Kelly grabbed her wrist. Before he said a word, the ground swallowed it up.

"My folks are going to kill me."

"No," the doctor looked up at her and despite his smile, his eyes began to water. "It's too late for me. You take Tobin and have him guide you out of here."

A new wave of tears rolled down Melanie's cheeks. "I'm not leaving without you."

Kelly reached up to wipe away her tears. "You can't carry me, Tobin can't carry me. The ground swallowed my cane a few days ago and it's swallowing me now. It will swallow you too if you don't get out of here."

A clap of thunder shook the ground as Melanie grabbed her head in pain. Tobin whimpered as he stood next to his master.

"This place feeds on the living," Dr. Kelly said. "It drains life. Listen to me little girl, you're more of a daughter to me than you could ever know. I couldn't stand the thought that I might be responsible for your death. Now get."

"And you're more of a father to me than my own dad, and I couldn't stand the thought of leaving you here to die."

Doc Kelly couldn't help but smile as Melanie grabbed his wrists and yanked as hard as she could. It felt as if she might tear his arms out of their sockets as the ground fought to hold him down. Slowly the earth loosened its grip, and with a gurgling sound, spit him out.

"I can't feel my legs," Kelly said. Crud covered him up to his chest. "I can't walk. Now will you listen to reason and leave me here."

"I don't mean to be rude, Doctor, but my head feels like it's going to explode. Now will you please quit being such a pain in the ass and hop on?" Melanie said. She turned her back to him and lowered down.

Kelly hoisted his arms around her shoulders and she lifted the old man off the ground. "Is that any way to talk to your father?" he said.

23

"I'm not usually this polite to my father," she grunted. "Which way?"

"I got lost just after I walked in," Kelly said. "Tobin, lead the way."

The mud softened as they walked, making a sucking noise with every step. Even Tobin strained against it. There was another flash of lightning, and as before, the meadow disappeared. Melanie stopped and looked at the endless bog, then, a fraction of a second later, at the long grass.

"I saw it too," the doctor said.

"Thank God. I thought I was going crazy," Melanie answered.

"Do you read the bible?" Kelly asked.

"Not since I was a kid in Sunday school. Why?"

Kelly smiled. "Not since you were a kid, huh?"

The eleven-year-old girl failed to catch the irony.

"Just thought I'd ask. I think Hell has come to earth."

The trio trudged on. Tobin marched, lifting each paw high to avoid getting stuck in the slog. Even though the doctor was all skin and bone, Melanie's back felt the strain of his weight. Deep down, she knew that she couldn't carry him much farther.

The ground came up to her ankles when Melanie fell forward landing with a splash. She tried to get up, but couldn't, not with the doctor on her back. Tobin turned back to see why they were no longer following. He marched in circles waiting for them to get up.

As Melanie tried to get on her feet, a crow flew down looking to grab a meal out of a puddle. They watched as the bird frantically cawed while it started to sink. It shrilled as its wings flapped wildly, shooting feathers in all directions until it became totally submerged. After a moment, an air bubble popped up to the surface, belching a stink of death.

"We both know you can't carry me anymore," Kelly said.

She wanted so much to argue, to tell him that yes she could. But he was right; her back ached and each step took all the effort she could manage. She couldn't lift him up again.

"I'll come back, with help. I promise," Melanie cried.

"I know you will," Kelly smiled. "Now get out of here."

She felt the bones sticking out from under his shirt as she bent down to give him a hug. He looked so old and frail sitting there. "I promise," she said again, then turned and disappeared in the grass.

Tobin stayed with his master. "Git!" the old man hollered.

"Tobin, come!" Melanie shouted.

The dog looked at his master one last time and trotted after Melanie.

~ ~ ~

After the pair disappeared and he could no longer hear their footsteps, Allen Kelly opened his pocketknife and made diagonal slices down his arms. The ground lapped up the blood as it dripped.

"I'll go my way, not yours," Kelly spat at the meadow.

~ ~ ~

The ground began to harden again as Tobin and Melanie made their own path. At first Melanie thought it was because she was so much lighter, but then she noticed the ground wasn't sucking at her feet anymore. Clouds started to break up and the grass turned back to green and gold.

Tobin started to run, and Melanie chased after trying to keep up when something caught her foot and down she went. A sickening crunch in her ankle sent intense agony searing up her leg as tar scraped her palms and knees. A deep howling, laughter mixed with suffering, started from Melanie's stomach and worked its way up her throat. She couldn't stop laughing and crying as she sat on the side of the road. The sky glistened bright blue, not a cloud in sight. Across the street sat the most wonderful sight – Dr. Kelly's house.

Branding-iron pain ricocheted up her leg as she put weight

on the foot. Thinking of hopscotch from years past, Melanie hopped across the road, all the way to the house, wincing only once as the tip of her shoe hit the ground.

Once inside, Melanie grabbed the phone. The line was dead. She and her folks were the closest neighbors, and unfortunately, they lived over a mile away. No way could she walk it now. She hobbled up the stairs and looked out over the empty road. *A car's got to pass soon,* she thought. *Then I can flag one down and get help.* Her head still ached and her body felt so weak, so tired. Already, Tobin lay exhausted. He rested on the easy chair, his head draped over the arm, watching Melanie's every move.

Melanie watched as a crow flew over the meadow and swooped down into the tall grass. It didn't come out.

Taking a quick break from lookout, Melanie crawled down to the kitchen to feed Tobin. Thinking of Doc Kelly, she started to cry. She felt too sick to eat.

The rest of the afternoon, until the sunset, no cars drove by. Melanie saw at least three more birds dive into the meadow. None reappeared. A star glittered in the sky over the meadow and she made a wish. More stars appeared and fighting fatigue, Melanie lost the battle, closed her eyes, and fell asleep.

~ ~ ~

Tobin raced up the stairs when he heard the scream. Melanie sat horrified, looking out the window. Dark gray clouds filled the sky even though her watch read 6:30 a.m. The sun should've been up over a half-hour ago. It looked like it could still be midnight. The road was gone. Black stumps replaced the trees that once lined the boulevard. Right up to the house everything was blackness and death, exactly what it looked like during the lightning flashes. It was as if the meadow no longer needed its disguise.

Tobin kept along side of Melanie as she limped to the top of the stairs. At the bottom, a black welcome mat, smelling of sulfur and rot, seeped in under the door. She staggered to the backside of the house. Outside the window, a little way in the distance, the sun shone past the clouds, illuminating the prairie as it swayed in the breeze. Melanie sat and watched with a frantic repulsion as she saw the grass, row by row, disintegrate into black goo. Tobin snuggled up against her. Melanie placed her arms around the dog and cried as the house sat alone in the meadow.

A HALLOWEEN STORY

He could no longer hear the footsteps chasing him. The full moon cast the only light in the woods as the boy's run slowed to a walk. Still peeking over his shoulder, he wandered, not sure, but hoping that he circled around and would soon be at the clearing, and back in his neighborhood. His mouth curved into a smile and he let out a sigh, as through the branches he saw light – back into civilization.

~ ~ ~

"Trick or treat?" It came out as a question.

Startled, Meg spun around and saw a wee nip of a Dracula, no more than 10 years old huddled in the open doorway. Standing on the hearth, she stopped stirring the bubbling brew in the cauldron. Its aromatic fragrance misted throughout the room. Layers of black veils attached to her black gown waved gently around her body. The brisk autumn air fought the heat from the fireplace, making the room of this small cottage comfortable.

"You startled me, good Count. I don't get many people coming to my door. How did you find my humble abode?"

Little Count Dracula, or Tommy Henkle as he was known

the other 364 days of the year, stared at the beautiful woman standing beside a giant pot. Long blonde hair swirled around her head, glowing from the light of the fire, making it look like a halo. Her blue eyes sparkled like diamonds. As she stared back, he felt his face blush and he looked away, noticing the room for the first time.

Across from him, bookcases lined the wall. Six shelves high, each one crammed with books that looked hundreds of years old, and papers, yellow with age. In front of that, a heavy oak table with only two chairs decorated the floor. Scrunched in the small space between the top of one shelf and the ceiling, a large black cat stared, its green eyes glaring into the boy.

"Are you a witch?" Tommy asked. He wouldn't believe her if she said no.

She laughed and Tommy melted. He could feel his face turn red, glowing through the white grease that covered his face.

"Do I look like a witch?" she asked.

Her words flowed like a song and Tommy knew she cast a spell over him.

"Yes," he said. "A lot."

"Well, as a matter of fact, I am. And my name is Margaret, but friends call me Meg.

"Are you a good witch or a bad witch?"

Meg's face lit up even brighter as she smiled. "It depends on my company. For young cute vampires, I'm a very nice witch," she said. "So let me ask you, are you a real vampire? You look like one – a lot."

"No," he grinned, looking down at his feet. "It's just my Halloween costume."

"Halloween? Is it Halloween already? My goodness, time certainly does fly by, doesn't it?"

"I guess," Tommy said.

"Casper," Meg said. "Don't be rude. Come down from there. We've got a new friend. You stay and entertain him while I try and find some treats."

A quiet thump landed on the hardwood floor and the cat padded its way to the small guest. Tommy knelt down as Casper rubbed himself against his pant leg. Its fur felt soft and thick as the vampire ran his hand down its back. Nice cat, he was about to say, but when Tommy looked up, Meg had disappeared. An open door just left of the fireplace lazily swung open a little wider as the breeze rolled in from the front. Tommy could see a corner of the kitchen, spotless white cabinets and counter against the dark brown floor. He heard a drawer open and some rustling about and thought about going in to see if he could help.

He felt as if the cat read his mind. The black ball of fur stepped back from him, blocking his way to the kitchen, and then Casper arched his back and hissed. Tommy understood the message loud and clear.

A biting blast of cold air flew in the front door and slammed into Tommy's back. The chill enveloped him and sent shivers shooting down his body. Maybe it would be best just to leave, he thought to himself. The cat made him feel kind of creepy and the wind felt like a warning. He remembered his mom reading the story of "Hansel and Gretel".

"Here we are, dear. Your timing was perfect." Meg came out carrying a tray stacked with cookies and two steaming mugs of hot chocolate. She set them on the table. "Would you be so kind to share some mead and ale with me?" She pulled a chair out for him.

Tommy looked inside the cup and saw small colored marshmallows dotting the top.

"After you're refreshed, I'll see what other kinds of treats I can dig up."

"Thank you," Tommy said. He took a sip of chocolate and closed his eyes as his mouth went into an automatic smile. Not too hot and not too cold, it slid down his throat like a warm breeze rippling velvet. Buttery goodness crumbled in his mouth as he savored the cookies.

"Tell me kind sir, how did you find a path to my door? For a lad out to collect as much candy as he can carry, you've certainly taken the wrong route."

He looked down into his cup and tried to think of the right words. How embarrassing, he thought. When she found out what a weenie he was she'd probably laugh in his face and then kick him out.

"I see you're uncomfortable," Meg said, her face full of concern. "If you just start to talk the words will flow. You'll find it easier talking to a stranger. Believe me, strangers are about the only people I talk to anymore."

Oh, he could listen to her forever. He loved the sound of her voice and the way she used words. He stored some of the strange words she spoke, like "mead" and "ale" and "abode," thinking how impressive they would be back at school.

"I got chased into the woods and got lost," he said.

"Oh my," Meg said. "Vampire killers, no doubt."

Everything the witch said made Tommy smile, inside and out. And she was right. The words soon came pouring out. He told how he and his friends had their bags almost full when some eighth grade bullies found them, stole their candy and began beating them up. "I got away and they chased me into the woods. I hid until they were gone, but I got lost. I saw your lights and thought I finally made it back to my neighborhood."

"And where were your parents through all of this?" Meg asked. Her face was stern and angry. Not at Tom, he could tell that, but mad at his parents.

Again, a sheepish look crossed his face. "I promised that I'd stay in a group and not go any farther than three blocks. It was the first Halloween they let me go without them. I let them down."

"You poor dear." Meg's face softened as she held out her arms. "Give Meg a hug."

Without hesitation Tommy got up and went into her embrace. She smelled so sweet and her skin felt like silk as she gently rocked him. He closed his eyes and snuggled as deep into her as

31

he could manage.

"What a terrible adventure," she whispered. "I know what will make you feel better. There's a box in the closet. Will you be so kind as to get it for me?"

"Closet?" he asked.

Looking around, he noticed for the first time, next to the shelves, an outline of a door. He reluctantly got off Meg's lap and walked across the room. The knob felt ice cold in his hand. A warning not to open it? Again, the thoughts of Hansel and Gretel haunted his mind. He looked back at the witch. Her smile was so beautiful. How could he not trust her? Tommy took a deep breath, closed his eyes, and opened the door.

Peeking his eyes open, he saw a plain cardboard box on the floor. He picked it up and brought it to Meg. She held her arms open and he crawled back into her lap.

"Open it," she said.

Tommy lifted the cover. Inside, filling the entire box sat a solid square of chocolate. "We couldn't let you have a Halloween without candy, could we?"

"All of it. For me?"

"Of course." Meg gave him a hug. "You rest for a few minutes if you'd like. When you're ready we'll journey back and return you to your parents."

"I almost thought that door was a giant oven and you were going to throw me in," Tommy said. He could tell her anything.

Meg gasped. "However did you ever get an idea like that?"

"Hansel and Gretel," Tommy said.

"Oh my. As if being a witch isn't hard enough. I hope you don't believe those fairy tales. They never were very kind to witches."

"I don't believe 'em," Tommy said.

"That's good," she whispered.

Meg began to hum a tune that Tommy never heard before. The melody danced on water as the young vampire drifted off to sleep.

~ ~ ~

Relaxed and refreshed, Tommy opened his eyes, ready to take Meg by the hand and head back home. The warm feeling instantly turned to ice. No longer in Meg's lap, instead, the boy found himself on a cold stone floor. Surrounding him, metal bars. He sat in a cage so small he couldn't even stand. On the far side of the room gleamed the sparkling white kitchen, but the cleanliness didn't even reach a quarter way in. The rest of the room was filthy. Smeared dirt and grease caked the walls, counter and floor. Bones littered the kitchen and cobwebs hung in every corner. At the counter an old hunched woman slashed at vegetables with a meat cleaver.

"Where's Meg?" Tommy shouted from behind the bars.

The old woman froze in mid-swing then slowly turned around and laughed. Tommy choked back a sob. The hag's face wrinkled like a prune. Her laugh could make dogs howl. Ratty blonde hair hung down in mats exposing patches of blistered scalp. Torn rags hung from what looked like a potato sack. It was the blue eyes that gave her away.

"Meg?" Tommy could barely spit out the word.

"No need for disguises now," she cackled.

Thinking quickly Tommy said, "I bet my dad's out looking for me right now. It's only a matter of minutes before he finds me. If you let me go right now, I promise not to tell him what you did."

Meg's laugh sounded like fingernails clawing a blackboard. "He can look all he wants. We're back in my realm now. I'm only in your world one night a year. He might find me, but he'll have to keep searching until next Halloween. And by that time, there'll be no trace of you."

"But you said you were a nice witch!" Tommy screamed.

"I said I was a nice witch to cute young vampires. You're not a real vampire, and to be perfectly honest, you're not cute. Now please be a good lad and shut up while I prepare dinner for

33

me and Casper." She looked down at the cat. "It's been so long since we had fresh, tender meat."

Next to the cage, Casper hissed. Tommy screamed as the cat licked his fangs, and in a very human way, smiled.

"Hansel and Gretel," she said to herself, and started laughing.

GRANDPA'S WATCH

A tear rolled down Milo Crane's cheek as the sun pounded its rays across the field. Jacob Crane sat on the rock looking sympathetically at his grandson.

"It's a fact of life, boy. People get old, they die. Ain't nothin' can be done about it."

"It's just not fair, Grandpa," Milo said. He wiped his nose with his sleeve.

"You're twelve years old now, boy. Old enough to know life ain't ever fair," the old man said.

Waves of heat danced up from the meadow. The long grass, dried and brown, swayed in the warm breeze. Off in the distance, an old pick-up kicked and bounced down the dirt road spitting a dust cloud into an otherwise flawless sky.

"That must be your Uncle John. S'pose we better be gettin' back to the house before we're missed."

"But can't they do something?" Milo begged. "Like chemical therapy or something?"

"It's called chemotherapy, and no they can't. The cancer's already spread too far. It's already infected the liver. Nothin' they can do but give me some pills for the pain, and even them's not

35

doin' shit no more."

Sweat rolled down Jacob Crane's face. Despite the agonizing pain in his gut, his lips parted into a smile exposing tobacco stained teeth as Milo came over and wrapped his arms around the now brittle frame of the old man.

"Before we go back into the house, I want to give you something for your birthday," Jacob said while gently pushing Milo back.

Reaching down, his liver-spotted hand undid the clasp that wrapped around the belt loop of his trousers. Very carefully the old man lifted the silver chain out of his pocket. At the end of the chain, the most beautiful pocket watch that Milo had ever seen was dangling in front of his eyes. A silver casing with an intricate carving of a small church decorated the cover. Next to the church stood a tiny cemetery inside a wonderfully carved little fence with six tiny headstones. Gold plating coated each one.

Milo's eyes widened to almost the size of the watch. The tears that had run down his face now looked like dried riverbeds.

"That's the neatest watch I ever seen."

"Open it up," his grandfather said with a sad smile.

Milo carefully took the watch out of his grandpa's hand and ever so lightly pressed the button on top of the crown. The church and cemetery snapped back on its hinge.

"Wow," Milo's voice shook.

Inside, the face of the clock was the deepest, darkest black Milo had ever laid eyes upon. Each number was made of hand-carved silver, the hour and minute hands were two squiggly lines of yellow that seemed to match the intensity of the sun. The second hand was curved like a scythe, blood red in color, which smoothly swept over the numbers. Between the center and the three was a little box that told the day and month, August 12.

"You're old enough now, boy."

"Wow," Milo echoed. "This is so cool."

"Y'know, it's been in the family for generations. My father gave it to me, his father to him. I ain't exactly sure how far back it goes, but my dad told me that this is the very first calendar watch ever made. Keeps perfect time and it don't hardly ever need windin' either. Fact, I remember when they first found the cancer I got so messed up I forgot to wind the thing for almost a week. Still kept runnin' smooth as silk."

Milo sat next to his grandfather totally absorbed with the watch. He lightly rubbed his thumb over the crystal while gently caressing the outer casing with his other hand.

"I suppose I shoulda gived it to your pa, or your Uncle John," the old man started to ramble. "Neither one of em ever seen it."

Milo instinctively held the watch tighter.

"But to be honest, I just don't trust your pa much anymore, and I think your Uncle John would sell it."

Milo loosened his grip.

"Your pa ain't a bad man, I ain't sayin' that. Well," the old man paused. "I guess he is a mean son-of-a-bitch. My fault mostly. Y'see, your grandma died when he was 'bout your age, and I guess I never was a very good pa after that. He pretty much had to grow up and learn things on his own."

Bad talk about his father didn't bother Milo in the least. People talked dirt about his dad as far back as he could remember. It used to get him in fights at school, but now it just rolled off. It didn't even faze him that it was his grandfather doing the sassing now. He didn't love his dad, but he didn't dislike him either. When he felt the back of his father's hand, he figured he must have deserved it. But mostly they just left each other alone.

Grandfather and grandson both sat in silence. Jacob stared out across the field, trying to memorize the beauty of the horizon, knowing there wouldn't be many left for him. He let the hot sun burn into his skin, fantasizing that the rays were eating the cancer inside. Milo couldn't take his eyes off the watch.

"I guess it's time we head back. They'll be callin' for us

soon."

Milo wanted to stay with his grandfather alone in the field, forever. Grandpa knew how to listen, and even more, understood. He never talked down to Milo, always spoke like they were equals. Milo loved the old man and figured the old man was about the only one who loved him back.

"Wait," Milo said. "How do you change the date on this? It says the twelfth of August, but it's really the eighteenth. It's six days off."

With a speed and strength Milo would have never guessed, the old hand snatched the watch.

"You got to promise me somethin.' Promise me to your grave, boy," Jacob glared at Milo. "You promise?" he almost shouted.

Milo nodded silently, looking shocked and scared.

Fear crept into the old man's voice. "You gotta promise never, never fix the date on this watch. Is that clear?"

"I promise," Milo whispered.

"Promise what?" Jacob snapped.

"That I'll never fix the date," Milo said, a little strength coming back into his voice.

"That's a promise to the grave," his grandfather said handing back the watch.

"I promise to the grave," Milo repeated. "But why not, grandpa?"

The old man heaved himself up and started walking away, "It's time we got back to the house," Jacob said while Milo sat watching. Finally, with a heavy sigh of resignation, the boy sprang up and chased after his grandpa.

The rooms in the Crane house were small and dark, the walls had the odor of mold. It was as hot inside as it was out, but more humid. Paul and John Crane sat on a rust color sofa. The springs were broken on the end John sat, so even though he was a good four inches taller than Paul, on the couch he only came up to his brother's chin.

The men were watching pro bowling on the old black-and-white TV when Milo and his grandpa walked in the door. Paul had already lost five dollars to his older brother on the first round and looked like he was about to lose five more. Jacob patted Milo on the shoulder. They both knew that in another couple of beers, Paul would lose his temper and another fight between brothers would break out.

The bitterness, resentment, and feeling of desertion still clung to Milo's dad even after all these years. He never forgave his brother for leaving to join the army after their mother died.

"Patty, I need another refill," Paul said.

Patty Crane stopped frosting the cake and ran into the living room with another beer for her husband. She smiled when her father-in-law and son walked in. "You two men wash your hands. Supper will be ready in a couple minutes."

"Hey, happy birthday. How's my favorite nephew?"

"Hi, Uncle John. I'm fine," Milo smiled.

"Don't get a swelled head," his father said. "You're his only nephew."

"For Christ's sake," John said. "Cut the kid some slack."

"Don't tell me how to raise my Goddamn kid," Paul spat. "Now double or nothin' on the final round."

"If you can afford it," said John. "I'll even let you pick."

"I'll take the white guy," Paul said as he popped open another beer.

"Hey," John said, trying to smooth things over. "Just let me know when you want help fixing the roof." He looked at the corner where water seeped in causing the wallpaper to bubble and peel.

"Yeah, yeah. I'll let ya know."

"Mom, look what grandpa gave me," Milo said as he handed her the watch.

"Oh my. Isn't that . . . interesting?"

"Let's see it, sport," John said. "Nice watch. I got ya something too. Why don't you get it, it's out in back of the truck."

39

"Can I, Mom?" He already started for the door.

"If you hurry up and don't get dirty. Supper will be on as soon as I set up the TV trays."

As Patty placed food in front of the men, Milo walked in wheeling a blue framed bicycle complete with racing seat and hand brakes.

"Thanks a lot," Milo beamed. "This is great."

"Happy birthday, sport. Glad you like it."

"Goddamn! The jackass can't even beat a Puerto Rican," Paul shouted at the TV.

"Good language around the kid," said John. "Real positive role model."

Paul sprang from the couch sending his TV tray across the room. "I told you once, asshole, don't ever tell me how to raise my kid."

Paul stood over John, clenching and unclenching his fists. The vein in his neck pulsated as the color in his face turned from pink to crimson.

"That's it. I'm out of here," John said. "Dad, you want a ride back into town?"

Jacob stood in the corner holding Milo behind him. Patty retreated into the kitchen.

"I told Milo I'd stay the night," Jacob said, trying to keep his voice calm.

"Sorry, sport," John said as he walked out the door.

"What a jackass," said Paul as he plopped back onto the couch. "Didn't even take the ten bucks. Hell if I'll pay him now."

"Pick that up for me," he pointed to the tray as Patty came out of the kitchen.

~ ~ ~

A cool breeze with a foul stench blew in through the window as Milo got ready for bed. Paul and Jacob sat on the couch watching wrestling while his mother stood at the kitchen sink finishing up the dishes.

"What stinks?" Milo asked as he came into the room.

"It smells like something died out there," his mom said.

Milo looked at his grandfather, watched him wrinkle his nose. He could have sworn the old man turned a shade whiter.

"Where's the watch, boy?" Jacob asked.

"It's right here," said Milo.

Somebody close the damn window," Paul shouted over his shoulder.

An odd look spread across Milo's face. "Grandpa, your watch changed," he looked up into his grandfather's eyes. "The gold is gone. And look at this, the gate to the cemetery is open. It wasn't open before, was it?"

"Open it up," the old man's voice croaked. "What's the date?"

Milo snapped open the watch. "It says the eighteenth." Startled and afraid that his grandfather might take the watch away, he quickly jumped in, "I didn't fix it. I swear."

"I fixed it," Patty said. "I noticed it when you went out to Uncle John's truck for your present. Are you ready for bed?"

"We gotta get out of here," Jacob said getting up from the sofa.

"What the hell are you talking about," said Paul. "Wrestling's on."

"It's the watch, it's cursed," the old man said. "We have to leave, now!"

"You gone loony, old man?" Paul sneered at his father.

"You gave my baby a cursed watch?" Patty stared incredulously.

"He was supposed to be its guardian, to keep this from happening," Jacob cried.

"To keep what from happening?" Paul and Patty asked in unison.

"I was going to explain it all to the boy tomorrow," Jacob said, mostly to himself.

Paul turned back to the TV, fed up with the old man's nonsense, while his wife continued to stare.

"Explain what?" she asked. Impatience and anger tinged her words.

Milo came into the room and sat near his grandfather. The air in the room was stale and the putrid smell permeated in through the kitchen window.

"Go get your clothes on, boy. We got to get outta here," Jacob said.

"You're not taking him anywhere," Patty said. "It's time he went . . ."

A bang on the front door made everyone jump. Milo looked at his grandfather and saw terror in his eyes.

"On the way to the door will you bring me another beer, Hon?" Paul said. "And close that damn window. It smells like the plumbing's backed up."

As Patty walked toward the door Jacob grabbed her arm with a trembling hand. "Don't answer it," he pled. "Take Milo and run out the back, and keep running."

Patty looked at her father-in-law and chills raced up her spine. His face was paler than she had ever seen and his touch was cold and clammy. She was afraid he might be having a heart attack.

"Why don't you sit down Jacob and I'll fix you some tea. You're not looking well." She tried to keep her voice gentle and in control.

Again a loud thump crashed into the door.

"I bet it's John wantin' his ten bucks," Paul said. "Well, he can go screw hisself."

She easily released the grip that Jacob used to try and restrain her and walked to the door.

Patty Crane let out a scream so deep and so thorough that Paul fell off the couch. He glanced at the wrestlers on the television to see if they heard the scream too, then whipped his head around just in time to see a skeletal hand grabbing at his wife.

Now it was Milo's turn to scream. A skeleton with mummified flesh dangling from its bones tried to drag his mom out of the house. Paul rubbed his eyes as he tried to make sense of what he saw, or what he thought he saw. Patty screamed again as she tried to break away from the hand that clutched her shoulder.

Jacob ran over and slammed the door, breaking off the creature's arm. Patty let out a cry as she knocked the bones off her blouse. Outside, they heard a clicking and rattling, then a loud crash into the door.

"What the hell is that!" screamed Patty.

"Paul, where's your hunting rifle?" Jacob yelled.

Paul never got up off the floor. He ignored the TV and just stared at the door.

"Snap out of it, boy. Where's the gun?" Jacob shook his son.

Milo's father didn't budge. He could have been a statue except for the drool that ran down his chin.

"It's in the closet," Milo screamed, then raced to get it.

Patty grabbed Jacob by the shoulders and looked pleadingly into his eyes. "What did you do?"

The old man's eyes suddenly filled with hate. "It was you, you stupid woman," his voice built with strength. "You had to meddle in things that were none of your business."

A sharp slap across his face stunned both of the adults. Patty couldn't believe she just hit her father-in-law. The hate drained from Jacob's face.

"I'm sorry," he whispered.

Patty nodded as Milo ran back into the room with his father's shotgun and a box of shells. The door kept shaking but held firm, at least for the moment.

"The story goes," Jacob started like it was story time and he had found just the right moment to tell one of his tales. "My grandpa's, grandpa's, grandpa saved a witch from a stonin' once, a long time ago. As thanks, she made him this watch."

Again there was a slamming into the door, as he popped shells into the rifle.

"She told him that the day he dies, the watch will stop for twenty-four hours. That he should leave instructions to his kin to right the clock and he'll come back to life. That he can live forever. The legend goes that he knew he was dealin' in evil and wanted no part of it. Instead of leaving instructions to right the watch, he told his son never to fix the date. It seems that through the generations the watch stopped for a day every time its owner died. Until now."

Milo and Patty just looked at each other, then back at Jacob. Just as Patty was about to tell the old man how ridiculous his story sounded, the front door flew off its hinges. Splinters of wood flew into the room. Patty screamed as she grabbed Milo and just through motherly instinct, pushed him behind, using her own body as a shield.

The walking skeleton came in the door missing half an arm. Shredded cloth hung from its petrified flesh. The deep sockets that once held eyes glowed red with devilish hate. Jacob raised the rifle and tried to level it. He shook so hard that the barrel looked alive as it danced. Jacob squeezed the trigger.

The creature's rib cage exploded into dust. The force of the shot knocked it off balance and the thing fell. The three watched as if hypnotized while the monstrosity tried to right itself. Their gazes snapped back as another figure moved in through the door. Behind it, they could see more of them coming up the path.

"You two get in the bathroom and lock the door," Jacob said. He let off another shot.

A skull of the thing coming through the door vaporized and its body flew into the creature behind it. Both bodies fell to the ground. It would have been comical if the Cranes weren't fighting for their lives.

Patty dragged Milo toward the bathroom. He grabbed the watch off the table, lifted its crown and frantically spun it backward. He looked up half expecting to see the dead magically disappear. Nothing. Milo looked down at the watch. Not only had the date not changed, but the hands weren't even moving.

Just the second hand glided across the numbers.

Another blast echoed off the walls. Milo wasn't even able to see if it did any damage. His mother had him hidden behind her body, pushing him farther back into the house, toward the bathroom. They made their way around Paul, who was still on the floor. With his legs crossed he rocked back and forth. He wrapped his arms around himself like a romantic embrace. He ignored the wrestlers as they bragged about how they were going to mutilate their next opponents. Instead, he stared silently at the door as another rotted body came through.

"Grandpa," Milo shouted. "Shoot the watch."

He was about to toss it over but Jacob stopped him. "Can't do it," he said. "If we destroy the watch, we'll never be able to stop 'em."

"But it won't go backwards," Milo pleaded.

"You'll have to take off the crystal, boy, and do it by hand. Now get away from here."

The entire house reeked of death as Patty slammed and locked the bathroom door. Milo sat on the counter, his fingers like sausages as he tried to pry off the crystal. They both jumped when the gun went off again. Patty reached out and embraced her son. Milo felt tears splash on top of his head as they rolled off his mother's cheek. They hugged even tighter when another blast rang out.

They tried to pry the glass off the watch face. Patty cursed under her breath when she broke a fingernail. Suddenly, they heard an old man's scream, and then silence. Milo's eyes filled with tears as he grabbed the watch away from his mother and smashed it on the counter. Not even a scratch.

Outside the door they heard a scratching and shuffling sound, and it was coming closer. Patty looked around frantically, like there might actually be someplace to hide in the bathroom.

"Milo, get in the tub. Lay flat and don't move. Don't make a sound. I'll cover you with towels. If they can't see or hear you, maybe they'll leave you alone."

In desperation Milo swung the watch by its chain. Faster and faster it circled until he brought it down on the porcelain sink. The crystal shattered as tiny bits of glass sailed across the bathroom. Milo cut his finger picking slivers of glass off the watch face.

A deafening smash came from the other side of the bathroom door. The cheap lock would never be able to stand many hits like that.

"Milo, quick, into the tub," His mother whispered urgently.

Milo put his finger on the hour hand. It felt burning hot. He tried to push it backward but it wouldn't budge. Another bang on the door and a splinter of wood broke off. He pushed the watch hand with all his might and felt it starting to give when the second hand swept by.

"Milo, NOW!" his mother screamed.

For a moment Milo was numb. All of a sudden, his hand throbbed as he saw blood pouring onto the face of the watch. It took another second to realize that the scythe second hand severed the very tip of his finger. He wanted to scream, actually tried, but nothing came out. All of his feelings, his emotions, were all choked up somewhere inside.

A blast snapped him back as the bathroom door came crashing in. Patty screamed as she tried fighting the creatures. Every ounce of her strength went to protecting her child.

Milo grabbed his toothbrush off the sink and as hard as he could, jammed the handle into the hour hand. His mother fought with a fury Milo had never seen before, as he pushed the clock hand back hour after hour. Every time the second hand swept by, another piece of toothbrush sliced off.

Patty went down under three of the creatures. Then, a rush of air that sounded like a moan came out of one of the skull mouths as it disintegrated into dust. There were only two creatures on his mother now. Milo had pushed the time back twenty-four hours.

The hour hand became loose and moved easier now. Milo spun it back faster and faster with his toothbrush handle. The second hand cut through it so easily it didn't even slow him down. Soon there was only one monster getting up from his mother, then with a groan, it turned into a pile of dust like the others. The toothbrush handle was down to the nub but Milo didn't stop until the date said the twelfth.

The house went quiet. No scratching or clawing, no screams, just the noise from the television set. Milo looked down at his mother. Her eyes were open but she didn't move. Scratches and gouges littered her body and her neck bent in a way that necks weren't supposed to bend.

Milo wanted to scream but found he didn't have the strength. He leaned down to hold his mom when he thought he heard the sound of breathing from the living room. Cautiously he stepped out of the bathroom. There were no walking skeletons, just two piles of dust in the hallway.

Paul Crane still sat on the floor staring into the night out the missing front door. It was the first time in twelve years that Milo hated his father.

"Grandpa!" Milo raced over to the man lying on the floor.

Blood was everywhere. It seemed to be coming from his chest, but at least he was still breathing. Milo knelt down and put his grandfather's head in his lap. Next to him sat another pile of dust just like the ones in the bathroom and hallway.

"You done good, boy," an old tired voice whispered. "Now you keep that watch. You guard it and make sure this never happens again. Let me rest in peace, boy."

Red foam bubbled out of Jacob's mouth. He closed his eyes and died. Milo looked down at the watch. It had stopped.

~ ~ ~

Milo had a good feeling about living with Uncle John. The police figured that in a drunken stupor, Paul went berserk for some reason and killed his father and then his wife. When the

47

realization of what he did sunk in, the man went comatose. If he ever came out of it there would be a trial.

Uncle John had packed all his things while Milo recuperated in the hospital. With just one more box to unpack, he had no idea what he had left. The box was full of odds and ends. He reached in blindly and the first thing he pulled out was the pocket watch his grandfather had given him just before he died. Milo remembered that he broke it, but couldn't remember how.

He opened the clasp and saw amazingly enough that the curved second hand still swept around the clock. It even had the right time. The only thing wrong was that the calendar was a day off. He was about to fix it but a warning from deep inside told him to leave it be. He closed the cover and gazed at its church and little cemetery with seven gold plated tombstones.

MOSQUITO TIM

"Do you feel fear? Pain? Are you aware of death? Probably not. Your brain can't be much larger than the point of a needle."

Timothy McMahon watched the mosquito with fascination. It crawled through the fine red hairs on his arm. Its tiny head flicked back-and-forth then stood in place. An unfeeling sting, more like a tickle, and the mosquito began to draw blood.

God's little vampire, Timothy thought. No, that wasn't true. Crucifixes didn't scare them, and sun certainly didn't dry them to dust. Holy water would only drown them. "But mostly," he said. "Is that you're not immortal." He slapped his hand down on the insect.

Timothy brought up his arm and drew his tongue across his skin, reclaiming his own blood. Pretending to be a vampire, he bit into the fresh bite and sucked out more blood. Oh, how he wanted so much to believe. After all, myth was based on fact, wasn't it? *Who's to say that they really don't exist?*

He'd read all he could find on Vlad Dracula and Elizabeth Bathory, from the fiction of Stoker to Rice. There's so much about them that they have to exist.

49

~ ~ ~

In the quiet suburban neighborhood the McMahon back yard faced the Walden back yard. Tina and Trish Walden, home for the summer from their first year at college, lay sprawled out on towels, collecting the last of the sun's rays for the day. Their miniature schnauzer, Lucy, stretched between them. Her front paw touched Trish while her butt rested against Tina.

Three years older than Tim, and if asked, he'd say they were the typical suburban snobs. In high school both had been cheerleaders, dated jocks exclusively, and were as beautiful as they were cruel. Every chance to harass, tease, embarrass or generally humiliate Timothy they did, and they did it with zeal. Because he was only 5'3", they made fun of his size, his carrot colored hair, his pasty white skin, his awkwardness around girls, and anything else they came up with whenever they passed him in the hall.

The worst came two years ago, when he was a freshman in gym class. Timothy twisted his ankle playing basketball. Mr. Cassidy allowed him to shower and change early, get a pass, and go to the nurse's office. On the way back from the shower he walked into Cassidy's office. There were no passes on the desk so he opened the drawer. No passes in the drawer either, but there was a copy of Playboy. No harm in looking – until the rest of the class walked in.

That had been the beginning of the end for any decent life Timothy McMahon would ever have at high school. The next day, between classes, it seemed as if everybody stared. Even his friends hid their smiles behind notebooks. Whenever he made eye contact the person quickly turned away and started to giggle. Until he made contact with the Waldens. The senior girls stared back and it was Timothy who averted his eyes. He knew they wouldn't let him off without comment. He was right.

Staring at the floor Timothy walked into Tina. His eyes were level with her chin. He lowered his gaze and noticed bra lines through her yellow sweater.

"We hear you got a hard-on in the boy's locker room yesterday. Do boys turn you on?" Tina said. An evil smirk spread across her face.

Timothy looked away and noticed the entire hallway was still. Filled with people and no one moved – and everybody smiling.

"I don't know how anyone noticed," Trish said. "I bet your little pee-pee's so small it's hard to see."

Tina shouted her triumphant dig, "Tiny Tim playing with his little Thumbelina!"

The hallway erupted. Through the noise Trish said, "Show us your little Thumbelina, Tiny."

The laughter intensified.

"If you show me yours," Timothy snapped.

He knew it was a lame comeback even before the words left his mouth, but he couldn't help it. He felt pressure and more humiliation than when he got caught in the locker room. He needed to get away from everyone.

Tim pushed his way through the girls and his hand accidentally pressed against Tina's breast. His first cop-a-feel and it fit in his hand so perfectly. Despite everything, he couldn't resist giving a little squeeze as he ran by. Even through the sweater it felt wonderful. He felt Thumbelina move.

"You pervert!" Tina screamed. She took a swing at him but he was too quick. "Did you see what that little asshole did?"

~ ~ ~

The happiest day in Timothy's life – graduation day for the Waldens. "Tiny Tim" stuck through the grades, and he couldn't walk into the boy's room without some jerk yelling "It's time for Tiny Tim to take Thumbelina out on a date." It became so ingrained that he couldn't help but think of it as Thumbelina, himself. God, he hated that.

Now the twins had returned from school. Back and not

more than 100 feet away, they were going to ruin his summer. He sat in his yard and watched as Tina swatted a mosquito, and then Trish did the same. They said something and both of them got up. Trish leaned over picking up the towel and wiggled her shapely ass in Tim's direction. Thumbelina stirred and he despised the twins even more.

Timothy wished he were a giant mosquito. He'd fly over there right now and pin them both to the ground and suck out all of their blood. He'd laugh while gorging himself as their beauty shriveled and they died.

The window behind him cracked open. "Timmy, come in and help set the table. Dinner's about ready," His mother quickly closed the window to keep the cool air inside.

Trish and Tina looked over and for the first time noticed Tim. They didn't say a word, just looked at each other and started laughing. Lucy jumped up to join in their fun.

That's it, Timothy thought. He bit at the mosquito bite on his arm and broke the skin. Sucking the blood he tried to plot ways to get back at the Waldens.

~ ~ ~

Time sped and summer was sailing by too quickly. Already the days were noticeably shorter. Soon bitch Tina and bitch Trish would head back to college. The entire summer spent fantasizing revenge would amount to nothing. Either Timothy the giant mosquito or Timothy the vampire, it didn't matter which, it always ended the same. He'd be intoxicated with their blood and they'd be lifeless shells.

A mosquito bit Timothy's arm. He watched his blood fill the tiny sac. "What a wonder of nature you are. So frail. Your stinger is smaller than a strand on a piece of string, yet it can go through all the layers of human skin." He squashed the bug and sucked his wound.

Timothy stopped and began to shudder. Swallowing the warm blood on his tongue, he had to consciously slow his breathing so as not to hyperventilate. Days and weeks of trying to come up with a revenge plot and now it just popped into his head. From a mosquito.

~ ~ ~

Long after dinner and the dishes done, Timothy went to the kitchen and grabbed a straw. Down in the basement he found everything else he needed. He took a small funnel and attached a strip of elastic to the wide end. He jammed the straw all the way through the narrow end and duct taped it to place.

The elastic band clung tight around the back of his head. That was good. It held the funnel in place over his mouth. He looked in the mirror and smiled from behind the mask. Timothy the Mosquito Man. He grabbed an exact-o knife from the toolbox and dashed out into the night.

"Where are you going, Timmy," his mother called after hearing the screen door slam. "It's almost ten o'clock."

"I won't be out too late." Even Timothy couldn't understand his muffled voice from behind the funnel.

"Don't stay out too late," his father shouted. "And shut the door."

The cool breeze couldn't stop Timothy from sweating with excitement. Looking back-and-forth he searched for a victim to test out his invention.

Sometimes things work out so well that you have to believe in a higher power. Mr. Walden opened his back door and out trotted Lucy. Timothy had seen the routine hundreds of times. The dog would sniff around the yard for a few minutes, do her nightly business, then scratch at the door until someone let her in.

"Luuuuucy." Timothy was on his knees holding out his hand. Lucy looked up and started running toward the voice that called her name. "You sure are a stupid dog," Tim said in a friendly voice.

The schnauzer sniffed his hand and started to lick. Timothy had no trouble picking her up and carrying her next to the central

AC of his house. He held the dog down on her back with one hand and opened the exact-o knife with the other.

As soon as Lucy was on her back she realized this man meant her harm. She squirmed and kicked but the hold was too tight. She yelped but was drowned out by the air conditioner. She lay still, submissive, hoping then that he'd let her go.

Timothy made a small slit in her stomach. Luck still held. He must have hit a vein or artery the way the blood gushed.

Lucy found new strength and kicked frantically as Tim tried to put the straw into the cut. Finally, holding the dog with both hands, the straw found its target. He sucked up one mouthful of blood, then another. It tasted salty and coppery and wonderful. Then it didn't. A volcano rumbled in his stomach and shot up his throat.

Dog blood came up first, then vomit. It filled the funnel then backed up into his mouth. Timothy choked and gagged as he tore at the funnel. Like a bullet, Lucy shot away.

Timothy emptied his stomach on the lawn; the funnel hanging from his chin. Gasping the warm air he finally lifted his head and froze. In front of him were two legs wearing black slacks. Fancy slacks. Black leather shoes shined in the darkness.

Oh God. Caught. How could he possibly explain this? A new missile of bile launched up his throat. Maybe he could puke himself to death. It was the only way out that he could think of.

Still on his knees and with his stomach empty, Timothy looked up. The man looked about thirty. Tall and slender, he had blond hair parted down the middle, reaching down to the middle of his ears. His eyes were large and looked black in the night. He had a hooked nose and thin lips that seemed to stretch across his face. A vest, that matched the pants, covered a long-sleeve, white silk shirt. Cradled in the arm of the shirt was Lucy. She shivered like it was below zero. Her blood soaked into the man's sleeve. He didn't seem to care.

He looked down with a sad smile, slowly shaking his head. "I've been around for a long time and traveled the world extensively, but I have never seen a spectacle like this before. I must confess, I had thought I had seen everything. You, young sir, have proven me wrong."

The man had a slight accent, but Timothy couldn't tell from where.

"Ivanov Ramkowski." The man held out his hand.

"Timothy McMahon." He took the man's hand. Ramkowski helped him to his feet. Vomit still drained from the straw and splashed the ground.

"Ah, Irish stock," Ramkowski said. "I should have guessed by the hair."

"Yeah, I guess," Tim said.

"I'm Ukrainian descent myself. Son of a hog farmer, but that was some time ago."

The two stared at each other. Timothy wanted to run and hide. He couldn't believe he'd been stupid enough to give his real name.

"Young Timothy McMahon," Ramkowski said. "The human mosquito. No. Better yet, Mosquito Tim." He raised his free arm in the air.

It sounded as if this man wanted to tour with Timothy, flaunting him as a sideshow freak.

Ivanov looked at Timothy. "I know the world is changing. Certainly faster than the likes of me can keep up with. But don't you agree, Irish, that some things just work out best the old fashioned way?"

Timothy shrugged his shoulders. "I guess so."

Ivanov smiled. As he did two huge fangs grew from his mouth and glistened off the moonlight. Timothy's eyes grew wide. His jaw dropped and leftover vomit dribbled down his chin into the funnel. With a quick snap the man bit into Lucy's neck. She let out a small whimper then stopped shaking. She looked so calm and peaceful, as if in a comfortable sleep.

Timothy took over shaking where Lucy left off. "You really do exist," he whispered more to himself. Then louder, "You're a vampire!"

Tim knew he should have been scared, should have run, but he felt more of a nervous exhilaration. This was what he'd waited his whole life for – proven existence of vampires.

Ivanov ignored the remark and casually tossed the dog's body in the small space between the air conditioner and the house. "Hors d'ouevres," he smiled.

Ramkowski licked the blood off his mouth and looked at Timothy with glowing eyes. "Well, Mosquito Tim, I must say you've been a most interesting person. One of the most entertaining I've seen in quite some time. Very creative, indeed. But alas, I'm afraid the show has ended and it's time for the main course."

Ramkowski took a step forward and Timothy tried to take a step back. He tried again but his legs didn't seem to be working. Looking into the man's hypnotic eyes, Timothy felt a wave of calm wash through him.

"I want to be like you," Timothy said with his remaining strength. "I want to be a vampire."

Ivanov stopped, smiled, and then broke out in laughter. "Then you're a fool, young Irish. Why in God's name would you prefer my existence over death?"

The spell was broken and Timothy involuntarily took a step back. "Well," he started to stammer. "I like the night." He never could think well under pressure.

Ramkowski's eyes shined with delight. "I should make you a vampire because you like the night?"

"And I want to live forever."

Ivanov laughed. "We're not alive, boy. We exist. I must say, you are a wonder Mosquito Tim."

"All right. Exist forever, then."

The Walden's back door opened and Mr. Walden, using his Ricky Ricardo imitation called for Lucy.

"That?" Ivanov cocked his head at the carcass behind the AC.

"Yeah," Timothy nodded.

"Lucy, come." Ricky's voice was gone, now Mr. Walden sounded between irritation and urgency.

"I do so hate interruptions," Ramkowski said. "Let us go to my abode and we'll talk. But please, take off that silly mask."

Down the block Ivanov opened the door to Gladys Simonson's house. He flipped on the light and Timothy followed him in. Gladys was 87 years old and a widow for the last thirty. She was also on the couch. If it hadn't been for the blue skin, the two holes in her neck, the stench, and the flies crawling on her body, she would've looked asleep in the midst of a wonderful dream.

Ivanov looked at the horror in Timothy's eyes. "Believe it or not, she was almost grateful." He closed the door. "So this is what you want to do, Mosquito Tim?"

Timothy shook the fright from his eyes. "Uh, yeah."

"You know," Ivanov said while looking at the body. "As long as I keep picking up her mail and leaving an envelope every Saturday for the boy who cuts the grass, who knows how long I can keep this place? That is, of course, if I can trust you. And let you live."

"You can. For sure you can," Timothy said.

"Okay, Irish. Let's talk business." Ivanov pulled out a chair for Timothy at the kitchen table then took a seat across from him. "Say I grant you your wish. What's in it for me?"

Timothy thought. What could he possibly have that a vampire could want?

Ivanov had his elbows propped on the table, resting his chin in his hands and noticed Tim's struggle.

"It used to be you could find pure maidens by the score. There seem so few this day and age. Do you think maybe you could lure one of your female classmates into my possession?"

Timothy thought for a moment then his eyes widened and a smile broke across his face. "How about twins?"

Ramkowski gasped, "Virgins?" He sat up straight and

clasped his hands.

"I think so." Timothy shrugged.

"Mosquito Tim, bring them here tomorrow night just after the sun goes down and I'll be greatly in your debt."

"Finally, my revenge," Timothy whispered to himself.

~ ~ ~

Tina answered the door. Her eyes were red and puffy. They looked for hope when the door opened and went to hostility when she saw who stood opposite. "What do you want?"

"I think I know where your dog is," Timothy said.

For a brief second he thought he saw a glint of thanks. Then it was gone.

"If you did anything to our dog . . ."

"Hey, I'm just trying to help. All right?"

"Who is it?" Trish came to the door. "Oh."

She too looked as if she'd been crying.

"He says he knows where Lucy is," Tina said.

"Where?" Trish looked at Timothy with a face that said "tell me now or I'll rip every bone out of your body".

"I think she's at widow Simonson's house," Timothy said.

The girls were out the door without question.

A full moon lit the way as they jogged over to the old woman's house. A man they'd never seen before answered the door.

"Where's Mrs. Simonson?" Tina asked. "Are you her grandson?" Without paying attention she tried to look past him.

"Indeed I am," Ivanov said. "Are you the owners of the little schnauzer I found relieving herself on our lawn this morning?"

"We sure hope so," Trish said.

They followed him into the house. Timothy followed them in then closed and locked the door. He thought he'd enjoy this even more than Ramkowski.

Ivanov crinkled his nose. "They're not virgins. Very disappointing."

Tina saw Mrs. Simonson on the couch and began to scream.

"Shut up, bitch," Timothy yelled.

She stopped. Three pairs of surprised eyes stared at Timothy.

"Irish, a new side of you I've never seen before," Ivanov smiled.

Before the twins could react, the vampire stood between them. He placed an arm around each. His hands covered their mouths and he had their heads twisted exposing their frail slender throats.

"They're not virgins, but they are beautiful. You've done well Mosquito."

Ivanov sank his fangs into Tina's neck. Trish struggled but the grip held her tight. Her eyes pleaded toward Timothy. Tim was giddy in his own thoughts. After tonight that would be him. *It's a shame I can't have those bitches for myself*, he thought.

Tina's eyelids fluttered. Her eyes rolled back so only the whites could be seen. Her breath slowed to almost nothing. Ivanov pulled out of her and started on the sister.

With Trish in the same state, he stopped and let out a satisfied purr. The smile vanished from Timothy's face. He'd read enough stories to know as Ramkowski bit into his own wrists and held them to the girls' mouths. Like babies, they started to suck.

"What are you doing?" Timothy cried. "You promised you'd turn me into a vampire."

Ivanov ignored him. The girls' skin turned from golden tan to pale white to dead ash. They were getting strong. Ramkowski yanked his wrists from their mouths. "Enough!" Then he placed his arms around their shoulders and held them close, like lovers.

"You promised me," Timothy said.

"I promised you nothing," Ivanov spat. The friendliness and charm had vanished from his voice. "No sane person wants to be a vampire."

"But I do," Timothy pleaded.

"Then you're a fool." Ivanov cursed at him. "You have no idea what it's like knowing you will never be able to feel the warmth of the sun on your skin. Knowing that someday you will cease to exist and know that you will never see the gates of heaven, but burn for eternity in the bowels of Hell.

"Oh, Irish," his voice softened. "I do like you and I'm doing you a favor. Really. I smelled the hate you had for these two. So, for you, not only did I kill them but I gave them a sentence worse than death." He took a deep breath. "But, unfortunately for you, I am a very even minded man."

Ivanov took his arms off the women. Tina stayed in front of Timothy and hissed. Trish sped behind him to cut off any escape. They looked ravenous. Their eyes burned into him as they slowly crept closer.

"Oh my," Ivanov said. "The first meal is always the messiest. Well, Mosquito Tim, you've had your revenge. Ladies, now it's your turn".

OLD ENOUGH TO KNOW BETTER

IS THAT MY REFLECTION
IN THE MIRROR?

I did it. I was finally going to make it out of this little rat-hole town. Fly to L.A., do the audition (a formality, my agent guaranteed), sign the contract, then get a big fat check. Stan, my agent, told me it was a done deal. He showed them my portfolio, a couple of reviews and the underwear commercial that I did. They loved me; they really loved me. They told Stan that I was exactly what they were looking for – a fresh face and a new name. I knew it was worth the extra five percent to get a Hollywood agent. I thought that once I flew out, I might never come back.

Outside, the temperature held at 80 degrees, not a cloud in the sky. A perfect day all around. I climbed up the fire escape of my apartment building and lay out on the roof, letting the sun fuel my already tan body. Couldn't hurt. I dreamed of fame and big bucks. My God! I'll be able to buy anything I ever wanted, sleep with any woman I choose. Have two or three hanging on my arm as we walk up to the front of the line at the fanciest nightclubs for instant service.

"Stop it right there, Douglas Powers," I said it out loud to myself. "That's not how you were raised. Us Midwesterners got us a reputation for clean livin' to uphold."

I couldn't lie there any longer. I felt too giddy with excitement. The Hollywood rags were already abuzz with rumors and speculation about who would play Lance Race (the American version of James Bond). James Bond nothing. This guy was going to make Bond look like Gandhi.

The deal was, if the movie grossed over one hundred and fifty mil (and how could it not with all the hype, and they hadn't even started shooting yet), I'd have a contract for five more films over the next ten years. Even if they didn't shoot 'em, I'd still get paid. It was a risk on both sides. If they quit after making two, I'd still be a multimillionaire. If all the movies were incredibly successful, I'd only be a multi-millionaire instead of a billionaire. I could live with that. I read there was even talk of Spielberg and Lucas teaming up again, taking the special effects world bounding into the 22nd Century.

The entire scene had been played out in my mind dozens of times. The reporters and camera folks would be packed in the auditorium, everyone wedging themselves to get closer to the stage. The executive producer would step in front of the curtain and thank everyone for coming. "Ladies and gentlemen (the curtain would come up), meet Douglas Powers, or should I say Lance Race."

There'd be stunned silence, then whispers of "Who the hell is Douglas Powers?" But in no time the uproar would start, and by the next morning, my name would be a household word.

I had to do something. No way would my mind let my body sit still. "Take a walk," my brain said. What a perfect idea. Stroll through the neighborhood one last time as a nobody. After today, everyone would be gathering around me asking for my autograph, remembering when I was a little tyke, how cute I was as I rode my bike across their lawns.

Strolling along, I noticed the air. It smelled so clean. Probably wouldn't be treated to that again for a long time. The sun reflected off a window across the street, and I stopped. The little antique and novelty shop had been there for years. I'd passed it so many hundreds of times, but I'd never been inside. When I was small, it used to give me the chills whenever I walked by. As I got older, I just quit noticing it all together. Well, maybe it was about time I went inside. Last chance sort of thing. Fare-thee-well, ta ta, don't call me – I'll call you.

Inside, I knew the musty, moldy smell was going to play havoc with my sinuses. The store did fascinate me, though. Counters lined the wall with old junk jewelry and metal windup toys that would bring instant lawsuits nowadays. In the corner stood a shelf with Civil War memorabilia and, next to that, Nazi paraphernalia. Maybe if I held my breath, I could make one quick run-through.

I felt like I was walking in a maze. One cubbyhole led into another. An old woman stared at some teacups and server tray with a look in her eyes that went back to another time. There were cast-iron muffin tins, old baseball gloves, trays of thimbles, and kitchen utensils that could now pass for lethal weapons. Everything seemed scattered around with no rhyme or reason. Hats sat next to jewelry that rested against radios complete with vacuum tubes that still worked. Not kitchen stuff over here, sports stuff over there. Everything just jumbled together.

Squeezing through the narrow aisles, my knee met with an old rain barrel full of canes, umbrellas, and a couple of old carved sticks. I couldn't scream and swear. There weren't many people in the shop, but all it took was one to talk to the tabloids. *"He just beat up that poor little defenseless barrel. I think he's on drugs."*

Looking around to see if anyone was watching, I saw only one face wincing at me. He had rugged good looks, a chiseled chin, Roman nose, and the most piercing blue eyes. He was the star of the future. It was me, now smiling back at myself.

The mirror sat on the top of a bamboo pole that ended just under my chin, making the glass a perfect height for my face. A tarnished frame full of indentations and curly-cues had looked to be quite fancy at one time. It could be again with a little tarnish remover and elbow grease. Hell, I could buy it now, and then pay somebody to work on it next week.

As I stared at my face, I noticed a couple of things. One was the reflection of a woman's smiling face behind me. She looked to be around fifty with black curly hair, thin lips, and one nasty shiner. Poor thing, probably served her husband's dinner too cold or something. Anyway, let her look. Maybe she thinks I'm vain. So what? If her face was going to make her millions of bucks, then she'd stare at herself, too.

The other thing, which I found quite a bit more fascinating, went past my reflection. Deep in the glass, there were other faces. Sad faces. Scowling faces. Familiar faces.

My God! This was incredible! Holographic images of famous movie stars were embedded in the glass. Derrick Marsdale, tough guy from the thirties and forties and my personal hero as I was growing up and watching old movies on late night TV, stood in front. He could play good guy or bad to perfection. In fact, I had quite a few of his movies on disc at home. I don't think a month goes by without me pulling at least one out and sticking it in the DVD. And if I'm not mistaken, behind him was Gary Oslund, another one of my faves from way back. My my my, if that wasn't Bruce Tenneson, great comic actor from the silent era. And to round it off, the beautiful Margo Merriweather, sex goddess and vamp, also from before the talkies.

"I've got to have this," I said out loud. That was until I saw the price. EIGHT HUNDRED DOLLARS? "You have got to be kidding." It's not like I couldn't afford it. Well, I couldn't yet, but by the time the check cleared, it would be pocket change. But that wasn't the point. The point was EIGHT HUNDRED DOLLARS. I dropped it back in the barrel and was about to walk away.

"Douglas?"

I turned around, and the lady with the black eye was staring at me.

"Do I know you?" I asked.

"No."

"Do you know me?"

"No."

"Okay, is there something I can do for you?"

She smiled. "It's only eight dollars," she said.

"Huh?" I turned back and looked at the tag. Sure enough, between the eight and the zero, half the size of a pinprick, sat the decimal point.

I broke out in a smile and said my thank-yous to the woman. "What are you? A psychic?"

"Yes," she answered. "Among many other things."

Couldn't be a very good one, or you would've seen that punch coming, I thought, but was too polite to say.

"Like I haven't heard that thought a million times," she said.

"My God. You really are."

"Chalk that one up to being able to read your face," she said.

I felt myself turning red as she stared. Thinking of nothing else to do, I held out my hand. "Douglas Powers."

She took my hand and smiled. Her skin was hot to the touch. "I know. I saw you perform last week."

So much for her psychic ability to know my name.

"My name's Rhiannon, like the Fleetwood Mac song."

She looked too old to be named after the song, but again, I held my tongue.

She let out a sigh. "I am too old." Then she looked at me with raised eyebrows. "Maybe the song was named after me."

Again, I felt myself blush. "Either you're very good or I've got the easiest face in the world to read."

"I wouldn't become a professional gambler if I were you." She smiled and started to walk away, then stopped. "And just to settle your curiosity, no, we don't hear all and see all. And sometimes we even walk into doors."

I let out a long breath after she walked back to her counter.

The woman was beginning to give me the creeps.

I slid the mirror-on-a-stick out of the barrel, past the umbrellas and eagle-head canes. Paying the eight dollars, I got out of there. I decided the whole place gave me the willies, let alone what the air was doing to my sinuses. Was that what living out in L.A. was going to do? What the heck. Between movies I could always buy a ranch out in Montana and be Ted Turner's next-door neighbor. Maybe I'd be tired of the mirror by then, and Ted would like to buy it for eight hundred bucks.

The sun was down, Letterman joked on the tube, and I was packing my bags for Successville. My new find leaned against the dresser, next to the mementos that I wanted to take with me: my dad's Purple Heart, a dagger he got off some dead North Vietnamese guy, his gold pocket watch, the Bible that my mother made me promise to keep when she was on her deathbed, and the framed, four-leafed clover next to a copy of my first paycheck as a professional actor.

A knock on the door startled the bejeebies out of me. Through the peephole stood the black eye of Rhiannon staring back at me. I knew she couldn't see back into my apartment. I'd tried that before. But the way she glared back, you'd think she could.

I opened the door and she slid by me without even waiting for a "please come in." She walked past the kitchen, through the living room, and straight to the bedroom. I had no idea why she came, but it didn't look like for fun and frolic.

"We have to talk," she said.

The words stung. Long ago memories from a girl who had dumped me, the girl I wanted to marry, cascaded in my mind. "We have to talk," she started out . . . Snap out of it, Powers. What the hell was I thinking? Here and now.

"If you don't mind," I said, pointing to the open suitcases, "I've got a seven o'clock flight out of here tomorrow morning, and I'm a bit busy right now."

She stared at me, looking deep into my eyes, ignoring my

words. "It's about the mirror."

I knew it. It really was eight hundred dollars, and now she wanted it back. Uh uh. I bought it, they accepted my cash. A deal's a deal.

It felt as if she read my thoughts as she smiled. "It's funny," she said. "I was sent to try and dissuade you from buying it in the first place. There are so many bigger and better ones out in Hollywood. In fact, I don't know how this one got out in the first place. This is a very early one. One of the first. It got misplaced somewhere along the way, and if we ever trace it back to who grabbed it, there'll be hell to pay."

My entire body began to shiver. I had no idea what she was talking about, but I got that same creepy feeling that I had in the novelty shop. "So let me guess," I said. "You want this back to return to its rightful owner."

"Quite the contrary. You are the rightful owner."

Now I was getting downright scared. What did she want?

"When I saw those faces, and how lonely they looked, I made an executive decision," she said. "I figured what the hell, they're some of Doug's favorite actors, and I bet they would really love some new company. It's not like they're fighting for room in there."

I began to get a very sick feeling in my gut. I was shivering and sweating at the same time. I still had no idea what she was talking about, but I knew I wanted her out of my life.

"Actually, this works out quite well," she said, approaching the mirror. "You'll be able to return it to its rightful place."

"Wait a minute," I said, then froze in mid-sentence.

She took hold of the bottom part of the mirror's frame and pulled. Like a window shade, the glass stretched. I rubbed my eyes, not believing what they were taking in. When they opened, Rhiannon was attaching the frame to the bottom of the pole, and I was standing in front of a full-length mirror.

Through all the drama classes, rehearsals, and plays, I couldn't have acted more shocked. My jaw hung open, my eyes bulged, and my tan faded to white.

The holographic images had grown to life-size. The pain and despair were etched clearly on all their faces. Tough guy Derrick Marsdale looked like a child with a grown man's face, wanting to cry. There was nothing comedic about Bruce Tenneson, nor anything sexy about Margo Merriweather. Only Gary Oslund seemed recognizable. Probably because he always had that forlorn look on his face. It's what made him famous.

"Normally, we wait until after the contract is signed," Rhiannon said. "But in your case, details got a little screwed up and I decided to take things a bit out of order. I hope that's not a problem."

She looked at me like we were doing a regular business transaction.

"C'mon, Mr. Powers, you've got a plane to catch, fame and fortune to reap. I certainly don't want to be the one to hold you back."

After a moment, she must have analyzed the dumb expression I wore. Rhiannon let out an exasperated sigh then placed her finger in the middle of the mirror.

Amazingly, the glass started to ripple where she touched it. A still pond catching a tossed pebble, the mirror wavered and a slit opened up. There was a blackness of never-ending night on the other side and moans that wouldn't cease.

Suddenly, a force wrapped itself around my body and pulled me toward the opening. I looked to and reached out for the psychic. "Help me!"

She stood there and smiled. "Well worth the eight dollars."

I fought with every ounce of strength I could muster, but the force kept dragging me closer. Just as I reached the mirror, there was a 'whumph' and I was released.

Totally drained, I dropped to the floor. It felt as if something had been ripped from my body. I felt like a shell.

"That wasn't so bad now, was it?" Rhiannon said. "By the time you sign the contract tomorrow, you won't even notice it's gone. Trust me. While you're rolling in dough, you won't miss it."

Catching my breath, I looked up into the mirror. Past my reflection, past my idol, Derrick Marsdale, there I was. I looked like I was going to throw up. Frozen in eternity stood my soul. The look of horror and torment surpassed all the others.

"I want it back," I was able to groan.

"Like you say, or at least think, a deal's a deal," she said.

She walked over to the mirror and bent down to unlatch it from the pole.

"NO!" I screamed as I got to my knees.

Using her bent body for balance, I grabbed my father's dagger and plunged it into the glass. Now it was the psychic's turn to scream.

Time seemed to move in slow motion. A hole punctured the glass, and we both watched as the cracks slowly moved their way to the frame.

The cracks widened, and my soul slipped through and like a shot snapped back into my body. I could picture a tiny me, shivering and curled up, hiding in some corner of my being. But at least I felt whole again.

The other souls weren't as lucky. With nowhere to go, they melted down the mirror like a Salvador Dali painting. The only thing left of them were puddles on the floor. As I looked up, the glass shattered, dropping to a pile of dust.

"You don't know what you've done," the psychic whispered in deadly quiet.

She stormed out of the bedroom, and with renewed strength, I got up to follow. She flung the door open.

"Wait," I called.

She stopped and looked back.

"You fool!" Rhiannon screamed.

She turned around and walked smack into the door, banging her face along the edge. She yelled an obscenity and slammed the door behind her.

I winced. That must have hurt. I ran after her, but by the time I got to the door, she had disappeared. I ran down the hall, but she was nowhere to be seen.

The phone was ringing when I walked back into the apartment. I picked it up. It was Stan.

"Sorry, kid. They'd promised me it was a done deal. At the last second they decided that they wanted a 'name.' They're going with Brad Pitt. Nothing I could do."

My heart sank. Brad Pitt? That hack?

"You gonna be all right, kid? That's Hollywood, I guess. Nature of the beast and all. We'll get 'em next time."

"No, we won't," I whispered after hanging up the receiver.

With only one thing to do when I feel that depressed, I pulled out the vodka (wouldn't need a glass tonight) and a disc of "The Little Tramp." If he couldn't cheer me up, at least I'd pass out trying.

I slipped the movie in the DVD, sat back, and took a long, heavy swig off the bottle. I don't remember if I swallowed any of it. Most, if not all of the vodka, came spraying out of my mouth. The movie that I'd watched so many times looked different. It wasn't a remake. Everybody was the same, except for one. Some guy named Chaplin had replaced the late, great Bruce Tenneson. What a dink. Who thought anyone could ever hold a candle to Tenneson?

Someone was playing with my head. I ejected the disc and examined it. It was mine all right. Still had the nick on it from when I dropped it on the floor. Something definitely wasn't right.

I pulled out another movie, "The Maltese Falcon." My blood chilled as I put it in and pressed the play button. "C'mon, Derrick."

A bomb exploded in the pit of my stomach. Who the hell was Humphrey Bogart? And what the hell kind of name is Humphrey? I couldn't believe what I was seeing. Lorre and Greenstreet were there. Everyone but Sam Spade were who they should be.

My God. What had I done?

My hands shook as I ejected the disc. I had no movies of Oslund or Merriweather, but I sprang to my feet as I remembered I had a Hollywood movies encyclopedia.

There was no reference to either one. I choked back a sob when I couldn't find Marsdale or Tenneson either. Then I remembered, page 66, a beautiful picture of Merriweather dressed as Cleopatra. "What the hell is a Theda Bara?" After staring at her for a minute, I had to confess that she wasn't half-bad.

Although Oslund wasn't in the book, I did a cross-reference with my favorite Oslund movie, "The Wild One." As I had feared, the starring role was with some strange guy, a Marlon Brando. Where did they come up with these names?

I plopped back onto the couch, took a long swig from the booze and stared at the ceiling. It began to sink in what I had just done. I thought about the four lives I'd ruined and the four lives that I'd made into stars. Eight lives nothing! I started thinking about their families, friends, and agents; then, producers, directors, the list went on. My God! What had I done?

It took the rest of that bottle then three-quarters of the next pint before I was safely back into self-pity. "The hell with them," I rationalized in my drunken state. "Look what I just did to me?" I'd just thrown away what I'd worked my whole life to achieve. As tears rolled down my face I thought of my favorite Oslund line – "I coulda been a contender."

A PEACEFUL LAKE

The week had been hectic and laboring. Mandatory overtime had everyone on edge. Kyle Holmes couldn't remember how many times his boss had threatened to fire him. He calculated at least once per day since the accounting error on Monday. When Friday finally came, after his two hours of overtime, Kyle got into his car, and drove. With no family to speak of, and no close friends, the weekends were his own. Many Friday evenings he'd get in his car and cruise until the sun came up. It became a ritual he defined as relaxation.

He drove north. Not because he had a particular destination, but because as rush hour slowly eased, northbound on the freeway had the least amount of traffic. Into the night Kyle drove. Stars speckled the black sky, and only the outlines of the trees could be seen as his car sped farther and farther away from Minneapolis, and his office.

It worked like magic, as it always did. With each mile, the tightness in his chest loosened and the tension around his head relaxed. Instead of becoming tired with the passing hours, he became invigorated – more alive.

The sun peeked above the horizon and Kyle realized he

hadn't a clue as to where he was, lost somewhere in the north woods. Sometime during the night he had exited off of the freeway and onto a paved road, then later a dirt road that had slowly narrowed to nothing more than a path, barely wide enough for his car.

Must have been an old logging road at one time, he thought. That was okay, the drive had done its job. Clean forest air and no distractions had cleansed his mind from work. The week of stress had eroded down to peace.

Find a nice spot to park, take a short nap, then head for home and still have a day to relax before another week of memos, faxes, meetings, and missed deadlines.

The road ended. Kyle stopped, got out of his car, and looked around. He stood in a small clearing of tall marsh grass. It would take a little maneuvering, but he could turn the car around. Before worrying about that, he climbed up on the hood, resting his back against the windshield, and relaxed while looking up at the clouds. His imagination turned them into a rabbit being chased by a kangaroo in one part of the sky, and a man with puffy cheeks staring back at him in another.

A soft wind rattled the leaves, and Kyle filled his lungs with deep woods' air as he sat up. He felt the knot of his tie still pressing against his throat and tugged it loose, snapping the top button of his shirt. He didn't care. Life felt too good at the moment. Before closing his eyes, he looked around one more time. The only thing to complete this picture of serenity would be a deer or two entering through the trees to nibble on some grass.

Instead, a gust of wind blew in. Kyle looked in awe as the grass blew in opposite directions, opening a small path. A soft voice he felt rather than heard whispered his name. He couldn't resist. Kyle slid off the car and entered the woods.

After no more than a five minute hike, the trail ended. Before him stood a lake so clean that he could see the sand under the water. It wasn't a big lake – the far shore looked close enough for a relaxing swim if he'd felt so inclined. But, there didn't seem to be much across the way to entice him. Only pine, spruce, and birch lined the other side. He had the exact same thing here. Shifting his attention back to the water, Kyle thought he might have discovered the last untouched lake in Minnesota.

Jutting out from the shore, a large rock of granite towered out and above the water. Kyle took off his shoes and socks and boosted himself up, sitting like a king on a throne surveying his kingdom. Pieces of sun glittered across the lake. Kyle let his legs dangle over the edge, his bare feet inches above the water that gently slapped the shore. He had no idea the name of this lake, if it even had one, but the only thing that mattered was its quiet peacefulness. And he was alone.

Kyle could have been dreaming; that's what he thought as he looked over the water and saw the crystals of reflected sun gather together. He tried to shade his eyes with his hand as the brightness took shape.

The blinding light slowly sank into the lake. Then, as if it wanted nothing to do with the sun, the water spewed it up like a geyser. As the lake settled, standing in the middle on top of the water, he saw a woman.

Kyle had to rub his eyes. Could he be in a dream? He had to be. She had fair blue skin with white hair that flowed down her shoulders in soft waves. A robe draped over her body like a gentle waterfall. Her eyes, like two ice crystals, stared into his.

Unlike King Arthur's the Lady of the Lake, there was no Excalibur in her hand as she reached out to him. Part of Kyle wanted to run, jump in his car, and never complain about work again. Instead, he sat mesmerized as the woman floated toward him. After all, this had to be a dream and he wanted to see where it would lead.

She stood in front of him, her arm reaching out to be taken. Hesitantly, Kyle took her hand. The skin felt cold, but so soft, like he could squeeze his fingers right through her.

Gently she pulled, and Kyle surprised himself by letting her guide him. He convinced himself it didn't matter. If things got too scary, he would force himself awake. He'd done it before during nightmares. He'd probably find himself back on the hood of his car.

Instead of floating above the water, like she had before, they sank deeper and deeper as they waded in. The water felt warm and inviting as it lapped up to his thighs, but as they went farther down, it turned cold and demanding.

As the water reached his chin, Kyle tried to force himself awake, struggling for release. As the water came above his nose he panicked, but the woman hugged him, keeping him trapped.

Something clicked in Kyle's brain. Not even knowing if he really was asleep, he gave up the thought of waking, gave up the thought of fighting. There was no need to resist. He could feel that this was right.

~ ~ ~

The lake had sensed a new presence – another lost child looking for a home. The family had grown over time, but there was always plenty of space for the lost.

It chose the form of mother to greet its new adopted son. Children wanted a mother figure to welcome them.

She saw the child sitting on the big rock, alone, sensing that he wanted a family. She felt his loneliness, his need to belong. She reached out to him. It pleased her that he took her hand. So many others had tried to run, thinking that they had changed their minds. But this one knew.

It came as no surprise that he put up a small struggle at first. Everyone had a right to be frightened in the beginning. But quicker than most, this one knew he had found home.

EDGING PAST REALITY

A lvin Hershey couldn't explain the feeling that crept over him. Not fear exactly, more like an eerie trepidation. *Gotta be the turbulence,* he decided.

"I have you pegged for a Scotch on the rocks." The flight attendant smiled as she stopped her cart, blocking the narrow aisle.

Alvin looked up and the feeling passed. "Never really developed a taste for it." He used his flirtatious smile. "I'll take a beer, though."

The vacation was over. Los Angeles in December felt like Eden compared to Minneapolis. For two weeks he and his best friend since before high school, Jeffery Carpenter, bummed around Hollywood doing touristy things, hanging out at strip bars, going to fancy restaurants and looking for famous faces. They even scored a couple of tickets to the L.A. Kings. Unfortunately, the Minnesota Wild were playing in Calgary. Their only appearance in L.A. wouldn't be until the end of February.

On the days his friend had to work, Alvin would go to a museum, or sit at the beach and draw.

An artist by trade, an artist by genes, Alvin could not help but draw. He relished the feelings of free drawing now that ninety percent of his work had to be the noncreative crap strictly for the ad agency. Eight hours a day, Monday through Friday, hunched over a drawing table, Alvin buried his creativity to draw the 'perfect' picture for lame copy. They told him what to draw, and even how they expected it to look. But the work was steady, although short lived.

Aaron Wright, Executive Vice President, fired his twenty-three-year-old secretary, Brenda Stein, when she not only refused his advances, but had the audacity to complain. The sexual harassment lawsuit she brought against the company had been nothing exceptional from any other lawsuit, except Brenda's boyfriend worked at the Star Tribune. A reporter ready to prove to his editor, and to the world, that he could write a damn good story, he went after the V.P. with zeal.

When the lawsuit went public, six of their top clients decided to go elsewhere. Speculation rumored that more would follow.

Of the four artists, Alvin had least seniority in the art department. Three had been there over five years, Alvin just one. The gossip from upstairs filtered down that the art department could easily get by on three artists, if not two. Now, a lay-off seemed inevitable.

Thinking tomorrow would be pink slip day, he conditioned himself not to take it personally. Having been laid off before, he kind of liked the idea. Unemployment compensation was a gimme.

~ ~ ~

The remote control clicked through the cable channels and the phone rang, interrupting Alvin's idling mind.

"Hello?"

"Alvin. Is it really you? This is Jerry."

His friend's voice sounded unusually excited.

"Jerry, how ya doin'?"

"I just got a thank-you note. It was your handwriting. I couldn't believe it."

"Yeah? Why?" Alvin couldn't understand the enthusiasm.

"I mean I was thrilled that you were alive. But the note, what the hell?"

"What do you mean? I was just thanking you for putting me up and showing me around all last week."

"Alvin, what kind of joke are you playing on me? Months ago . . ." his voice cracked . . . "I hear you died. First time I cried since I was a kid. Then I get this crazy note from you. You weren't here last week, at least not with me." Jerry sounded as fazed as Alvin felt.

Now Alvin's voice carried on his friend's animation.

"What do you mean died? What kind of joke are you playing on me, Jer? Ain't funny, man."

After a long silence, Jerry's voice had changed. "Am I on some new reality show? What's it called, 'Fuck with your friend's mind'?"

"I could ask you the same thing."

"Alvin, you're pissin' me off. The joke's over, okay?"

Alvin's voice verged on panic. "Jerry, you took me to a Kings game. We went to the Improv, and threw bread crumbs to the gulls on Venice Beach. Now what the hell are you talking about?"

"I went to the Kings game last week, but it was with Rhonda, not you. I haven't been to the Improv for years, and I haven't been to Venice Beach since I was mugged there over two years ago. For the last time, the joke's over. Tell me what's going on or I'm hanging up."

"I don't know what you're talking about . . ."

So uncharacteristic of his friend, Alvin could only wait for Jerry to let him in on the joke.

"I thought it would be a thrill talking to you again. I was wrong." Jerry hung up.

As if in a trance, Alvin stuck the phone back in its cradle

and blankly stared at the TV. He finished the beer and got his senses back just long enough to get another. The twelve-pack sat empty before the clock hit ten.

The next morning, Alvin went into work and like always threw his jacket over the chair. Only half jokingly he looked at his fellow artists. "I did go on vacation to Los Angeles, right?"

"You tell us," Jack said. "You weren't here for a week, and you did say you were going to L.A. Did you?"

Senior Artist, Jack Hafter, also did freelance exhibits. Forty-five years old, he had been with the company for eight years, and was unquestionably the most talented of the four. He'd even won awards for the company.

Alvin sat at his desk, looked around conspiratorially, and motioned for Jack to come closer where they could talk in whispers. He felt most comfortable with Jack and often confided his more personal insecurities.

"Something happened to me," he said. Alvin trusted Jack. He told him about the phone call knowing that their conversation would go no further than that room. Alvin finished and waited for Jack to start laughing.

Jack's face went blank. A door opened that both of them ignored.

"I've heard about this once before." Jack's voice eerily lacked any hint of emotion. "A couple of years ago there was this case about . . ."

"Sorry Alv, Gard wants to see you right away." Shelly Mouse stood in the open doorway with the most pitiful look on her face. A fellow artist, next lowest on the seniority list, Alvin knew that she felt sorry for him, but more importantly to her, she was the next artist in line if more layoffs were to follow.

"Sorry Alvin. You're a damn good artist. I'm sure you'll have no trouble getting a new job. Feel free to use my name as a reference." Jack put his hand on Alvin's shoulder. "We'll continue our conversation later."

Alvin looked at both Jack and Shelly, put on an artificial

smile, took a deep breath and walked out the door.

Sixty-three years old and founder of Ad-Gard, Inc., Gary Gard was hard working, honest, and a man who didn't believe in delegating work unless absolutely necessary. His poor business sense kept Ad-Gard, Inc. from becoming the foremost agency in Minneapolis advertising. His latest faux pas had been ignoring the sexual harassment complaints, publicly backing his vice president, and calling Miss Stein a money-hungry liar.

Alvin knocked. "You wanted to see me Mr. Gard?"

"Come in and shut the door." He paused to look at the three by five card on his desk, "Mr. Hershey . . ."

~ ~ ~

Alvin opened the door back at his office. Helen Stier, the fourth artist, had arrived making the foursome complete.

"He told me I was doing a great job and gave me a fifty percent raise," Alvin said.

"I thought you were going to get laid off." Shock radiated from Helen's face.

Alvin grinned "You are so gullible."

Alvin looked over at Jack for a confirmation of an 'I gotchya' but Jack sat at his desk and stared blankly at the wall.

Alvin became somber. "He said I could finish the day and gave me three weeks' severance. But if you all don't mind, I think I'd rather just take off."

Andrew packed all of his belongings in one box. On his way out the door, Alvin gave Helen and Shelly a hug and shook hands with Jack.

"Give me a call and we'll finish our conversation," whispered Jack.

"You can count on it." Alvin walked to the door and stopped. He put down the box and went back to Jack, embracing him.

A cold bite in the air nipped at Alvin as he stopped at the liquor store on the way home. By the time he got to his apartment the pint of vodka was half empty.

~ ~ ~

Selling sidewalk art and doing caricatures at birthday parties, Alvin had eked out an existence until enough time had elapsed that he could apply for unemployment. He enjoyed the lifestyle and would have liked to exist that way, but rent and food kept kicking him in the ass, reminding him that his savings was nearly depleted.

Alvin looked up from his drafting table at the ringing phone. He sensed who it was before he picked up the receiver. It had a government ring to it. The unemployment office told him to report the following morning at 8:15. *So much for sleeping in.*

By 8:00 a.m., Alvin sat fuming in a hard plastic chair at the unemployment office. Once again he'd woken up with a queasy feeling in his gut, a feeling he'd had a number of times now since he returned home from vacation. And now some pencil-pusher had told him that they had no record of his appointment. In an effort to be accommodating, a Mr. Simon would forego his break and get a file on Alvin together.

At 10:10 they called his name. "Please follow me, Mr. Hershey."

Alvin followed the overweight, gray-haired man to a little cubbyhole of an office with faded-green cubical walls.

"Mr. Hershey, I'm having a little problem with your application for unemployment."

Alvin raised his eyebrows. "What seems to be the problem?"

"I'll get right to the point."

Alvin placed his hands on his lap, cracking his knuckles. "Please do."

"Mr. Hershey, I tried to verify your employment. They have no record of your ever having worked at Ad-Gard."

For the second time in as many weeks, Alvin felt stunned. "But I worked there. Call Gary Gard! He laid me off himself!"

83

He slammed his hands on Simon's desk.

"I talked to Mr. Gard," Simon said, unfazed. "He said he never heard of you. He checked his files and said that you've never worked there."

"That's impossible." Alvin's voice brought the attention of security.

"Do you have any verification, like check stubs? Anything like that?" Simon waved away the officer like he'd been in this situation too many times before. The officer stood by the doorway.

"Ask any of my co-workers. They all know me."

"Any other verification?" Simon asked again.

"I cash my checks and toss the stubs. I just don't save things. Listen Mr. Simon, my mother was a pack rat. She saved everything. It drove me crazy." Alvin bit his tongue to keep from any further babbling.

"I suggest you talk to your bank. Or the IRS should have records."

"I'll do that," Alvin lied. He didn't think it would be wise to tell a man who worked for the government that he never filed tax returns and never held money long enough to open an account. He cashed his checks at the pawn shop, for a hefty fee, and made a deal with his landlord. He paid cash and got a ten percent discount while the landlord collected unreported income.

"You know," Simon said while staring suspiciously into Alvin's eyes. "I have heard of small illegitimate companies destroying records of employees, but they always paid out cash. I thought I had heard everything, but to be quite honest with you Mr. Hershey, this is a first for me. The only reason I'm not going to report you to the police is that I can't believe anyone would be so stupid as to make up working for a company when they know it's going to be checked out. I think you really believe you worked there. But then, I don't work in mental health."

"Good Lord," Alvin jumped up from his chair. "I'm being lectured to by a civil servant. Life is just fucking wonderful."

He looked for something to throw and saw a stapler sitting on Simon's desk. That would do well for starters.

"Is there a problem in here?"

Alvin whipped around. Inches from his face, a brick shit-house in a cop's uniform looked ready to kick some artist ass.

"If you could escort Mr. Hershey to the door, please," Simon said calmly.

After retreating to the sanctity of the liquor store, Alvin decided there was no better place to spend the rest of his cash. Alvin never drank before noon but today he would make an exception.

That goddamned feeling now washed over him like waves.

Locked in his apartment, Alvin felt ready to tie one on. Chugging his second brew, the conversation with Jack Hafter popped into his head. They never did get together, but now Jack would be able to tell that government flunky that Alvin had worked there. As he reached for the phone, it rang.

"Hello?"

"Alv, this is Jerry. How ya been doin'?"

"All right," he answered cautiously. "You okay?"

"I'm fine. Just called to check up on you. I haven't heard from you since you left." Alvin froze, he didn't know for how long. "Hey Alv, you okay?"

"What about the thank-you note?" he whispered as ice seemed to envelope his body.

"What thank-you note?"

"I sent you a thank-you note."

"Never got it. Musta got lost in the mail."

Alvin began feeling sick to his stomach. "Let me call you back, Jer, I'm not feeling too well right now." He hung up the phone before getting a response.

Alvin made a dash for the bathroom. After emptying his stomach, he picked up the phone and called his old work number.

"Thank you for calling Ad-Gard. May I help you?"

85

"Helen, this is Alvin. How are you?"

"Do I know you, sir?"

"Helen, it's me. Alvin. Quit kidding around and let me talk to Jack."

There was silence for a few seconds then Alvin heard, "Jack, there's an Alvin somebody on the phone for you. He sounds kind of strange. You want to talk to him?"

Another couple seconds of silence. "Can I help you?"

"Jack, it's me, Alv."

"Do I know you, sir?"

"Don't do this to me Jack, I'm in no mood. I was just rejected for unemployment because that jerk, Gard, has no record of my employment."

"Then I suggest you call personnel, sir. This is the art department. Would you like me to transfer the call?"

"This isn't funny, Jack. C'mon now, this is Alvin you're talking to."

"Sir, I'm very busy . . ."

"Wait." Again, panic crept into Alvin's voice. "Don't you remember our conversation? I told you about my friend in California. He didn't remember my visit just a couple days later. You said you heard of something like this. You were about to tell me about it then Shelly came into the room. You said you'd tell me about it later."

After a long pause, Jack asked, "What did you say your name was?"

"C'mon Jack, it's Alvin. Alvin Hershey!"

"Mr. Hershey, there's a bar just a couple of blocks from here . . ."

"I know the one you're talking about, Jack. You always stop there after work for one Manhattan."

Again there was a pause. Finally, "Meet me there at five-thirty. I assume you'll know who I am."

What the hell did he mean by that? "I'll be there, Jack."

Alvin hung up the phone, opened the Scotch, and took a

couple swigs from the bottle. His throat closed and he coughed up the last mouthful. For the first time in three years he had a terrible urge for a cigarette.

~ ~ ~

The neon Coors clock showed 5:15. Alvin nursed his second glass of water trying to ignore the glare of the bartender. He'd found enough money in his apartment to pay for a pack of cigarettes. Already, the girl at the corner store, the girl he took out once last summer, didn't recognize him. This was the girl who wanted to stay just friends, but still liked to flirt and exchange obscene jokes when he came into the store. Bedroom jokes, she used to tease him. Today when he told her his latest joke, she threatened to call the police.

At 5:35, Jack Hafter walked in and sat at his usual stool at the end of the bar. For the first time in Alvin's life, he noticed that Jack looked nervous. The most laidback, in-control man Alvin had ever known, looked nervous.

"Jack." Alvin half ran, half stumbled over to the bar.

He looked into Jack's eyes and saw no sign of recognition.

"You're Alvin Hershey?"

Alvin wanted to cry. This man had been his mentor for the last year.

"Yes," he replied as calmly as he could.

"Have a seat Mr. Hershey. I'm going to tell you a story that I doubt you're going to like. In fact, I highly doubt you're even going to believe."

Without exchanging a word, the bartender brought a Manhattan and placed it in front of Jack. "Another water for you, sir?" His voice dipped in sarcasm.

"He'll have what I'm having," Jack said. He looked at Alvin. "You'll need it."

Alvin nodded his head.

Jack took a large swallow and let the vermouth and rye slide down his throat. He took a deep breath and began picking at his cocktail napkin.

"Tell me everything that's happened to you. At least since the strange things started."

Alvin told him about L.A., the two calls from Jerry, the unemployment office and the girl at the store. He talked about the strange feeling that would suddenly creep upon him and the thoughts about his going insane.

"Maybe you are going insane," Jack said while tearing his napkin. "First, let me tell you, if it's what I think it is, things will get better. The bad news is I think it will get worse first."

The bartender set the Manhattan in front of Alvin. He downed it in two swallows and looked at Jack with pleading eyes. Jack nodded and Alvin ordered another.

The television set at the end of the bar came on, and a group of five men in business suits gathered to watch the pre-game show. To Alvin's amazement, the Minnesota North Stars were playing the Boston Bruins. A friendly argument could already be heard over the outcome of the game. More men and women in business suits filtered in and the noise level rose.

"The North Stars? They moved to Dallas!" Alvin said, bewildered.

Jack shook his head, "What the hell are you talking about?"

"The North Stars. Norm Green bought em and moved the team to Dallas. Years ago." Alvin's voice verged on hysteria.

"Hockey in Dallas? How many drinks have you had before I got here?"

Sweat rolled down Alvin's face. "Can we move somewhere else? Between this and the noise, I'm getting a little spooked."

"You'll be all right."

Concentrating at what his fingers were doing, Jack spoke softly. "I'm not sure when it started or how long it took, but I first noticed it about ten years ago. Old friends knew me, but they remembered a different past. New friends had no idea who I was. I went to my job to find out I had never worked there. I'd get a new job and found out I didn't work there. I saw a guy who I knew and he knew me, then he didn't, then he did and asked me why I stopped showing up for work from the job I had, then didn't have." He looked up from his napkin. "Is this making any sense?"

Alvin didn't disappoint. His jaw hung slack while his eyes looked like they were in a hypnotic trance.

"I committed myself, Mr. Hershey. For two months I stayed in a hospital. The doctors summed it up to a nervous breakdown. They had me almost believing it too, until today. Then you called."

Alvin couldn't tell if it sounded like vindication or regret in Jack's voice. A shout reverberated down the bar. The North Stars scored the first goal. Jack Hafter did something for the first time since becoming a regular at the bar. He ordered another Manhattan. The bartender raised his eyebrows, picked up the empty glass and shredded napkin and replaced both. Alvin switched back to his water.

"I started thinking today where I left off when I entered the hospital. Mr. Hershey, I don't know how, I don't know why, but I do believe I did, and maybe you are, walking a line between parallel dimensions, or worlds. Right now I believe you're hopping back and forth just like I did years ago. It felt like all my nerves were tingling at once. Maybe similar to those strange feelings you're having. It lasted a few weeks then went away. Pretty soon you'll settle in one side or the other. I don't know. For me it was the other. Maybe for you it will be in the one you started in. If you're lucky, it will be this one. Who'd want to live in a world where they play hockey south of the Mason Dixon line? Do they even know that ice can be used for something besides cooling drinks?"

Alvin choked and water sprayed out his nose. Jack stopped picking at his napkin and smiled at the sight.

"Normally I'd say you should be recommitted, but this is just hitting too close to home," Alvin said while wiping his nose.

"What do you suggest I do?"

"All I can say is try to roll with the flow without going too crazy."

Alvin nodded. "What about your other self?"

"All I can guess is that when I cross that line, so does he. Who knows? There might be two, three, ten, ten million Jacks on ten million different planes. Whatever the case, I've never seen myself."

"If it's any consolation, I have. At least one of you, anyway. He's also working at Ad-Gard, and he also seems to know something happened. He was about to tell me but we got interrupted."

"I don't know why, but that makes me feel a little better," Jack said. He began tearing at his new napkin. "Well Mr. Hershey, I've had one drink too many and it's time for me to leave. I wish you the best. If you end up here, give me a call and we'll talk. Next time maybe you can give me answers." Jack Hafter got up from his stool, laid some money on the bar, and walked out the door.

Without warning, Alvin was very tired. He thought of staying to watch the rest of the game, just out of nostalgia, but decided to watch it at home instead. Home still had a few beers, and there he could drink it for free.

~ ~ ~

Turning the key, Alvin opened the door and stepped in. He flipped on the light and froze. He'd walked into his apartment, of that he was sure, but the furniture didn't belong to him. He looked around and from out of nowhere, a piercing scream scalded his eardrums. He looked into the face of an hysterical woman. A man came running out of the bedroom wearing only pajama bottoms and carrying a pistol. Alvin couldn't move. His legs felt as if they were embedded in concrete.

"How'd you get in here?" the man screamed. "Laura, call the police."

Alvin got his feet back and made a mad dash for the street expecting a loud crack in the air and to feel a bullet shatter his spine. Neither one happened. He finally stopped running when he reached the park four blocks away. He sat on a bench staring up at the sky for the remainder of the night. No one had ever pointed a gun at him before. Alvin knew that there would be no sleep tonight.

At six o'clock the following morning, the sun rose orange in a cloudless sky. Alvin hugged himself, shivering. Fortunately, the weather gods had looked after him and kept the overnight temperatures in the twenties, a blessing for early March.

He had more questions than the night before and fewer answers. If what Jack said was true, if there were a parallel world, or worlds, what different paths had the other Alvin, or Alvins, taken? Why did no one recognize him? Had he moved to another city? Alvin's mind felt like a computer ready to crash. Too many questions and nowhere to look for answers.

It hit him. "How could I be so stupid?"

He remembered his conversation with Jerry. "I'm dead. At least in this world, the other me is dead."

With his adrenaline pumping, Alvin made his way to the library. Closed. He ran to get some breakfast, went back to the library, and went half-crazy waiting for the doors to open. At nine the doors unlocked and he raced to the microfilm machine. *Please let me be on the other side.* He knew he was. He could feel it.

After three and one-half hours of scrolling through microfilm, Alvin found what he'd been looking for in the Star Tribune obituary section. This other world stuff began to make sense.

"Murder Victim Identified As Local Artist"

The other Alvin Hershey died from a stabbing outside his apartment just over a year ago. Nothing remarkable, just an innocent victim of a robbery. Tried, convicted and sentenced, a three-time-loser went to prison, for life. *What a waste. Well, life*

91

should be easier now. As long as I stay in this world, all I have to do is start over.

~ ~ ~

A new life needed a new name. He liked 'Alvin'. That would have to stay. His parents said they named him after Alvin the chipmunk. Alvin Monk had a ring to it, middle name Charles. He laughed to himself as he imagined passing out business cards, 'A. Chip Monk'. *If that doesn't say 'artist' what does?* "I love it!"

Alvin applied, but couldn't get a job at Ad-Gard. He did get work at another ad agency, but he felt a bit like an outsider. The other two had been working together for years. They tried to make him feel welcome and went out of their way to include him, asking for his input. They invited him to join them for lunch and even bought him a present for his birthday. *Yup, this is going to work out just fine.*

Payday Friday, the artists ritualistically went to the bar to unwind from another exhausting week at work. They drank, talked about real art and the galleries where they'd like to show their work, and drank some more. After a couple Scotch and waters, Alvin excused himself from the table. As he wove his way between tables, heading toward the restroom, a woman sprang up, and without looking turned right into him, spilling her rum and Coke down the front of Alvin's shirt.

"I'm so sorry," the girl said.

A disgusted Alvin looked up from his shirt, ready to let go a few obscenities. Then he saw her eyes. The most beautiful blue he'd ever seen. The sun reflecting off the clearest lake didn't sparkle as much.

"It's quite all right," Alvin smiled. "Alvin Hershey." He momentarily forgot about his new name and held out his hand. "But friends call me Chip." He tried to recover. *Oh God. Chip Hershey, chocolate Chip. Ugh.*

"Linda Ellis." She took his hand and held it in hers.

The way she smiled, Alvin knew she'd made the same

connection, but she didn't say a word about it. After he thought about it, was it really any worse than Chip Monk?

"Actually, I kind of like Alvin," she smiled.

"Then Alvin it is."

Linda worked as a computer programmer in a small accounting firm down the street from Alvin's office. Since that first meeting, they met at the bar every evening after work. Alvin, acting sentimental, tried to reserve the table where they met. They talked for hours and were both amazed at how much they seemed to have in common. Politics, religion, marriage, they both wanted children, but not yet. Linda even dabbled in art. Every Sunday afternoon, Alvin would be in Linda's apartment offering his expertise and guidance. He told her he would always volunteer to look at her etchings any time at all.

For three months they saw each other almost every day, and it was Linda who brought up the discussion of living together. Alvin reached across the table. "Twist my arm."

Just as Linda rested her fingers on his arm, Alvin shouted, "Okay. You win, we'll move in together."

The next day at work, Alvin couldn't sit still, giddy with excitement. Not only was he going to move in with his love, but at lunch he had picked up a ring: a half-carat diamond with a thin gold band that swirled around the mount.

"Think she'll say yes?" Alvin danced between the artists' tables.

His co-workers couldn't resist smiling at his goofy grin, the faraway look in his eyes, and the way he couldn't sit still for more than two minutes at a time.

Five o'clock finally came. He felt a bit off, but figured it to be nerves. Alvin raced to the bar. He had to dash to make sure he could snare "their" table. He had it planned perfectly in his mind. Her rum and Coke glass balancing on a small box that, when she lifted her drink, Alvin would reach across the table and pop open, exposing the ring.

With Linda's drink across the table, Alvin stared at the

people as they entered the bar. A bundle of nervous energy with nowhere to go. Six o'clock came and went; no Linda. Concern turned to anger, to confusion, to worry. As Alvin looked down and saw the shredded cocktail napkin at his fingertips, the memory of Jack popped into his head. Alvin knew and it hit him hard.

"It's not fair!" he shouted. "I built a new life here!"

Customers stared as a wild man raced out of the bar, leaving an untouched drink sitting on top of a small box.

Alvin pounded on the door to what he prayed was Linda's apartment. The door opened a couple of inches, the chain keeping it from opening any wider. Linda peered through the crack. A wave of relief washed through Alvin.

"Yes?"

The relief drained instantly away as he looked at her blank stare. He reached into his pocket and realized that he didn't have the ring.

"Yes?" she said, this time with a little less patience.

"I'm sorry." The words choked their way up Alvin's throat. "Wrong apartment."

As Alvin walked down the hall, he heard the door close and the sound of a bolt sliding into place. He had to stop and catch his breath. He'd swear to anybody who would listen that hearts do cry. Out on the street, a cool breeze slapped Alvin in the face. He turned around to look at his new world, wondering if this was where he was going to stay.

Back at the bar, he sat down at his table. A sympathetic waitress handed him his box with the ring.

"I kept it safe for you," she said.

Alvin tried to say 'thank you' but the words caught in his throat. He ordered a Manhattan, gulped it down and ordered another before the waitress had a chance to walk away from the table. He drank four more before they cut him off.

Accounting firms advertise don't they? Of course they do, and they'll need an artist too.

He stuck the ring in his pocket and passed out for the night.

THE WITNESS

It was against company policy, but Francis didn't care. The feeling of freedom outweighed the risks as he unhooked the safety line from his harness belt and sat on the platform, his legs dangling over the side. Thirty stories below he looked at the little dots that were people scurrying to get to their cars in a vain attempt to beat rush hour traffic.

"You're already too late," he shouted down to no one in particular. From his vantage point he could see that there had been an accident on the freeway. Already cars were backing up, east because of the wreckage, and west because of the gawkers.

Francis wiped the sweat from his face, the start of evening cooled off the day's heat. The sun still sat above the horizon and cast a carrot glow from his red hair. Freckles merged with the lobster colored skin from his broad shoulders.

Smiling, he picked up his shirt that lay next to him and reached in his breast pocket, pulling out a pack of smokes, and a book of matches. Francis knew better than to leave his shirt lying like that on the scaffold. He had already lost three, but it was too bothersome to tie around the safety bar.

The sun started to set and there were a few wispy clouds

in the sky, reddish orange against a darkening blue background. He loved watching the sun go down, almost as much as taking his squeegee out of the bucket of dirty water, and flick it on the people below.

But not tonight. He was in too good a mood. It was Friday, payday, and tonight he was going to take Donna out to a fancy restaurant and ask her to be his bride. He had an appointment after work to pick up the ring.

Sweethearts from high school, two years more to grow up, he decided it was time to live together and start a family. She had been dropping hints for almost a year waiting for the question – "Will you marry me?" Everything was right with the world.

Francis hoisted himself up and went to press the button and begin his slow descent. As the scaffold began its way down, a wind whipped around the corner of the building. The safety rope that dangled over the edge, snapped up. The metal clasp smacked him painfully in the knee. His leg buckled and Francis lost his balance. The cigarette flew from his mouth as he slipped into the safety bar, and like a gymnast, did a flip over the top.

His eyes went wild as he somersaulted off the structure. He flailed his arms blindly for anything to grab onto that wasn't air. Miraculously, his hand smacked into the safety rope. Fist instantly clenched, Francis held on, literally for his life. The evening shade cast its shadow over a face in agonizing pain as Francis felt the rope burn into his hand. A twisted arm felt as if it was being pulled from its socket.

"Don't look down, don't look down, don't look down," he kept repeating to himself while staring up at the bottom of the scaffold.

Uncontrollably, he looked down. The burning fist clenched tighter around the rope, fingernails dug deeper into his palm, drawing blood. The street, the cars, the people, all seemed to be moving in circles as the wind spun Francis like a tangled coil. He jerked up his head and concentrated on the platform above.

The scaffold crept down the building but Francis knew he

wouldn't be able to hold on nearly long enough. With all his strength he brought his other arm around and started to climb the rope.

"Don't look down, don't look down," he kept saying to himself, his gaze fixed on the structure above his head.

Hand over hand he climbed. Wet hair plastered to his face by the river of sweat running from his brow, stinging as it rolled into his eyes.

"Don't look down." He sounded like a broken record until his hand finally reached the metal structure. With adrenaline strength, Francis heaved himself up onto the scaffold. Once on top he lay there on his stomach, arms spread-eagle, each hand grasping opposite sides of the platform. His knuckles were white as he hung on as if his life were still in danger.

As the scaffolding slowly inched its way down, Francis looked into the building and saw a man standing behind his desk staring out the window. The man's horrified look matched the way Francis felt. *He must have seen the whole thing, at least most of it*, Francis thought. He wanted to wave to the man, let him know that everything was okay, but his hands were frozen to the scaffold. Laying flat he was stuck in that position until the platform safely touched the ground.

It took a few minutes before Francis could pry his fingers off the boards and get himself to stand. As he stood with wobbly legs, he looked up and saw a little man in a black suit walk rapidly toward him. His hair was cut short, and his eyes were dark brown. There was intensity in his stare as he approached. It took a couple of seconds but Francis recognized him as the man in the building about fifteen stories up he saw just a few minutes ago.

The man came beside him and put an arm around Francis' shoulder. "Come with me, window washer."

Still in a daze, Francis let the man guide him into the building and into the restroom.

The cold water felt like a drug as Francis cupped his hands in the sink and let his head fall in his palms. Looking up into the mirror he saw the reflection of a gun pointed at his back. The color that had just started to return to his skin instantly vanished again.

"It was the perfect crime," the man said. "Months of planning, an unshakable alibi. Everything mapped out to the smallest detail. Only one thing I could possibly have overlooked – a window washer.

"I thought, maybe he didn't see anything. I mean you were moving down and all, I didn't know how much you saw. But then I saw you lying there like you were trying to hide, and that look on your face. I knew then that you saw me kill her."

Before Francis could utter a word, the man pulled the trigger.

THE SCREAM BOX

Business had picked up a little, but for a Saturday night it was still slow. Brad placed two drinks on the bar, and then, quick with a lighter, he lit the lady's cigarette. At the other end, Gary stared dreamily at table number five. His gaze was on a blond, a brunette, and a redhead, enthralled with their conversation.

"Do you believe this is my first night out since the baby?" the brunette said.

"It's been too long," said the blond, rolling a straw between her fingers.

"You have no idea how good it feels just speaking like an adult for a change. I mean I wouldn't trade Emily for the world, but sometimes I just want to scream."

The jukebox played the Rolling Stones as Gary gazed over the babes.

"Hey, Dreamer, a little help?" Brad shouted over the noise.

Gary smiled from behind the tap.

"You know what I need?" the mom said.

"Sorry, you're married," said the blond. She broke into a giggle.

The brunette ignored the remark. "I need a private room

99

where I can lock myself in and just scream my lungs out. I suppose it would have to be soundproofed so I wouldn't scare the baby."

Gary felt like a cartoon character when the light bulb pops on above your head when you have a brilliant idea.

"What on earth for?" Diane asked.

"You've obviously never had a baby," she answered.

~ ~ ~

"I tell you, this could work," Gary said.

Brad rolled his eyes and continued sweeping the floor. He couldn't count the number of schemes and dreams his partner had come up with over the years to increase business. The few they'd tried turned into disasters.

"We can give the winner some cash, or a free pitcher." Gary turned the chairs over onto the tables.

"It didn't have to be much when we had bowling with frozen turkeys, either. It almost cost us the bar." Brad felt the anger rise in his voice. "And nothing could go wrong with that except some ice melted and that drunk asshole slipped and decided to sue."

"Nothing like that can happen. They just go into a giant box and scream. What can go wrong?"

"I don't know," Brad sighed. "But with our track record, something will."

"I'll build it myself, and we can advertise with fliers. The whole thing will hardly cost any money at all."

Brad shook his head and turned away from his friend. As he pushed the broom, goose bumps broke over his flesh. He tried to come up with reasons why they shouldn't be doing this. Nothing came to mind.

The next morning, Gary paged through the ads and saw exactly what he was looking for: 'Planks of pine and mahogany, already polished, best offer.' He called the number and asked if he could bring the truck later in the day.

~ ~ ~

It had been the best Saturday night crowd the bar had seen in months. Brad had to admit that the fliers had worked their magic. In the back corner by the fire exit stood a large black box on a small stage. A bit larger than a phone booth, the colored lights reflected off its shiny surface. One of the sides swung out on its hinges as a woman, deep crimson in the face and taking heavy breaths, stepped out. Wearing a giant smile, she squinted her eyes to readjust for the light. The crowd roared in approval as she took a seat on the stool and waved in acknowledgment. A small decibel meter attached on the outside was projected on a big screen so everyone in the bar could see.

"We've got a new leader," Gary shouted. The crowd cheered even louder. "Janet peaked at one-hundred-and-eight-point-two decibels. Let's see if Bob can beat it. Bob, come on up."

There were jeers and catcalls from around the bar. The predominantly male crowd wanted short skirts and long legs. Bob had neither but smiled as he took the hecklers in stride. He wasn't the first guy to pay the two-dollar entrance fee and he wanted the fifty-dollar prize as much as any woman there, no matter what the crowd thought of him.

The door closed behind him and the crowd stared at the meter in silent anticipation. Brad stood behind the bar and smiled at his partner. Thirty people had entered the contest, which meant a ten-dollar profit after they awarded the prize. That was nothing compared to the increase in business. Besides, the mob was having a great time. It seemed as if Gary had finally scored with one of his ideas.

The crowd screamed and taunted as the meter reached 105.9 decibels. Bob walked out, red-faced, reaching his arms above his head like he just hit the winning homerun. The mob hollered, hooted, and threw popcorn and peanut shells at him. Gary shook his hand and thanked him for being a good sport.

"We've only got one more!" Gary shouted. The multitude

groaned in unison before Gary cut back in. "Let's see if Helen can snatch the fifty dollars away from Janet."

The men screamed in delight as a woman, a little tipsy, stumbled up on the platform. Helen wore a short denim skirt and black fishnet stockings. Her blouse was thin white silk that covered a black lace bra. Gary wished her luck as he held the door open.

~ ~ ~

She stepped inside the box. What looked like gray egg cartons made of foam padding covered the walls. In the middle of one wall a small pick-up microphone jetted out. She giggled. It reminded her of an erect penis.

The door closed, and she stood alone in total darkness. Grabbing the foam wall to regain her balance, Helen took a deep breath. Just as she was about to release a scream, a hand reached around her head and clamped over her mouth. It pulled her back into the body of a man.

She fought with all her strength against the hand until she felt the flat end of a knife rub against her cheek. Her body froze. The box suddenly reeked of old sweat and stale cigarettes.

"No scream." The voice had a thick Spanish accent.

She nodded her head and he removed his hand from her mouth, but the knife remained stiffly at her throat.

His callused hand moved from her face and down to her breasts. She started to protest, to plead, until she felt the tip of the knife break into her skin. In blackness she stood silently, tears running down her face as the hand fondled her breasts then slowly moved down her stomach.

The man's breathing became heavy as he moved his hand to between her legs. Helen started to gag as a rotten garbage smell flowed from his mouth. He lowered the knife as he pressed his hand between her legs. She felt his bulge press against her ass. All the terror that had welled up in her body exploded.

102

~ ~ ~

"One-hundred-and-ten decibels! We have a new champion!" Gary shouted.

The crowd erupted in cheers and applause as Gary swung open the door. The people closest to the box noticed first. A hush quickly spread throughout the bar. Helen stared out from inside the box, not moving. Her skin matched the white of her blouse except where the eyeliner streaked down her cheeks. Her eyes, open wide, stared straight ahead with an insane look. Gary reached in to help her out of the box. Without moving her eyes she grabbed his arm, digging her fingernails into his skin.

"I guess she's a little afraid of the dark," Gary tried to laugh.

No one in the room laughed back.

~ ~ ~

"We can't give up on it. The scream box will make us a fortune," Gary pled.

"Until the next person who freaks decides to sue us," Brad said.

"They wouldn't have a case. We've got over a hundred witnesses saying she was the only one in the box, and twenty-nine other contestants who came out of the box smiling."

Brad rubbed his eyes and shook his head. "I don't know," he mumbled. "I just don't like it."

"Listen, I'm not going to give up on success because of one unstable broad."

"Okay, okay. But if it happens again, we take it down. Agreed?"

Gary smiled, having chalked up another victory. "Maybe I'll put in a light," he said as an afterthought.

~ ~ ~

Sunday evening brought in a mixture of new faces and

103

repeaters. Brad had already overheard conversations referring to last night, and it gave him an uneasy feeling. More people filled the bar now than the night before. It seemed as if everybody wanted to enter the scream-box contest.

"How y'all doin' tonight?" Gary shouted from in front of the stage.

The crowd whooped and hollered and shook their fists in the air.

They're like lambs and I'm their shepherd. Gary raised his hand in a gesture for the mob to settle down. "Can I get a volunteer to help me out?" he shouted. Again, the noise started up, and almost every hand shot in the air. "Someone who's not entered in the contest," he tried to speak above the roar.

A loud groan echoed off the walls as hands went down. About a dozen hands remained in the air when Gary's eye caught a hot blond about twenty-five years old. He pointed, and she excitedly wove her way through the crowd, careful not to spill any of her drink.

"And what's your name, pretty lady?" Gary asked as he gave her a hand up onto the platform.

"Elsa," she said with a wide smile. The men whistled and cheered.

Elsa's thin golden hair hung down to the middle of her back. She was a little taller than Gary, with small breasts and long legs packed tight in blue jeans that looked molded to her skin. Her crystal green eyes sparkled in the spotlight.

Gary lifted a shoebox and held it above his head. "Elsa, what I need you to do is be my name caller. Just reach in the box and pull out the first name." *And after the bar closes, come home with me and fuck me 'til my brain explodes.*

Elsa gulped the last half of her drink, much to the delight of the crowd.

"Emily Hobson," she called out.

A woman, even taller than Elsa, pushed her way through the mass of bodies shaking her fists in the air like a boxer entering the ring. She was a dark-haired beauty who was big without being fat.

Elsa and Emily, my E girls, Gary thought. *E for ecstasy, erotic, endearing, ecstatic. . .*

A fresh round of applause and cheers snapped him back from his ménage-a-trois fantasy.

"One-hundred-and-seven-point-seven," he said in quick recovery. "Good job Emily. She's setting a high pace folks, one that's going to be tough to beat. Elsa, who's the next contestant?"

Brad smiled from behind the bar as his partner hammed it up. He looked like a natural, a born showman. Brad could have been pissed off being stranded alone at the bar, but the customers didn't seem too upset. Besides, if business kept up at this pace, they'd be able to afford a waitress in no time.

As Elsa read through the names, the atmosphere in the bar seemed pleasantly soused. Laughter carried out through the door, which brought the curious in from the street.

"I don't get it," a woman said as she filled an open seat in front of Brad. "What's the point? Just let em scream in the open."

In all his years working bar, Brad had never been so fascinated by a woman. She wore black boots, black stockings, an incredibly short, black leather mini skirt, and even though it was at least seventy degrees outside, a black leather jacket. Her black hair was moussed in spikes and she wore black lip stick and black eyeliner. One ear was pierced twice in the lobe, and her other ear was pierced all the way around with colored rings. She had a thin gold ring in each nostril. Behind all the decorations, she had the smoothest, whitest, softest looking skin he'd ever seen. Brad was captivated.

"For one thing it doesn't hurt the ears," Brad said. He tried to act macho and nonchalant at the same time. "Besides, people like to go into the box. They probably enjoy the few seconds of silence. In other words, I don't really know."

The woman pulled out a thin cigar, and before she could stick it in her mouth.

"Sorry, no smoking," Brad said.

She shrugged her shoulders and put it back in her purse.

"We could get fined, even lose our license," he added.

"No big deal." She gave him a wink.

Brad stared back while trying to wipe the impish smile from his face. *God, I think I'm in love.*

"Roland Sorenson," Elsa hollered.

Gary smiled as she jumped up and down on the small stage. She was really getting into the act. Of course the now-free alcohol might have helped a little bit.

A young roly-poly man tried to squeeze between people on the crowded floor. As he bumped and grinded into the mass of flesh, they shoved back. Had it not been so thick with humanity, Roland would have gone down. Finally the mob pushed him up to the platform.

"Ewwww, gross. Butt-crack," a girl from the front yelled out.

The mob reveled at the remark as Roland yanked up his pants, his face bright red. A few in the pack started to chant "Go Butt-crack, go." Within seconds the whole floor joined in.

~ ~ ~

Roland tried to be a good sport and laugh it off, but the scars from years of humiliation ran deep, and once again he felt like the tubby little boy in grade school. I'm too old to cry, he kept repeating to himself, as he felt the tears well up in his eyes.

Gary held up a hand, motioning the crowd to ease up. He leaned over to whisper some encouragement, but before he could say a word, Roland darted inside the box and slammed the door.

Dark, warm, and stuffy, but so very quiet, a reminder of those many times as a child he spent hidden in the closet. A click of the door and the outside world went away. Eyes opened or closed, it didn't matter; there was nothing to see, nothing that could be seen. Roland sniffed back the snot that ran from his nose and used his sleeve to wipe his eyes.

He worked himself into a frenzy. His heart beat faster as he took deep, labored breaths. *Have you ever heard the scream of a man who felt all alone in the universe?*

Roland took a deep breath, and then he suddenly stopped. His spine tingled as he felt that not only wasn't he alone in the universe, he wasn't even alone in the box. Staring into the blackness, he stuck his hands out in front of him and out to the sides. All he felt was soft foam padding.

He let out a sigh and tried to calm his racing heart. Shutting his eyes, he took a long drawn breath when a powerful hand grabbed his hair and jerked his head back against what felt like a huge man's shoulder.

From nowhere, the room started to smell of rot and decay. As Roland's face pointed upward, a God-awful breath permeated his nostrils.

"What do you want?" Roland whispered. He couldn't scream now, even if he'd wanted.

A spasm started in his gut and shook through his entire body as an ice-cold piece of metal pressed into his neck. It turned just a fraction and an edge, sharp enough to shave with, caressed his skin. Roland started to whimper.

"Es su tiempo a morir," a low crusty voice whispered.

Even as his mind panicked, Roland recognized the language. He took Spanish in his final two years of high school.

"I don't understand," Roland said. His voice shook and he could smell his own fear as it mixed with the stench. He let out a tiny yelp as the blade poked through the skin.

"Okay, okay," his breath became jagged. "Tiempo, that means time, right? And es su, that's your, right? Okay, it's my time for what? I can't remember morir."

Roland felt the blade slide across his throat. It tickled as the river of blood rolled down his chest and over his stomach.

"To die, Amigo," a Mexican voice said.

With little pain and even less emotion, Roland dropped to his knees.

~ ~ ~

Impatience slowly replaced Gary's sympathy. The mob gave the poor guy a pretty rough time and now he was paying them back. The crowd was getting antsy, and Gary didn't want to lose control of the situation. Elsa looked at Gary, and they shrugged in unison.

"Everything okay in there?" Gary asked as he rapped on the door. With a smile on his face he turned to the crowd. "It brings back memories," he said. "I used to say the same thing when my little sister used to hog the bathroom."

"Maybe he fell in!" a voice shouted.

That seemed to break the tension as the room erupted in laughter. While the mood was still jovial, Gary knocked again. Still no movement from the needle.

The humor evaporated and Gary let out a deep sigh. "I think we have a disqualification here," he said.

Applause and cheers shook the bar.

Gary swung open the door.

"Sorry, Roland, you ran out of time, buddy." He choked on the last word.

Roland was on his knees leaning back against the wall. His eyes bulged from their sockets, looking up toward heaven.

Gary's stomach curled and a lump lodged in his throat. He stepped in the box to check, if by some miracle of a chance, the man still had a pulse. As he leaned over the body, the door behind him swung shut. All alone with a dead body in total darkness, his heart skipped a beat.

"Elsa, you drunk bitch," he said under his breath. "You think this is a game?"

Gary felt around and his fingers found Roland's face. He slid his hand down to the neck and felt no sign of life. As Gary stood up, something made him freeze. The sound of breathing came from somewhere.

A severe case of the willies engulfed him, and he jumped

out of the box. The door flew open and almost hit Elsa, making her lose her balance.

"Quick! Call an ambulance! I think he still might be breathing."

~ ~ ~

The police finally finished with their questions and inquiries. The coroner had just left with the body. He spoke with Gary and Brad, explaining that he had to do an autopsy, but was willing to bet a week's pay the guy died of a heart attack. One of the cops said he didn't think there'd be charges.

Brad leaned against the bar, cradling his head in his hands. Gary sat across from him and downed another shot of Southern Comfort.

Both sat in silence waiting for the other to say something when Gary felt a tap on his shoulder. Brad looked up as Gary turned around. Towering above them both stood Emily.

"So, where do I pick up my fifty bucks?"

~ ~ ~

By three a.m. the two owners finally cleared everyone out.

"You can take off," Brad said. "I'll close up. I think I need to be alone for awhile anyway."

"No problem," Gary said, as he slid off the stool. "I think I need to drive around and clear my head."

Brad knew better than to argue. Gary always said he was more careful when he drove a little drunk. Brad had actually driven with him when he was, and damned if it wasn't true. He had never been in an accident, never even gotten a ticket.

Brad sat alone at the bar, hand-washing the glasses. This was his favorite time as the night closed in around him. He looked at the room where just hours ago were wall-to-wall people, where just hours ago a man had died. Now it was so empty, so peaceful.

"I hate the cops."

Brad jumped as he whirled around. He dropped the glass he was holding and it shattered on the floor. Standing by the restroom door was his woman in black.

"I hid out in the can 'til I was sure the cops were gone. Hope you don't mind."

Brad wasn't sure what to say. "You must've been in there for hours."

"No problem, just powdering my nose," she said with a sniff and a smile.

Brad didn't need to ask.

She walked over and sat on one of the stools, propping her leg up on the bar. Brad leaned over and casually looked up her skirt. He could see her thigh between the top of her stocking and where it connected to a garter. Her thigh was smooth and alabaster white and soft.

"You like me?" she asked, and sniffed again.

Brad could feel himself getting hard. "I think you're very nice." *I can't believe I just said that.*

"You want me?"

There were aggressive women before, but never had he experienced anything like this. "I don't even know your name," he said. "My name's . . ."

"Shhh," she reached over and placed her finger on his lips. "Let's see how good you are first."

Oh my God. Sweat rolled from under his arms and soaked through his shirt. His heart worked furiously pumping blood to the right place.

The woman stood up from the stool and boosted herself up on the bar, then swung her legs up and lay across the counter. "Want to make it in the box?" she asked.

Brad's jaw dropped. "My God. A man died in there tonight."

"Makes it kind of exciting, doesn't it?"

"No. Uh Uh. No way." Brad realized he was in way over his head with this one.

She twitched her eyebrows and cocked her head. "Okay then, ever make it on your bar?" she asked.

"You want to make love on top of the bar?"

"For starters."

~ ~ ~

As Gary drove around the city, the night became a blur. He'd never touched a dead body before; the only one he had ever seen was at his grandfather's wake.

The streetlights seemed to dance around the car as he sped down the highway. The wind felt cool on his face, but his stomach began to gurgle. He knew it was only a matter of seconds before the puke would rush up his throat like an active volcano. With the next exit still another mile away, he decided on the ditch. With the car safely in park, he rolled out the door with no seconds to spare as the sickness washed through and out of him.

~ ~ ~

Walls of wood stole the air. Taking giant breaths, the walls seemed to suck each other closer. Gary sat in the middle of the shrinking room watching passively as he tried to gulp the little oxygen that remained.

"Are you superstitious?" a voice asked.

Gary turned around, and standing behind him was the guy who sold him the wood.

"What did you sell me?" Gary asked.

"Superstition," the man answered.

Gary turned around and was alone in the room again. The walls were close enough that he didn't need to move to touch any side. "I'm not claustrophobic," he said to no one.

The air vanished as the wooden planks took one last breath. Gary began to struggle as he tried to inhale. The walls, now padded, pressed into his body. He fought but they closed tighter and tighter. Soon he couldn't move but could feel the walls sucking the life out of him.

~ ~ ~

111

Gary's eyes snapped open in blinding sunlight from the nightmare. He let out a small scream as the foam padding of the seat pressed against his body. A jarring pain ricocheted through his leg as he jolted up. He grabbed at his knee and smashed two of his fingers against the steering wheel.

"Jesus fucking Christ!"

The sun beat down and it felt like jackhammers were playing a symphony in his head. The air smelled too damn fresh to be in the city. Gary sat and let his vision return and the pain in his limb subside. The landscape looked vaguely familiar. *Another blackout episode?*

The key glistened in the ignition, and with a turn of the wrist, the car purred to life. The clock on the dash said it was already past noon. *Oh shit, Brad's going to kill me.*

Still not sure of his bearings, he just followed the road. Off in the distance, a pack of dogs barked. Something clicked, and Gary knew exactly where he was. Less than a mile away from the wood seller's home.

The man was digging by the side of his house as Gary pulled up. A rottweiler ran up to the truck.

"Whadda you want?" the man said.

Hostility accented his words and Gary knew he had to be careful or the guy just might pull him out through the window and give his dog a snack. In truth, he had no idea why he was there, but as the sweat glistened off the man's tattoos Gary figured he had better think of something quick.

"I just gotta know what the hell you sold me," he said, conviction in his voice.

It struck a nerve. The man's whole personality seemed to change. "You want a beer?"

Gary's head still pounded from the hangover. He was already late, and the last thing he needed was alcohol. "Sure."

The man jerked his head toward the house and walked away from the car. The dog got up and trotted after his master. He didn't even bother to look back as Gary opened the door.

When they reached the house, he motioned Gary to help himself to a chair that sat in the yard. The door creaked open, and a scattering of yips and claws echoed through the walls as the man went inside. A moment later the two men were drinking beer and looking out over the horizon.

The man broke the silence. "Lost two of my best fightin' dogs."

"Sorry to hear that," Gary said. *What does that have to do with squat?*

Like a mind reader, the big man continued, "Woke up one morning and found 'em dead. They was sniffin' by that pile of wood I sold ya."

A chill raced up Gary's spine. He waited silently for the man to continue.

"You ever been to Mexico?" the man asked.

"What?" Gary asked. "Mexico? No. Why?"

"Know anything about it?"

Gary had no idea where this guy was going. "I like the food."

The man ignored the remark. "They got cemeteries down there."

Oh Lordy, Gary thought. *I'm sitting next to a rocket scientist.*

"They don't buy plots like we do here, they rent em."

"Yeah?" Gary now seemed interested.

"Can rent 'em for generations. Then when the family can't pay no more, they dig up the bodies and rent the hole to someone who can. That wood you bought was the coffin parts they dug up. That's why I asked if you was superstitious, remember? You said no."

Gary felt sick all over again, and just nodded his head.

"I think it's possessed," the man rambled on. "I think whoever was buried in it left his spirit in the wood, and it killed my two pups. Hell, I probably woulda given it to ya anyway. I jus' wanted it off my property."

The hangover made Gary's temper snap. "You're nuts!"

he shouted. "A fucking loon. I've heard crazy-ass stories before, but this beats em all." He stopped and collected himself. "Sorry, I guess I'm still hung over from last night. You caught me off guard." No way was he going to tell him about Roland dying and a woman claiming attempted rape in the box he made.

Throughout the whole tirade the man never made a move to get up from his chair. "Maybe you're right. Maybe I am nuts, maybe I ain't. Either way, you got the wood now and I don't. And if something weren't goin' on with it, you wouldn't be here now, would ya?"

Gary looked at him but didn't say a word.

"And now I think it's time you got off my property. There was threat in the man's voice.

~ ~ ~

It was no surprise that the door to the bar was unlocked. What did send a shiver into Gary was that the bar appeared empty. Not only empty, but a mess. Dried beer and peanut shells still littered the floor. That wasn't good. Brad would never have left the bar like that.

"Brad. You in here?" Silence. "Brad?"

Out of the corner of his eye Gary saw the scream box door slowly open, just an inch or two.

A sick feeling ate at his gut. "You in there, Brad?"

Slowly he stepped over to the box. The door opened just wide enough to see inside. He wanted to turn and run, but something drew him closer. Swallowing his fear and taking a deep breath, Gary swung open the door.

The first body he saw was that of a naked woman. What stood out, aside from the pierced nipples, was how pale her skin looked. White as a ghost. By the frozen stare on her face, it looked like she had seen one too. Then he noticed Brad, also naked, curled in the fetal position, his face to the floor.

As Gary stepped over the woman to reach his best friend, the door slammed shut. He whipped around and tried to push it open. It wouldn't budge. He was locked in a giant coffin with two corpses.

"Who's out there?" he screamed.

He heard nothing. Of course not, the box was soundproofed. Then, through the walls came the sound of breathing.

"Brad. You're alive!"

"Habla español, señor?" a menacing voice whispered.

"Who the hell said that?" Gary hollered in the blackness.

"Habla español?" the voice said more forcefully.

"I don't understand what you're saying. Where are you?" Gary cried.

"Stupido," the voice said. "You wants me to keel you now?"

Gary felt around in the dark but could only feel the ice-cold flesh of his partner and the strange woman. "Who are you?" he pleaded.

"I can keel you or let you live," the voice said in broken English.

Gary had no trouble understanding the thick Mexican accent.

"If I let you live you make promise to help me."

"Anything," Gary said. He felt his skin turn as pale as the woman's.

"You must bring me persons, help me become strong. Then I let you keep your pitiful life."

The smell of death was so strong, Gary began to choke. "Anything," he gagged.

The door opened, and light streamed in. Gary tripped over the woman and landed hard on the floor. As quick as he could, he crawled away from the box. He stopped when he reached the other side of the room.

Totally out of his control, he started rolling back. He struggled and fought, but it was a losing battle. The box sucked Gary in, and the door slammed shut on him once again.

Gary clawed through the foam padding scratching to get out.

"In case you had thoughts of betrayal," the voice said with less of an accent. "You are part of me now and I am part of you. You will not be able to run away."

Again, the door opened and spit Gary out.

~ ~ ~

A young man, dirty and homeless, sat at the bus stop watching people and traffic pass by. He held up his sign "Will Work For Food." If someone gave him a chance, he would prove he wasn't a bum.

Ready to call it a day and head back to the shelter, a car rolled up to the curb. He looked in and saw a clean-cut man behind the wheel.

"Are you serious about work?" the driver asked, "or are you just looking for handouts?"

The driver had a slight Mexican accent. A smile spread across the homeless man's face. "I want to work, sir."

The driver reached over and opened the door for him. "Hop in amigo, my name's Gary," the driver said. "I hope you don't mind, but this job is very temporary."

PEEPING TOM

As she undressed, Amanda seemed unaware of the two blue eyes staring into her window from the trees just outside the cabin. The eyes belonged to Tom Perkins, who wiped the sweat off his forehead with his sleeve as he watched the redhead brush her long, silken hair. His eyes were locked onto her breasts as they slowly and rhythmically moved up and down with her brush strokes in time with his own hand deep inside his pants.

"Ready for bed, Hon?" Paul said as he toweled off his hair, walking in from the bathroom.

"God, I love this cabin," she answered. "I'm going to sleep great tonight. That breeze feels wonderful."

Tom's heart raced even faster as the man stepped up to the window. Less than three feet separated them. Tom's spine went cold as Paul seemed to look right at him, just the blackness of country night blocking his vision.

"I love the smell of outdoors after a rain," Paul said. "It smells so clean."

Instinctively, Tom took a step back, quietly sneaking behind the widest tree. As he crept backward his foot caught on root growing above the ground. Landing hard on his tailbone, Tom splashed in the mud and muck. Pain rocketed throughout his body as he froze in place, trying not to scream.

"Paul, is somebody out there?" The beautiful Amanda asked.

"I can't tell. Turn out the light."

Tom tried to get up, but the ground hugged him, not wanting to let go. Finally, with a sucking sound, the ground released its grip and Tom scrambled to his feet just as the light in the cabin went out. A shadow filled the frame of the window and Tom froze.

"I can't see anything," Paul said.

A breeze picked up and Tom closed his eyes and began to sway like the trees around him. In perfect unison his body quivered and shook, making him one with the forest.

His memory floated back to when he was a child, teaching himself the ways of the woods. He taught himself to stay hidden in the trees after his parents got drunk and fought. To be a hidden tree in the forest while they looked for him the next day, shouting apologies and promises to never fight again, and then turned to threats when he didn't appear. He always marveled at how majestic the trees looked. Branches reached out in all directions proudly flaunting their leaves, showing off their colors in the fall, and finally resting in the winter, only to start all over again in the spring.

Tom opened his eyes and noticed the shadow in the window had disappeared. The light remained off, but to be safe he waited another two minutes before moving like a human, just to be certain no one was going to come back for a second peek. Silently he wove his way through the trees and back to his home while fantasizing about Amanda.

~ ~ ~

Tom owned six cabins, inherited from his father, on Seagull Lake, up on the Gunflint trail in northern Minnesota. Each cabin stood behind a sandy shore, surrounded on the remaining three sides by trees of birch, pine, and maple. The woods were still Tom's sanctuary, and even though he was only twenty-four, Tom had already made provisions. Upon his death he left instructions to be cremated, and his ashes scattered in the forest, becoming part of the earth.

~ ~ ~

Amazed at the people who rented his cabins, Tom had become fed up with humanity. He'd spied on gay couples, child molesters, what he thought had been women, but were in fact men. But it was on certain rare occasions that made his life worth living. This weekend it was cabin #3 – Amanda Hyatt.

His body shivered in excitement when the redhead had first walked into his office/cabin door. Her green eyes sparkled as she filled out the registration card. Amanda had worn a pink blouse open just wide enough to show off the tan freckles that dotted her cleavage. Tight jeans clung to her long, slender legs.

Tom's senses exploded with delight as she stood in front of him. The clean smell of her skin, the herbal scent of her hair, he wanted her so much it hurt. His rapture diminished when a tall man with dark hair walked in and put his arm around Tom's new fixation. They looked like they were posing for one of those "I Love You" greeting cards. Still, Tom brushed the woman's hand as he took back the pen. Lingering for just a fraction of a second, he would've sworn she intertwined her fingers around his. Their eyes locked and he felt as if lightning electrified his heart as he pushed the key to her cabin into her velvet soft hand. She silently mouthed some words that Tom could only interpret as "I love you." And those perfect lips. She smiled as she and her husband left for the cabin. She wants me too, he thought. Night seemed an eternity away.

~ ~ ~

The morning sun was up and the temperature had already passed seventy degrees. A warm breeze flowed in from the lake.

Tom woke up in a sweat, voices from a dream hidden in the back of his mind. All he could remember was that the voices wanted him to join them. He couldn't remember why. Then he thought of Amanda brushing her hair and the dream faded.

Tom sat up and gasped as he looked down his body. The memory of Amanda faded as quickly as the dream. Red, scaly patches covered his flesh, dead skin flaking off like a shedding dog. He fought to remember if he'd ever seen anything like it before. He couldn't.

Damn, I must have rolled in poison ivy when I went down last night, he thought. As soon as poison ivy popped into his mind, Tom's body began to itch. His feet felt like they were walking on broken glass as he walked into the bathroom. A shower seemed to help as warm water splashed upon his body.

~ ~ ~

Amanda was stretched out on the beach wearing a red bikini while her husband sat in a canoe in the middle of the lake, casting his fishing line into the calm water. Two cabins away, Tom peeked around the curtain. His breath came in heavy gasps as one hand held the binoculars focused on Amanda. He drooled at the way the suntan oil glistened off her skin, the way the sun reflected off her hair. His other hand worked below the waist, intermittently stopping to scratch the rash that had turned deep red and now looked like sunburn.

~ ~ ~

A cloudy darkness crept over the woods as Tom wove his way between the trees to look in on cabin #3. His body ached, his joints stiff, as he trudged through the mud and growth. Walking seemed more like a chore, knees not wanting to bend. Every step was a concentrated effort, but at least the itching had stopped.

A drizzle turned into a light rain as Tom took his position behind the birch just outside Amanda's window. He felt the water soaking into his shoes, and decided to take them off, letting the wonderful feel of mud squish between his toes.

The cabin light was on. Paul and Amanda were on the top of the bed in a tight embrace. Tom's heart raced as he watched Paul slip Amanda's blouse tenderly down and off her shoulders. The peeper's breath came out in short gasps as he stared through the window. They undressed each other ever so gently, caressing each other's bodies.

Paul lay on his back as Amanda mounted him. She rocked slowly back and forth, letting out tiny gulps of pleasure as Paul emitted a satisfying purr. Both enthralled with the other, and drowning in the rhythm of their lovemaking, an agonizing scream from outside broke their spell.

"What the hell . . ." Paul said as Amanda rolled off. She grabbed a sheet to cover her body.

Tom doubled over in pain and jerked his hand out of his pants. It felt like a grenade went off in his groin when he came. He tried to run back to his cabin, but each step was a struggle as his dick felt pulverized while the mud grabbed at his feet.

"I can't see a damned thing." Tom heard Paul's voice behind him. "Where's the flashlight?"

Tom made it home and plopped onto his bed. The room spun as he stared at the ceiling. He decided if he didn't feel better by morning it would be worth the fifty-some mile drive to Grand Marais to see a doctor.

~ ~ ~

The clouds were low and a fine mist hung in the air. Tom Perkins woke up from the same dream he'd had before. Again, he couldn't remember who was calling, or why. Still on his back, Tom's entire body felt sore. Every muscle knotted and cramped. He tried to sit up. It felt as if a medicine ball had been thrown onto his stomach.

Groaning into a sitting position, a scream caught in Tom's throat. Large black patches crusted over his body. His arms were bent and twisted. A flash of pain zigzagged up his body. Tears rolled out of his blue eyes when he put his feet on the floor. He fell back onto the bed, and with great effort bent his knee. Black warts had popped out of the bottoms of his feet. Out of each one a tiny black thread poked through the middle. He went crazy trying to figure out what he'd done to himself. This wasn't poison ivy.

Wincing after every step, Tom dragged his way into the bathroom. Ever so carefully he undid his pants. He looked down and held back a scream. His legs were worse than his arms. The skin was hard and black, scabs reaching down to his ankles. But worse than any nightmare, his most prized possession had turned into a short hardened stump. And even worse – there was no feeling in it.

Rain drummed on the roof as Tom pulled himself in front of a mirror. He couldn't scream, couldn't utter a sound as he stared mortified into the glass. Tufts of hair were gone, replaced with black welts spread over his scalp. His face reminded him of a fish. Gray scales covered his cheeks and forehead. The only recognizable features were the two frightened blue eyes staring back at him.

A knock on the door interrupted Tom's terror. He heard the door swing open.

"Anybody here?"

He recognized Paul Hyatt's voice. Tom took a deep breath and prayed that he could keep his voice steady. "I can't come out right now."

He heard Paul tapping his fingers on the front desk.

"I heard a scream by our cabin last night. You know anything about it?" Paul called down the hall.

A new fear belted Tom in the gut. He tried to think of something, but it was so hard to concentrate. "The woman in #5 thought she saw a bear," he blurted out.

"Really? It didn't sound like a woman's scream."

"You haven't seen the woman in #5," Tom said. He eased a little bit when he heard Paul chuckle. Still he kept thinking about how beautiful Amanda looked last night.

122

"Even with all the rain we really enjoyed our stay here," Paul shouted back. "In fact, if it's possible, we'd like to stay an extra night."

"That's fine. Just leave the money on the desk."

Tom stayed in the bathtub all day. He found that soaking in warm water provided the greatest relief, and made it easier to bend his limbs. The water invigorated him. He hadn't thought about the doctor, in fact he hadn't thought about anyone except Amanda. Physical problems now seemed petty. Amanda was the only thing that mattered.

It was dark before Tom crawled out of the tub. A clear night and a full moon lit the path to the cabins. Too warm for clothes, Tom crept out of his cabin. The soft ground still grabbed at his feet as he slowly made his way to #3.

Leaves applauded in the breeze as Tom stood transfixed, gazing into the window. He didn't notice, or even care that the tendrils on his feet were worming their way into the ground, rooting his legs in place. The urge to play with himself became as faded as his dream.

He saw the woman with red hair standing before him.

"This witch knew you were a pervert the moment I laid eyes on you." She stroked his arm that now sprouted buds. "But this is what you wanted, wasn't it? To be one with the forest? And now you can spy on the cabin all you want and never again have to worry about getting caught."

"Are you talking to someone?" Paul stepped out of the cabin carrying their bags.

"Just communing with nature." She gave a quick kiss to Tom and joined her husband.

"That's the strangest looking tree I've ever seen," Paul said. "How could I not have noticed it before?"

"Guess you had your mind on other things." Amanda tweaked his butt.

As the couple walked away laughing, two blue eyes disappeared behind bark eyelids.

IS THIS A MID-LIFE CRISIS?

ANYBODY GOT A SMOKE?

An old man stood before the solid gold gate that seemed to reach the sky. The man, tall and lean, had long white hair and a bushy white beard. An anorexic Santa, Albert thought, as he approached. The man wore a red robe that had faded orange with age. It was frayed at the bottom where it had been dragging across the ground for eons.

Hello . . . My Name Is Pete.

It was one of those stick-on nametags. In parentheses after the name, was "Saint." The old man smiled as he stuck out his hand.

"Albert Henney, welcome to the Here After."

He handed Albert a stick-on that said the same, except Albert instead of Pete, and no saint in parentheses. Albert stuck the paper on his lapel, the same ratty brown tweed coat he'd been buried in. He shook the old man's hand and then automatically reached into his breast pocket for a pack of cigarettes.

The pocket was empty.

Even with one lung, Albert had continued to smoke until the cancer devoured the remaining one. By the time he finally

127

went back to the doctor, it had already spread to his liver and kidneys. He smoked his three packs a day, until at fifty-four years young, he died during a coughing fit in an abandoned warehouse he called home.

Peter pulled out a folder, almost a ream thick, and with a wide smile said, "Albert Henney, this is your life."

Albert shuddered. He knew that there would be no way he'd ever see the other side of the Pearly Gates. He fumbled through all of his pockets with shaky hands, unable to find a cigarette anywhere.

The old man thumbed through the folder with a rapidity that would have made a speed reader jealous. "Well, everything seems to be in order here. Just put your John Hancock right here, and in you go."

Albert stared at him with wide eyes. A smile brought out the shine in his brown stained teeth.

"You're kidding," he said. "I never thought I'd make it into heaven. I haven't lived what you'd call a stellar life."

Peter looked at him with sorrowful eyes. "Mr. Henney, it's not so much what you did by your actions, but what you felt in your heart. You never considered yourself an evil man, did you?"

Albert thought for a moment. "No," he stammered. "I guess not. I just did what I had to do."

"That's right," Peter said. "You never really wished anybody any harm. But in the world that you lived in, you did what you had to do. Remember, God helps those who help themselves."

"Oh yeah. That's right," Albert said. His hand stopped shaking long enough for him to take the pen that Peter offered and sign on the dotted line.

"That's it then." Peter stuck the paper inside his robe. The Gate silently swung open. "Just follow the green line until it crosses the blue. Turn left. Take the blue line past the yellow until you see the red, then turn right. Follow the red line until you hit the park. Cross the purple bridge, then pick up the brown line. Go three blocks to the tan line, turn left again until you see the white stucco house. That's your abode. I think we've supplied it satisfactorily. If there's anything we forgot, just come back and see me and I'll get it rectified right away." He held out his hand, and Albert shook it.

Pristine was the only word Albert could think of as he entered the gate. The only word he could remember from Sunday school all those years ago. The word Sister Angela had always used to describe heaven. Immaculate lawns in perfect squares dotted cobblestone streets. Foliage of every color, the likes of which he had never seen, decorated the boulevards. The only thing where Sister Angela was wrong: the streets were streaked with colored lines instead of paved with gold.

Albert looked back at Peter.

"Green, left blue, right red, purple bridge, brown, tan, white stucco house. It'll be easier than it sounds," Peter said. He smiled at Albert and gave him a Boy Scout salute.

Albert closed his eyes, memorized the colors and started his trek. Along the way, a young woman carrying a bag of groceries crossed his path. "Excuse me, ma'am. You wouldn't by chance have a cigarette you could spare, would ya?"

The woman shook her head and kept walking. Up ahead, a man about Albert's age was looking at his watch.

"Sir," Albert called as he ran over. "Got a smoke?"

"Sorry. Don't smoke," the man answered.

Albert was across the purple bridge when he saw a group of three men sitting in the shade under a giant elm. "Hey guys, bum a smoke?"

They all answered in the negative.

"God Damn," Albert said. He realized what he said and slapped his hand over his mouth, sneaking a glance around to see if anybody might have heard him. None of the three seemed to notice. There was no one else around.

Peter was right. Albert found the house without any trouble. A white picket fence lined a lawn that was as perfect as any he'd seen on the walk over. At the gate stood a mailbox. Stenciled on the side was "A. Henney." Unfortunately, his mood had already soured due to lack of nicotine. He had seen no other people, not even a car on the roads. He wondered if they even allowed cars in heaven.

As he approached his front door, the smell of roses massaged his nostrils. This was all so foreign. No garbage in front yards, no smog, no sirens or screaming – just quiet. It wasn't natural.

An ache, slowly turning into a throb, began to echo in Albert's head. "I need a cigarette," he said to no one in particular.

The front door swung open, and Albert's headache temporarily vanished. Across the white shag carpet, Albert eyed a sofa with fluffy blue cushions. On each side rested an end table. On top each one stood a crystal ashtray. Inside each ashtray lay a pack of Camel straights under a book of matches. Across the room, a big screen TV, complete with DVR, invited further inspection. On the wall behind the couch stood a painting depicting the Last Supper. Each disciple, even Jesus, was enjoying a cigarette with their dinner.

Albert plopped onto the sofa and tore open a pack. He could taste the tobacco before the match was lit. His remaining lung rejoiced as smoke replaced air. With no more worries about cancer and all the other health related propaganda, Albert leaned back and blew a cool, gray cloud toward the ceiling.

Two cigarettes later, Albert felt alive again. He walked over to the TV, found the remote, and flipped it on.

"All right, sports."

A hockey game was in progress, the Blues were beating up on the Devils. Between the first and second period, he found his way into the kitchen and opened the refrigerator door. Behind the head of lettuce, pound of sliced carrots, and other foods that Albert hadn't tasted in years, a twelve-pack of beer sparkled. "Sweet," Albert said as he carried it back to the couch.

By the end of the game, six beers and a pack of smokes

had disappeared. Drowsy, Albert decided it was time to seek out the bedroom. He grabbed the remote to turn off the TV, but his finger slipped and touched the wrong button.

"Porn!" He was instantly wide awake.

This wasn't the soft-core Playboy Channel stuff either. This was the down-and-dirty, in-your-face, Supreme-Court-banning Porn.

Subconsciously another lit cigarette found his lips, and another can of beer popped open. The last thing Albert thought before passing out was that he should have died a long time ago.

~ ~ ~

Albert awoke with a road construction headache, and a mouth that tasted a lot like the ashtray looked. He fumbled around for a new refreshing smoke, but found both packs empty. Rolling off the couch, he stared at his reflection in the blank television screen. He hadn't remembered turning it off, but that was nothing new.

"How can I be in Heaven, and look and feel like such Hell?" he asked himself.

Dragging himself to his feet, Albert explored his new home. All the comforts were there – washer/dryer, bed with a firm mattress, even an automatic icemaker built into the freezer. The only thing missing were cigarettes. No problem, Albert thought. There was that lady yesterday with a bag of groceries. There has to be a store around here somewhere.

Outside, the sunlight, with no smog to filter the rays, attacked Albert's eyes. Chirping birds made bombs explode in his head. He remembered fondly his days as a kid, taking his b.b. gun into Loring Park, wasting pigeons, pretending they were snitches.

Following the tan line running down the street, Albert saw an elderly gentleman bent over, trying to make sure he was on the right color.

Albert hauled himself to the front gate. "Excuse me. Got a smoke?"

The man looked up. "Have you seen my house? It looks just like the one I grew up in. He said follow the brown line and you can't miss it."

In Minneapolis, this would have been the type of mark Albert would have rolled. Usually lots of cash easy for the plucking. The idea sounded appealing, but he decided that kind of behavior would probably not be tolerated here.

"You're on the tan line, old man. The brown one is back there." Albert pointed behind the man. "Got an extra cigarette?"

"This isn't the brown line? It looks brown to me. Doesn't it look brown to you?"

Albert rolled his eyes. It felt like they were rubbing against sandpaper behind the lids. "A cigarette. Can I have a cigarette?"

The old man looked at Albert like he saw him for the first time. "A cigarette?"

"Yeah," Albert said, his voice starting to lighten. "Can I bum a smoke from you?"

Albert's eyes lit up as the man reached in to his pocket. The flare instantly went dead when the only thing coming out of the pocket was an old, used, hanky. The man blew his nose, and then stuffed the rag back into his coat.

"Nasty habit, that smoking. It'll kill ya. Doesn't this line look brown to you?"

"It sure does, old man," Albert said. "Just keep following that brown line."

Albert made it to the park. His head felt trapped in a vise while the little nicotine gnomes played his intestines like a base. He'd been up over three hours, and he was still looking for his first smoke of the day.

"Hey lady," he called to a woman crossing the purple bridge. "Please tell me you can spare a cigarette."

"Sorry," she said. "Don't smoke."

Albert dropped to his knees screaming, "Jesus Christ. Where can I get a damned cigarette in this place?"

The woman giggled. "If you see him, you can ask him. Actually, I think the designated smoking area is outside the gate." She started to walk away.

"Wait a minute," Albert called. "Sorry for the dramatics. It's been a rough morning. Do you know where that grocery store is?"

"Oh sure," the woman answered. "Take the yellow line past the post office. Turn left on the maroon, straight to the gray, and you're there."

"Thank you." Albert began to walk along the yellow.

"But I don't think you'll find what you're looking for, if all you're looking for are cigarettes. It's a health food co-op."

Albert sank again to his knees. Who would have thought it would be that hard to find a fellow smoker?

With trembling hands, an aching head, and a lung screaming for something besides fresh air, Albert made his way to the front gate. Even before he got there, his senses began to tingle. Cigar smoke drifted to his nose. With renewed energy, Albert ran to the Gate. Peter was in his place, his back to the door, holding at his side a cigar that looked and smelled Cuban.

"Peter," Albert shouted through the bars. "Can I join you? And where can I find me some cigarettes?"

Peter turned around. "Oh my. Didn't we supply you with any at your home? I'm sure that we did."

"Yeah. Two packs," Albert answered.

"Whew. You scared me for a second. I thought we screwed up. Of course you can join me. C'mon out."

Albert pushed at the gate, but the door wouldn't budge. "It's locked," Albert said. "You got the key?"

"Oh my. That does create a problem. I guess you're kind of out of luck," said Peter. "But I'm glad you're here. One thing I forgot to tell you. You might want to make those cigarettes of yours last. Those two packs are going to have to last you to eternity. And when they're gone, well, those withdrawal symptoms, they'll only get worse, and worse, and worse." A deep throaty laugh escaped his lips as his eyes turned from blue to blazing red.

"What are you talking about?" Albert said. In a hushed whisper, "You're not Peter."

An evil smile spread across Peter's face. "I have a lot of names."

Through laughter that made Albert's eardrums want to burst, the paper nametag burst into flame. "Ya know, I just don't feel like a Peter today," he said. The fire sizzled out, but the name-tag remained. In smoldering letters, "Pete" had been replaced with "Lucifer." "Saint" still in parenthesis.

A WALK IN THE WOODS

What he did know was if he stopped to rest he might die. A cold whipping wind stung his exposed face. He tried to look through the birch and pine for any sign that the cabin might be ahead. Snow fell in clumps, making it hard to see more than twenty or thirty feet. It covered his tracks almost as fast as he made them. Steve Blanchard was lost.

Looking around at his surroundings, despite his frustration, he thought what a great scenic postcard this could make. While watching the white cascade down upon the trees, he shouted out loud, "But not for a man to be stranded in!" The sound muffled in the blizzard. No echo bounced off the trees or rocks – a forest soundproofed.

As he walked through a cluster of trees, a branch snapped into Steve's face. The sting felt like the slap of a steel glove across his cheek. He screamed, and in a small fit yanked the brittle branch from the tree. In childish temper tantrum fashion, he stomped on it. "That will teach you, you son-of-a-bitch. And let that be a lesson to you others," he shouted at all the branches. The trees smiled back in silence.

"Gotta keep moving." Time turned into the enemy. He had

no idea how long he'd been wandering. Steve figured another half-hour more and then he'd better start looking for shelter. *The woods must be full of caves*, he hoped, he prayed.

Snow crunched under his boots as he trudged onward. Even with the heavy lining, his toes were past freezing and started to numb. He pulled his fingers from the tips of his gloves and balled them into fists, cramming them as deep as he could into his pockets. He sucked on the tiny icicles from his breath that formed on his mustache.

The snow turned into flurries as the tired lawyer concentrated on stepping one foot in front of the other. The wind picked up and daylight faded. The cabin now seemed a luxury that was out of reach. His hands, feet, and face were beyond feeling. White noise filled his mind, but he kept pushing himself on.

A rock, hidden by snow, caught Steve's foot. His ankle twisted. A jolt of pain raced up his leg as he grabbed his boot.

"Blanchard, you're an idiot," he cried. "City folk don't belong in the wilderness!"

He sat in the snow, chastising himself. During the tirade, he glanced to his left and choked on a gulp. Sanctuary? About fifteen feet away, a small opening in the rocks could barely be seen. Steve felt relief as he pulled himself up. His eyes watered and teeth clenched as he put weight on the twisted ankle. Each step held a new threshold in pain, but he was going to make it to the rocks.

At the entrance, the wind whistled a melody that sounded like a death wail. Inside it was a couldn't-see-your-hand-in-front-of-your-face darkness, but it would protect him from the cold and just maybe keep him alive. Steve let out a long sigh as he sat against the rock wall and closed his eyes as the weariness quickly caught up. He thought back to Janet, and three weeks ago when she concocted this devilish plot.

~ ~ ~

"You're going to kill yourself if you don't take some time

off," Janet said.

"What do you know about it?" Blanchard asked.

"The doctor's office called with the results of your physical. I told the girl you were in court, but that you wanted them to give me the results."

"And they did?"

Janet lowered her head and let out a little smile. "I think she was new, and I cajoled her with a bit of legalese."

Steve looked down at his paralegal. "Well, she'll be looking for a new job." He paused for effect, "And so will you, young lady, if you ever try that again."

"You'll do no such thing," she scoffed. "If you blame any-body, blame me. She thought she was doing the right thing, and I'm sure she'll learn in time. And you can't fire me. You've told me too many times I'm invaluable to this office."

"There's nobody in this office that isn't expendable," he snapped. "Including you."

He turned away, knowing she was right. Not only had she been a paralegal for over three years, but she was also a secretary and law clerk. Her legal research was as good as any he'd seen, but her biggest asset was her keen insight in pointing out the obvious while he lost himself in the intricacies of a case. Unfortunately, he realized, she knew he knew she was right.

"Anyway," she continued, "you're taking a week off. I cleared your calendar for next week. I talked to Jeff and he agreed you should stay at our lake cabin for a week and unwind. Read in front of a nice roaring fire. Take a nice peaceful walk in the woods. It's just what the doctor ordered."

Blanchard smiled, shaking his head. "Northern Minnesota in January, in the middle of nowhere? I'll freeze my ass."

"The place has indoor plumbing, electricity, and heat," she said.

"So, how do you expect me to get up there?" He started to sway.

Janet groaned and raised her eyes. "Take your 4x4 yuppie-mobile. Use it for what it was made for once in your life."

"It gets a good workout on these pot-holes," he said defensively.

"It's just north of Bemidji. I'll have a map for you by tomorrow. Trust me, it'll be great. This time of year, you'll be the only one on the lake."

"So tell me," Blanchard asked. "Do you have your husband as whipped as you've got your boss?"

"I'm working on it," she smiled.

~ ~ ~

In less than a week, Steve had missed the action of court, the fighting for custody, alimony, and assets, on behalf of his clients. He missed the high of outmaneuvering his opponents, the rush as the judge ruled in his favor. He'd studied every judge on the bench, learning their quirks and eccentricities. He knew when to stroke their egos and when to shut up. It made him the top divorce lawyer in Minnesota and one of the wealthiest. It also made him a workaholic with a blood pressure that hovered near stroke.

She was right. Looking out over the frozen lake, nature projected a scene begging to be painted. Trees lined the shore, each branch balancing an inch of snow across its length, making a beautiful contrast to the bright blue sky. The lake was a white sheet that sparkled as the sun reflected off the ice crystals like bits of stained glass.

The small A-frame cabin held a loft that housed a bed and dresser. On the main floor sat a couch resting in front of a small fireplace with a hearth made out of different colored rocks mortared together. Off to the side stood an oak table just big enough for two, a refrigerator, stove and oak cupboard finished the room.

Outside, Steve plodded through a snowed-in path to the firewood stacked as neatly as the papers on Janet's desk. Animal tracks led around the cabin and off into the woods.

The next morning, clouds rolled in from across the lake. The lawyer stepped outside to get more wood. He froze at the door. The biggest gray wolf Steve had ever seen (not that he'd seen many, in fact none outside of the zoo) sniffed at the woodpile. God, it was big. Big and half-starved. Its fur hung down flapping off bone. It had been a hard winter for the beast.

Steve felt sorry for the animal and immediately thought of all the insulting jokes told by his clients about lawyers with no conscience. His anger built toward humanity thinking how he busted his ass so one client could keep custody of his children, and how he spent three sleepless nights thinking up a plan that would keep another client from declaring bankruptcy. He wished they were all with him now as he stepped back into the cabin and retrieved a pound of hamburger that sat thawing on the counter. The door creaked back open. The wolf stopped and sniffed the air, then jerked its head and glowered into Steve's eyes.

"You hungry fella?" Steve asked, holding out the meat. "You're probably more deserving than most of my clients. You're nothing but bones and fur."

The wolf stared, not moving. Steve took a step toward the animal and immediately stood motionless. The wolf sensed danger and raised its lips in a snarl. It exposed its teeth, yellow and sharp, two fangs glistening in the morning light. Somewhere deep inside, the animal made a hellish gurgling sound that turned into a low growl.

"It's okay, boy," Steve spoke softly. "Just want to give you something to eat."

Steve took another step forward. The wolf raised its lips even higher as saliva dripped off its chin into the snow. The hair on its back stood straight, the growl turned to a snapping bark. Steve retreated back into the doorway. Safely inside, he tore off a piece of hamburger and tossed it in front of the wolf. The animal didn't move.

Blanchard finally gave up and shut the door. He peeked out the window and saw the wolf slowly move toward the meat. One second the hamburger was there, the next second it had disappeared. Cautiously, Steve opened the door. The wolf looked up. The lawyer tore off another piece of meat and tossed it. This time the wolf didn't wait for Steve to go back inside, but neither did it take its eyes off him while he ate.

Every morning for five straight days, the wolf met Blanchard at the door. It no longer growled or raised its fur. By the third day, it even took food out of Steve's hand. So far, the lawyer went through a pound of hamburger, a package of hot dogs, a chicken, and half a turkey breast. The wolf grew stronger each day as the man got thinner. What the hell, he figured; eating less could only be good for his blood pressure. Besides, his new friend needed it more.

"Tomorrow it's ham for breakfast," Steve said as he watched the animal chomp on the turkey. "After that I'm afraid you're back on your own. But I'll leave any extra food I've got."

He felt bad for the wolf, but he also knew the wolf was a survivor. He'd made it this far. As he watched the animal eat, Steve couldn't wait to tell Janet to be expecting a new visitor when she and her husband came up in the spring.

The fire roared as the flames licked the dry wood. Steve sat on the couch catching up on his reading. He'd brought up his unread issues of *Forbes*, *GQ*, and *Rolling Stone*. As he finished each one, he tossed it in the fire and watched, mesmerized, as the orange and yellow flames burst into blue and green, then slowly settled back down again.

God, I hate it when she's always right, he thought staring out the window at the lake. He knew when he got back to the office, Janet would see how great he felt, how much weight he'd lost, and not say a word. She would just walk around with that smug little 'I told ya so' grin. What could he do to repay her? He fantasized about what kind of bonus he could give her. He knew what he wanted to give her. No, that was just gutter fantasy and best to keep away, even from private thought. They'd developed a deep friendship that included trust. Even though Steve was

140

divorced, Janet was still very much in love with her husband. No way would he ever ruin that friendship with infatuation, or lust.

Close to the lake, nibbling on a shrub exposed above the snow stood a deer. A young one. Antlers had just started to sprout from its head and a light snow coated its tan back with a white gloss.

Steve sprang up from the couch and raced to get his boots. He grabbed his jacket and hat and was out the door before his arm went through the sleeve. Silence consumed him as he stood outside in the chill. The trees remained motionless as they tried to catch snowflakes.

The young stag ran before Steve could get down to the shore. All it left was a set of tracks that led back into the woods. The temperature felt tolerable and Steve knew that a walk would do him good. He followed the tracks blindly as the snow got heavy. Deeper into the woods he walked, enjoying the serenity, until a cramp knotted in his leg and told him it was time to turn back.

The snow fell thick as Steve followed his own tracks back. A mass of white dropped off the branches and pine needles. As he came upon a small clearing, the lawyer stopped. A shiver crawled up his spine that made his neck hairs stand straight. His heart pounded and his breath came out in short gasps. In the clearing, his footprints, his trail back, was gone, buried beneath the newly fallen snow.

~ ~ ~

A tiny gust of warm, steamy air that smelled like old meat woke Blanchard from a troubled sleep. A wet piece of leather lightly slapped his cheek. Automatically, he raised his hands to his face. Something blocked it.

Through a gloved hand, Steve felt a mound of soft fur. His eyes snapped open and he remembered where he was. His body became paralyzed. There was heavy breathing, and it wasn't his. Too scared to remember how to breathe at the moment, his heart tried to beat out of his chest as a jaw lightly clamped itself around his wrist. A jaw that could snap through bone with little effort.

The mouth tugged on his wrist forcing Steve onto his knees. He crawled until he was out of the sheltered rock and out in the open.

The wolf.

The jaw let him go.

His wolf.

A bolt of pain shot up Steve's leg as he put weight on his foot. His face twisted as tears welled up in his eyes. The gray animal cocked its head quizzically then turned and started to weave its way through the trees. About ten feet away, it stopped and turned around. Steve stared back. The wolf came forward a few steps then started away again, impatient.

"I went to law school you know," Steve said. "I can tell when somebody wants me to follow. But in the courtroom, I'm the wolf that people follow."

A snap cracked the air as Steve broke off a branch and followed the wolf using the stick as a cane.

"You come to save me?"

The wolf raced ahead then waited for the man to catch up.

"I think I'll name you Lassie. Lassie was really a boy, ya know."

When Steve got within ten feet, the wolf raced ahead again. It made sure Blanchard never lost sight of it.

"If you get me out of this alive, the rest of the food is yours. No sharing."

For a moment, the lawyer lost sight of the animal. Then, over the ridge of a small hill he saw its head staring at him, waiting. He limped up the hill using the stick as a crutch. His ankle throbbed, his body shivered, and his head ached. Snow fell in his boots, soaking his feet. He knew that when he took the boot off, his foot would swell like a balloon.

A lump caught in Steve's throat when he reached the top of the hill. About two hundred feet away sat his 4x4 waiting patiently next to the cabin. He tried to ignore the pain as he half-limped, half-ran. Tears flowed down his face, partly from pain but mostly from joy. When he reached the car, Steve noticed the cabin door stood wide open.

"Damn," Steve said. "I'm really going to have to build that fire up." He tried to remember if he had left it open when he went out to follow the deer.

Relief washed over him as he stepped into the cabin. It was when he started to unzip his jacket that he noticed. His blood froze and he felt his heart pound.

Two little wolf pups wrestling in front of the fireplace stopped to look at the strange intruder. An adult wolf looked up from where it rested on the couch. Another one slowly walked down the stairs from the loft, while yet another poked out its head from under the railing.

Steve slowly turned to make his way out of the cabin. Standing in the doorway the big wolf blocked his exit, drool sliding down its fangs. Steve Blanchard realized that his new friend had just brought home dinner.

THE BLUE LIGHT

Jacob Hardaway pressed his foot on the pedal a little harder even though the speedometer read twenty miles an hour over the limit. According to the map, he'd already traveled ten miles past his destination; but this was a single lane, and there hadn't been an exit in the last thirty miles.

Hungry, tired, lost, his bladder pressing urgently against his groin, Jacob debated with himself whether or not to pull off to the side of the road and urinate into the brush. His phobia made it an easy decision.

The dashboard clock read eight o'clock, and he already had the headlights on. The full moon cast a glow from above the tree line. Fear of the dark that he never outgrew fluttered his heart. *God only knew what might be hiding at the side of the road, waiting for a man to exit the safe confines of his car, leaving him defenseless to the night.*

He remembered the one and only time he dared step from the car – all those red eyes staring at him through the bushes; too real, too dangerous. Trembling and sweating, he couldn't even piss. Finally giving up, Jacob would've sworn he'd heard laughing from the other side of the thicket as he got back in the car. Never again, he told himself.

Five more miles, he thought. *That's how long I can make it. If I don't see a gas station, restaurant, something, I'm pulling over.*

At four-and-a-half miles, Jacob saw a soft blue light illuminating over the ridge. An inviting blue light. A blue warmth that said "Strangers Welcome."

"Finally." He pressed even harder on the gas.

The hotel stood alone in the middle of nowhere. An old boarding house structure with a sign hanging from a beam by the door gave the only clue that this was a hotel. It said "Hotel". Through the lower window, a yellow light cast an enticing shadow on the porch. Upstairs, the blue light that Hardaway first noticed glowed like a protective night-light.

Jacob felt like a child, holding his crotch as he stepped out of the car and walked into the hotel. *How embarrassing*, he thought, and looked around for a rest room.

"How can I help you, friend?"

Jacob whirled around, startled by the old man behind the counter.

"I'm sorry, I didn't see you. Where's the rest room?"

"Didjya say you wanted a room?" the man said.

"Oh no, nothing like that. But I'd be more than happy to buy a souvenir, a mug or something. Now if you could kindly tell me where the rest room is."

"All we gots is the one room, but ain't nobody using it. It's yers if ya wannit."

"No. You don't seem to understand." Jacob was melting now. "All I need is to use your rest room."

"The room comes 'quipped with a WC," the man said.

"A what? Listen, I just really need to go to the bathroom. Don't you have one down here? Please!"

"Sorry, friend. Thas jus' for employees only. There's one in the room, though."

Jacob couldn't tell if the man was teasing him, a rube toying with a city slicker, or, if the man was just simple. "All right. I give up. You win. How much?"

"You jus' wannit for the one night?" the man asked shoving a key and a card across the desk.

"I just want it for about two minutes!" Jacob snatched the key.

The man behind the counter shrugged his shoulders, "Fifty dollars, cash. Fer a whole night."

Reaching into his back pocket, Jacob pulled out three twenties. "I'll be down in a few minutes for my change."

The man pulled a fingernail full of wax from his ear and stared at it. "Hey Friend, ya forgot to fill out the card."

Jacob was halfway up the stairs, bounding three at a time, and chose to ignore the old coot. When he reached the top, he stopped and stared. The long hall stretched narrow and empty. Constricted enough that two people would have to go single file, long enough that they'd be winded when they got to the other side. But what made Jacob stare was the door halfway down the hallway and to the left. The only door on the floor.

Bare walls, dull white, reflected the light bulbs hanging from the ceiling. Three of them, spaced evenly apart, couldn't have been more than 40 watts each. The floor held a faded red carpet that looked worn down to the padding.

Jacob walked down the hallway. With each step the floorboards creaked. He feared he might fall through and land back in the lobby.

A sharp pang in his groin reminded Hardaway why he came here in the first place. Walking a fast gait down the hall, he fumbled with the key and almost dropped it. Perspiration glistened on his forehead as he thought about the agony of having to bend down.

With grave concentration, he fit the key into the lock. The door swung open. A blue light bulb glowed, dangling from a cord, like a noose. Hardaway stared momentarily. *Later*, he thought. To his right, an opening – the bathroom. *Thank God*. Stepping in, he reached behind for the light switch. Nothing there. *Forget it.*

The blue bulb cast enough light.

"Ohhhhhh God," he moaned as he drained. "Well, this is the most expensive whiz I ever took."

Feeling like a new man, Jacob zipped up his trousers and flushed. *Go downstairs, ask for directions, and see where the map screwed up. Find the right hotel, a presentation in the morning, back on the road by ten, and home before sunset.* He just had to remember no coffee until the interstate.

Jacob Hardaway's jaw dropped as he stepped from the bathroom. The room was totally bare. No desk, no table, not even a bed. No furniture at all. But that wasn't what made his eyes stare in amazement. He couldn't believe he'd missed it on the way in. Every inch of wall was covered. Small pictures, large pictures, pictures of all sizes showed scantily clad women in various dress of lingerie. Cleavage and thighs plastered all over the room. Bizarre didn't begin to cover it. Boobs and butt coming at him from all angles. But what made the hair on his neck stand, his nerves shiver, and his stomach knot, was that every barely dressed woman was missing her head – each photograph stopped at the shoulders.

"Whoa," Jacob whispered. "This is too crazy."

Whipping around to get the hell out, he didn't remember having closed the door when he entered. The knob turned but the door wouldn't budge. With a surge of adrenaline, Jacob shook and rattled the wood almost off its hinges. Panting and heaving, he pulled. A scraping wood sound made the skin on his arms turn to goose bumps as the door flew open.

"I trust everythin's ta yer satisfaction," the hotel keeper said.

Jacob gasped and grabbed his chest as he saw the old man smiling, his body filling the frame of the doorway. He held a tarnished silver tray with what looked like a peanut butter and jelly sandwich and a glass of milk. Peanut butter fingerprints marred the top of the bread.

"Ya looked like ya might be a bit hungry," he said.

Catching his breath, Jacob gave a nervous smile, "I thought you locked me in."

The man chuckled, "She warps when it gets humid, but just rattle 'er a bit and she'll be fine. Samwich?"

There was a glint of craziness in the man's eyes. His smile showed tobacco stained, rotting teeth, and his breath smelled foul.

"If you'll excuse me, I have to be back on the road," Jacob said. "I have a presentation at nine in the morning."

The old man made no move to get out of the doorway. "I took all these pictures myself."

"Very nice," Jacob said.

"Developed 'em, too. Gots me a darkroom down the basement."

Just the thought of this guy's basement gave Jacob the creeps.

The man balanced the tray on one hand and with the other took Hardaway's arm and led him across the room.

"Tha's my first wife, Doreen." He pointed to the black lace bra and panties. "An' over here is our daughter, Ruth. Named her from the Bible." It was a shot of a small torso wearing a Wonder-Bra.

This guy's gone way over the edge, Jacob thought. "A nice family," he said. "But I really do have to go." He started for the door.

A hand grabbed the back of Jacob's collar and flung him across the room. Jacob slipped, landed on his ass, and slid the rest of the way to the wall. This man was a hell of a lot stronger than he looked. Hardaway sat stunned as he looked up at the crazy old fool. The tray still balanced on one hand; he hadn't spilled even a drop of milk.

"Tha's not right friendly, son. I go to all the trouble a makin' you supper, showin' you my family, an' you jus' wanna up and go. You jus' sit there fer awhile an' think 'bout yer bad manners."

Jacob stared as the man set the tray on the floor and backed out of the room. As the door shut there was a gleeful chuckle and the sound of a key turning in the lock. It took a moment for Jacob to get over the shock and get to his feet. He walked over to the door and tried turning the knob. It was frozen. He pulled out his key and swore as he realized there was nowhere to put it in on this side. His worst fears were confirmed; he was being held prisoner.

Clouds rolled in under a gloomy sky, dimming an already dark room. Jacob sat on the windowsill, staring outside. Giving into his hunger, he nibbled the peanut butter sandwich and watched as drops of rain splattered on the pane. *What a view*, he thought. *Nothing but swamp*. His reflection gazed back, showing the face of trepidation. *What the hell is next?* He'd almost thrown his back out trying to open the window before realizing it had been nailed shut. *What good would it do anyway?* Looking down the two stories below, the hotel stood surrounded by a moat of small rocks, decorated with shards of broken bottles, the path too wide to leap past.

The rain started to pound as Jacob drained the last of the milk. He watched as water bounced and ran down his mirrored self. The road got harder to make out through the outline of the trees; the pictures inside the room seemed to get darker too. He clutched himself in under the blue light trying to keep back the night.

Is it getting warmer in here? He felt sweat bead on his forehead. When he squinted just right, he could make a picture of one of the big-breasted models jiggle under the bra she almost wore. He giggled while getting up to take a closer look.

The room began to gyrate as Hardaway stood up. His stomach churned, and sweat ran down his face as freely as the rain rolling down the window. Dropping to his knees, he let out a loud groan. He tried to crawl to the bathroom but collapsed halfway there. *The bastard's poisoned me*. He heard the sound of a key turn.

Yellow light filtered in, creeping from the hallway and mixing with the blue. It painted the hotelkeeper's skin the color of Frankenstein's monster. The way he smiled made him look more menacing than Karloff ever did.

The old man was a blur as Jacob stared up at him, totally helpless. He focused on the nostrils and watched in fascination as they grew and then shrank over and over again with each breath. His concentration snapped as something covered the geezer's face.

A blinding flash made Jacob want to cover his eyes but he was unable to move his hands. Lightning, he thought, but there was no sound of thunder to follow. Darker blue lights danced and snapped around the dangling blue light bulb. This is even better than the nostrils, Jacob thought, until the eclipse of the monster's head stood above his face.

Hardaway wanted to scream as he forced himself to look away. A giant boot sped in slow motion with a myriad of colors before it crashed into his side. He felt the wind rush out of his lungs, could almost see it in his mind, but there was no pain, just a whump in his side that kind of tingled.

Something tugged at him, and Jacob realized he was on his stomach, staring at the floor. The wood came alive, each grain dancing around a knot that seemed to pulsate with a nonexistent rhythm. Somewhere, far away, granite-like hands yanked down his trousers. Those same hands grabbed the love handles of his belly and jerked him up to his knees, his face still kissing the floor. Before losing consciousness, the last thing Jacob felt was a boot kicking his thighs apart and smooching sounds between heavy breathing.

~ ~ ~

Jacob could tell the sun was out even though his eyes remained closed. He dreamt of sewers and of his entire body itching, but someone held his arms down so he couldn't scratch. Slowly he forced his eyes open. Everything looked hazy as light flooded in, but he couldn't shake the smell of refuse. Sitting

150

in front of the window, he tried to rub his eyes, but as in the dream, his arms wouldn't move. Straining with effort, he forced himself to focus. His arms were locked inside a white sheet – no, a straitjacket. The ends of the sleeves, which stretched well past his hands, had been tied to the arms of the chair he was stuck on. Slits cut into the sleeves exposed black-and-blue inner arms peppered with needle tracks. Below the jacket he sat naked, degraded. Between him and the window, a small wooden bench now stood, big enough for one person to sit on and talk to him face-to-face.

Every muscle ached as he fought against the restraints. The heavy fabric scraped sensitive skin, making it burn. So weak, so tired, helplessness ravaged his mind as clouds cleared from his head.

Scads of headless women in their underwear lined the walls. Headless Patty and headless Jodi showed off their bodies, tacked on either side of the window. They were twins he remembered from somewhere. There was headless Doreen. She was married, he thought, or once was. Each one had a name and a story, but damned if he could remember many.

The door creaked and Jacob felt his nerve endings burst. There came the familiar smell of peanut butter and body odor. Cackling laughter from behind forced his eyes to clench.

"How's my sweet cakes doin' this morning'?" the hotel-keeper said, resting the tray on Jacob's lap. The cool metal felt good on his bare thighs.

Jacob looked down at his daily meal of a peanut butter and jelly sandwich, a glass of milk, a rubber strap, and only two hypodermic syringes this time. He racked his memory trying to remember if there were usually more needles.

"Ya hungry?" the captor asked as if he were in love.

He picked up the sandwich and held it in front of Jacob's face. A warning went off in Hardaway's brain and he tried to turn away. The old man started to laugh.

"I ain't done nothin' bad since the first one," he said between

151

snorts. "I'll shows ya."

He proceeded to take a bite out of the bread and a swig of milk. "Mmmm. Good." His mouth was full and drooling as he held the sandwich back in front of his prisoner's mouth.

Jacob's stomach growled loud enough for both of them to hear. That started the man laughing again, showing brown and white chew stuck on his teeth. A gagging reflex took over as Jacob fought with himself between hunger, stench, and revulsion. Hunger won out as he leaned his head forward and took a bite, then another, and another, until the sandwich disappeared.

"Ya done good," the hotelkeeper said, setting the tray on the floor. He came back up with a syringe and the band. Jacob stared as his kidnapper separated the slits from the jacket apart and pushed the needle in black-and-blue skin.

It felt like an out-of-body experience as he watched, rather than felt, the rubber strap being tied around his arm, the needle digging into his arm. It seemed to be a kind of ritual he was becoming accustomed to.

"Yep. Yer doin' real fine," he whispered. "An' this one to make ya feel better." He repeated the process with the other arm. "I'm a bit low though, so only half a dose today. All righty?"

It really did make him feel better. Jacob's head clouded up again. He watched in a semiconscious state as the man picked up the tray and silently walked out.

There was something wrong with the ritual, and Jacob frowned, forcing himself to concentrate on what he missed. A smile spread across his drug-induced face. There was no click after he left. The idiot forgot to lock the door. "I'll have to remind him," he mumbled before falling back asleep.

~ ~ ~

The blue light glowed like a full moon inside the room. Jacob's shadow looked weak and feeble staring up from the floor. He couldn't recall waking up at night before, and this was the first time he felt even close to clear-headed. Every muscle ached.

Whatever that sadist shot him up with, it was doing a number on his body.

He tried to swivel around in his chair. His ass screamed as he moved. It felt like raw meat. Realization hit. *That bastard's been raping me! I'll kill you, you fucking bastard* kept repeating itself in Jacob's mind while his eyes filled with tears.

The rage inside grew, hate building into strength. Jacob lashed back-and-forth trying to free himself from the restraints. The old pervert had gotten lazy. Hardaway had lost a lot of weight and the straitjacket hung loose. *If I could only reach my hand up through the slit*.

Sweat rolled into his eyes, his red face straining, trying to pull back an already aching arm just a little bit more. When it felt like his shoulder was about to explode, his thumb slipped through the bottom of the cut to freedom. Wedging the canvas material just a little bit further, the rest of his hand quickly followed.

One arm free, halfway home. Hardaway paused to look at his arm. The skin looked pale and clammy, corpse-like in the blue light. Even the hairs looked lighter and thinner. Quickly, he forced his mind back to the subject at hand. Numb fingers fumbled with the sleeve, trying to untie the rough fabric knotted around the arm of the chair.

It took longer than he thought it should have. Finally, both of Jacob's arms were free and he hoisted himself up. The two long sleeves dangled at his side, whooshing back and forth while his legs roared in agony, being awoken from their long sleep. He massaged one, then the other, trying to get feeling past the millions of stabbing needles. It did little good. However long he'd been sitting had taken its toll on his legs, too. Despite the pain, they even looked pasty. The firm thigh muscles, he always thought were the best part of his body, now felt soft and flabby. Even that hair looked thinner.

His first step felt stiff and disjointed. Pushing his weight back, Jacob plopped back into the chair. In a panic he grabbed the arms before he fell through. Struggling back to his feet, he looked down. The middle of the chair had been carved away. Under the hole sat a bucket. In the half-second it took Jacob to realize he'd been sitting for god-knows-how-long on a homemade toilet, the stench filtered down his nostrils and into his throat, making his stomach wretch.

Fighting back nausea, Jacob froze. A chill raced up his spine as floorboards from the hallway creaked.

The door opened on grating hinges. Jacob could feel eyes burning into his back. He bobbed his head forward, feigning sleep.

The footsteps came closer. Jacob's hands grasped the arms of the chair, clutching the jacket sleeves in his fist. Not daring to open his eyes, he prayed the material still covered his arms. There would only be one chance for surprise, and he had to make the first shot count.

The plan raced in his mind. As the hotelkeeper stepped in front, Jacob would take a swing. Hopefully, that would stagger him enough that Jacob could leap up and go for the eyes.

Warm, sour breath chilled the back of Hardaway's skull. Something wet and slimy ran its way from the nape of his neck to the back of his ear, followed by the sound of smacking lips. *Don't scream*, Jacob thought. *Please hurry up and walk around the chair.*

He cracked an eye open, tensing his body ready to strike. The shadow showed the man behind him like a monster ready to pounce. Jacob took a deep silent breath and held it.

Without warning, the chair tipped forward, and Jacob clenched onto the arms even tighter, not knowing what else to do. He landed with a whuumph against the wood bench, air rushing from his lungs. A heavy hand slapped his exposed butt and one of the sleeves dropped from Jacob's fist. It hung like a useless arm, and swished against the floor.

"What the hell. . ." The man stood up.

Wasting no time, Jacob let go of the chair and hugged the wooden bench. Moving from the hip, the chair flipped off to the side as he swung.

Crunching bone, then a scream shattered the quiet. Jacob raised the bench for another swing. He looked at the old man, dropped it and gasped. A worn, blue terry cloth robe lay wide open. Underneath, the pervert wore a black lace teddy. Varicose veins ran up his legs. He wore mascara and eyeliner, rouge highlighted his cheeks, and lipstick smeared across his mouth. It should have been comical, but it looked grotesque; the big strong madman/rapist was clutching his knee, crying like a baby wearing lingerie that looked obscene.

Jacob got to his feet, his knotted muscles fighting with each step. "Where are my clothes, you bastard?"

The man ignored him, still curled up around his knee, whimpering. Jacob limped to the bench, pushed it toward the hotel keeper, picked it up, and dropped it on the injured knee. A new howl pierced the night. "Tell me where my clothes are!" His anger rose.

"My leg," the man screamed. "You broke my leg."

"And I'll break your other one." Jacob picked up the bench, blood rushing to his head.

"Noooooo!" The man curled up into a tighter ball.

Had Jacob not seen him do it, he would've sworn the scream came from a little girl. "Last time. Where are my fucking clothes?" He raised the bench over his head, hoping his legs wouldn't give out.

"The basement," the old man choked between sobs.

Jacob dropped the bench next to the innkeeper's leg and started toward the door. It was amazing. He almost felt pity for the sicko.

"You're mean," said a little boy voice from behind.

Hardaway snapped. Fire blazed in his eyes as the old man looked at him with pouting lips, still grasping his leg. Without thinking, Jacob picked up the pail and swung. Shit and piss sailed across the room, splattering the provocative models to a satisfying thunk of metal to head. The old man was out.

155

With no modesty, Jacob carefully traipsed down the stairs. He had to laugh, thinking what kind of reaction he might get. What would somebody think if they saw a man with no pants, wearing a straitjacket with cuts in the sleeves and arms dangling out? Probably an escapee from the asylum.

His lifeline back to sanity sat on the front desk, an old rotary dial telephone. He picked up the receiver. Nothing. The cord draped over the side, so Jacob followed it behind the desk. No outlet and not even a hole in the wall, the connector rested on the floor.

A new set of shivers coursed through Jacob. *This IS an asylum.*

A tidy room behind the lobby housed an old television set sitting on a TV tray, a patched-up recliner, and a wall full of empty bookshelves. A door behind the chair led to the kitchen. It was immaculate. The linoleum sparkled, the cabinets shined. Jacob's stomach grumbled for food. "After we get our clothes on and we have the car keys in hand." His stomach growled louder in protest.

A blue light filtered under a door next to the stove. Apprehension smothered the air as Jacob opened the door. He hoped to never see another blue light. Making a U turn to go down the steps, a blue light bulb hung loose from a cord hooked to the ceiling. On the floor, next to an antique washer complete with rollers, sat a huge mound of clothes.

Jacob's stomach quit protesting and he instantly lost his appetite. It never occurred to him that this might have happened before. Judging from the pile of clothes, it had happened to quite a few others.

With shaking hands, Jacob picked up his crumpled pants and shirt off the top of the pile. His underwear was still inside the slacks along with his wallet. There was no sign of his shoes, socks, or car keys.

It felt good to wear slacks again – his own slacks. They were loose enough around the waist; he'd lost weight. But they still didn't feel right. As loose as they were, they felt tight around the hips and thighs. *Probably from all that sitting.*

Past the pile of clothes, a door caught Hardaway's attention. A sign in handwritten scrawl read "Dark Room – Keep Out." "You don't give the orders anymore, pervert," Jacob said.

His shirt was inside out, and he unconsciously pulled the sleeves back out while walking toward the door. Pulling it open with one hand, Jacob fumbled with the straitjacket, trying to pull it over his head with the other. Automatically reaching around inside feeling for the light, he pulled the jacket off just as he found the switch.

Jacob couldn't breathe. His face turned straitjacket white. His legs buckled, and he quickly grabbed the door for support and vomited what little was in his stomach. "Deep breaths, in and out," he told himself. He shut his eyes and prayed that he didn't really see what he saw. He opened them again, but the nightmare still laughed.

Breasts. He had breasts. Female breasts. Certainly not Dolly Parton size, but mature, definitely needing a bra, female breasts. The small amount of dark hair he once had on his chest was exactly like the hair on his arms and legs – lighter and very fine. *What had that monster done?*

Jacob quickly buttoned his shirt as if it would hide his embarrassment and shame. He took a deep breath and looked around. A small scream wound through his ears, and he realized it came from within. "My God!" he cried.

A group of snapshots were tacked to the wall. They were of him in various stages of development. He looked asleep or semiconscious in all of them, and in the later ones, he wore red French-cut panties and a red lace bra. Underneath his pictures was taped the name "Jacqueline." Down the wall there was Pauline, Jessica, Melissa . . . it kept going. They were all men, all unconscious, all covering each stage of their development.

As sick as it made him, Jacob could not take his eyes off the photos. It repelled and fascinated him at the same time.

Film hung on clothespins above the developing pans. Next to the sink sat gallon jugs of chemicals and next to them, dozens of small bottles. Jacob picked one up. "Estinyl." Underneath, in the same sloppy writing as the keep-out sign, was written "estrogen." "Oh my God!" he said in a whispered cry. There was also "Aygestin", "progesterone" it said under the label, and "Nizoral" an "anti-hormone."

"Anti-hormone!" Jacob screamed, and threw the bottle, shattering it against the wall.

Nausea washed over him again as he smashed bottle after bottle. He stopped when a sliver of glass cut into his foot. "I've gotta get out of here."

~ ~ ~

"You been down there quite some time, Jackie."

Jacob stopped cold at the top of the stairs. Sitting in the recliner now shoved in the kitchen sat the innkeeper with a double barrel shotgun pointed at Jacob's head. The madman took aim. He'd reverted back from the little child that Hardaway had left unconscious upstairs. Traces of make-up still outlined his face, but it looked as if most of it had been rubbed off. A cut glistened above his cheek, swelling his right eye almost closed. The robe cord tied tight around his waist, but the teddy still peeked through his chest.

"After all I done fer you."

Why didn't I kill him? Jacob looked up to the heavens. Something inside clicked off.

"I shared my food, kept you clean. Fer Christ sake, I only charged ya fer one night an' you been here well over a month. An' this is how my generosity gets repaid? I'd be within my rights ta blow yer Goddamn brains out."

The fight drained from Jacob's body. A transformation overtook him, and he just didn't care anymore. There was nothing to do but accept death. The barrel of the gun looked black and cold, and Jacob wondered if he'd see the flash before he got hit.

"Now what we're gonna do is march you back ta yer room, an' git you settled 'til I'm ready ta teach you a lesson. Clear?"

Surprised, but apathetic at the reprieve, Jacob nodded, put his hands in the air, and started toward the lobby. The hotel-keeper kept the gun ready and picked up a broom with his free hand. Using the handle as a cane, he hopped after his guest up the stairs, careful not to let his foot touch the floor.

At the top of the landing, down the hall, the door was open. A magic carpet of blue light rolled out to give Jacob a ride back to Hell. He stopped at the top of the steps and stared. Numbness faded, and the desire to live crept back in his mind. He would not go back into the blue room.

A sharp pain jabbed Hardaway's back. The tip of the gun pushed him a step closer. "Keep goin'."

Jacob closed his eyes and took a deep breath. "No!"

He spun around and accidentally knocked into the barrel. A deafening explosion echoed down the hall. Buckshot blasted a hole through a thin sheet of drywall, sending chunks of plaster and dust in all directions. The hotel keeper hadn't prepared himself for the backlash and put too much weight on the broom trying to catch his balance. The handle snapped, sending him tumbling down the stairs.

Jacob looked at the hole in the wall, then at the weapon at his feet, and then at the bottom of the stairs. The man's gray eyes stared at the ceiling but looked at nothing. His legs awkwardly apart, exposing the bottom half of the lingerie. One arm pointed toward the door while the other lodged behind his back. Jacob felt nothing. He assumed neither did the hotel keeper.

Slowly, he focused his attention to the hole in the wall. On the other side of the plasterboard stood a door full of buckshot. The knob had been removed and it pushed open easily. The smell of rot and decay rushed out from its long confinement. Jacob reached through and flipped on the switch. A blue light snapped to life.

The room looked like an exact replica of the one he'd been

159

locked in. The same pictures of headless women in lingerie, that weren't really women, covered the walls. A body, mostly decomposed, lie huddled in the corner. Jacob felt nothing for him either. He wondered how many other victims the old man had humiliated, raped, tortured, and then killed. He decided that he didn't really want to know.

~ ~ ~

He walked around the hotel grounds one last time, looking for his car. Not a trace. He assumed the old man had driven it into the swamp. He could only think of one thing to do.

The reflection smiled back. It wasn't great, but it wasn't a bad job for a novice. He used the hotel keeper's straight razor and never had a smoother shave. The eyeliner looked a bit thick, the lipstick a little too red, but it was the best available. He moussed his hair up and thought it looked chic. In the pile of clothes from the basement, he found a pair of tight jeans and a sweater a size too small. They felt good over the silk bra and panties. He convinced himself that this was the only way for a ride home. No one picks up guy hitchhikers anymore.

It took almost an hour, but the first car driving down the road pulled over. *I just have to remember*, he thought while the driver reached over to open the door. My name is Jacqueline.

A CRACK IN THE AIR

"Ya know how when you squint your eyes really tight you can sometimes see things that aren't really there? Like little lines that seem to float?"

Albert Ross stared into Dr. Hamensham's eyes, looking for any sign that the shrink might think him crazy. One thing that Albert couldn't tolerate was anybody who took him lightly. That meant disrespect, and that meant showing what happened to people who dissed Albert Ross. Two women and one man involuntarily sacrificed their lives as Albert made his point.

The doctor, calm and resolute, sat behind his desk and returned the gaze. "You mean like an eyelash," he answered softly.

"No! Not like a fucking eyelash," Albert sneered. He tried to stand up from the chair, momentarily forgetting about his wrists shackled to the metal arms. "Goddamn, son-of-a-bitch!"

The door behind Albert swung open and a uniform poked his head into the room. Hamensham held up a hand and the guard stepped back out, quietly closing the door behind him.

"We're not going to get overly excited again are we, Albert?" the Dr. asked.

Albert turned from the brain doctor to see if the guard was

within earshot. "Do you know what I would like to do to you, Dr. Quack?" Albert smiled.

It had been doctors that told the court his father was competent to stand trial; doctors that convinced the judge his mother was unfit; doctors that told his one good foster mom that the lump in her breast was nothing to worry about. In Albert's eyes, there was nothing lower on the food chain than doctors. Even lawyers were a step up. They just took money; doctors took lives. And what they didn't take, they made sure would be fucked up enough that it wouldn't be worth living.

Hamensham sighed. "You've been found competent, tried, convicted and sentenced." The doctor's cold blue eyes stared into Albert's icy grays. "Whatever is left of your life belongs to the Department of Corrections now. You'd better resign yourself to that fact because it's never going to change."

Albert glared back. "Like father, like son, huh?"

Hamensham stared back until Albert broke contact and slumped in his chair.

"Good," the doctor said. "Can we be friends now?"

"I saw a poster once," Albert said. "It said 'Too many people make the mistake believing that the court appointed psychiatrist is your friend.'"

For the first time in the interview, Hamensham smiled and began to write. "I'll have to remember that one. Now, tell me about these lines."

"Back to the subject at hand, fine." It didn't really matter. At first Albert thought that if he screwed around, controlled the conversation, the doctor would spend more time with him. He felt nothing but contempt for the sessions, and even less about the shrink, but every minute here meant one less minute in his cell. Unfortunately, just like the outside, when your hour was up, your hour was up.

"They're not really lines, more like cracks."

"Cracks that float," Hamensham said.

"They don't float, exactly." Ross could feel his agitation

162

rise. *Why can't this jerk understand?* "They're just there. And I can feel them pulling at me."

Hamensham flipped to a new page, still scribbling.

"It's hard to explain, but if I squint my eyes really tight, and concentrate as hard as I can, I can make the cracks widen, and I can see inside."

"And what do you see?" the doctor asked.

"It's hard to tell. Everything is fuzzy. Kind of like looking through crumpled up wax paper."

"No beautiful women in bikinis, holding pina coladas and waving at you to come over?" Hamensham asked.

Albert glared. "And no megalopompous, fuckhead shrinks, doubled over a bar with their pants around their ankles and blood draining out their assholes, either."

The smirk vanished from Hamensham's face. "Guard!" He set his notebook on the desk. "I don't believe we can make any more progress today, Mr. Ross. If you can manage to keep yourself out of seg, I'll see you again next month."

The guard unlocked Albert from his chair and roughly grabbed him at the armpit, hoisting him onto his feet.

Even upside-down, and through the chicken-scratch the doctor called handwriting, Albert could make out a few of the words . . . deluded, intelligent, sociopath.

Hamensham saw him looking and quickly grabbed his notes. Albert started to laugh.

"Hey," he said to the guard as they left the office. "The shrink thinks I'm smart."

~ ~ ~

With just a couple hours to go before last head count and night lock-down, Albert tore the foam padding off the stainless steel shelf the State called a bed. Midsummer heat baked the men in their cells, making tempers short and violence all too easy to fall into. The metal would feel cool, at least for a few minutes. Two cages down he heard muffled screams as boots and mal-

163

let fists tenderized new meat. If the guy was lucky he wouldn't survive the beating. Albert saw the kid when he checked in three days ago. Small, young, and stinking of fear – he showed not even a front of bravado.

Too bad for the kid; mugging in the zoo was a science. Anybody who knew anything knew where to cause the most pain with the least amount of damage. Ninety-nine percent of the time they knew how far they could take it – just this side of fatal. By wake-up tomorrow, everybody on the block would know new meat was anyone's bitch until he became property.

Albert thought back to his first days. It had been easy to ignore the prisoners' taunts, but he had to draw the line when some asshole spit on him. Albert had grabbed the offender through the bars, and before anyone could react, sank his teeth into the man's face like a pit bull.

With his eyes rolled back into his head, only the whites showed. The guard had pummeled Albert in an effort to get him off the inmate. Albert finally let go when the man's cheek separated from his face, bloody flesh dangling from Albert's mouth. It took four guards to carry Albert away to the cheers of the crowd, each one showering him with saliva as he passed by. The injured prisoner went to the infirmary while Albert got 90 days in seg before he even set foot in his new home. It didn't matter – his reputation had been made.

Bells screamed, bringing Albert back to the here and now. Footsteps pounded down the tier, and Albert quickly rolled on his side, his face almost touching the wall, eyes straight ahead. Normal procedure from the Sgt. Schultz school of staying alive – Rule number one: I see nothing.

While guards shouted orders, inmates whooped and hollered around the open cell door trying to create a diversion for their comrades. Albert rolled onto his back, scrunched his eyes, and waited. Waited and searched.

A white hairline fissure crackled in the air. A tiny bolt of lightning seemed to suspend just out of Albert's reach. Through eyes barely open, Albert concentrated, blocking out the mayhem outside his cage. Beads of sweat formed on his brow as he willed the crack in the air to grow.

Slowly, like watching the minute hand of a clock move, the crevice opened a tiny slit wider. Carefully, he reached out his hand. With no more than the sting from a tattoo needle, his finger penetrated the small abyss. Albert snapped his eyes wide, hoping to catch a glimpse of the other side. But as his eyes sprang open, the vision and the sensation in his hand had disappeared.

He laid back on his slab and stared at the ceiling as the doors all thundered shut in unison. Metal clashing against metal echoed throughout the tier, and Albert could feel each door banging inside his head. He reached for a small bottle of aspirin, a half-day's wages, and popped four tablets onto his tongue. He focused on the bitter taste in his mouth, rather than the blood soaked man that the guards carried past his cell.

"I got to get outta here," he told himself.

Again, he tried to bring back the cracks. He had to send his mind somewhere before the walls closed in on him again, giving the claustrophobia control. Albert squinted and scrunched his eyes until the lines reappeared.

Minutes went by, maybe hours. It didn't matter. What did matter was that Albert was almost free. With sheer scrutinization, he brought the opening to him and combined with willpower, opened the crack wider than he ever had. He stuck in both arms, all the way up to the elbow, still concentrating. He couldn't see his hands; they were buried in a light gray fog. The tingling in his arms felt like a massage. He had to concentrate – fight the excitement, fight the temptation to jump up-and-down, screaming in triumph. Just concentrate until he could get to the other side. Just a little wider and he'd be able to squeeze his body through.

Slowly, Albert brought his face to the mist. He could smell the electricity, feel the pins jumping out to caress his face, inviting him to come in, gently pulling him. His body rose off the bed and in an instant was sucked through.

~ ~ ~

Albert sat on the concrete floor, his head spinning. Dazed and confused and saturated in sweat, he looked around at his new surroundings then screamed obscenities until his throat felt raw. He hadn't traveled anywhere. The toilet, the sink, and the bed, were all within reach. The cage door – still locked shut. Something was different, though. Something not quite right, unsettling, but he couldn't place a finger on it. Not yet.

The floor felt cool and Albert decided he would sleep there until the morning bell sounded and the doors would slide open. Once the rage subsided, sleep came almost instantaneously.

Albert woke up to silence and waited for the bell. His body alarm knew it to be seconds away. He waited. Once he had settled in and his life was a daily routine, Albert never woke up more than one-half minute before the wake-up call. And he waited in the eerie silence.

Silence! That was it. When was the last time he had heard nothing? Before the joint, that much was certain. You could always depend on someone yelling or screaming or banging on his bars. Twenty-four hours a day one of the animals had something to say. Albert was an expert at blocking out noise. A jailer could scream just inches from Albert's face, but when Albert put his mind elsewhere, he'd never hear a word. He might not hear it, but he always knew it was there. It became a comfort, a security blanket, a knowledge that he wasn't in this hell alone. As much as he hated the noise, he'd grown dependent on it. Silence scared the hell out of him.

Could he have slept through the alarms and missed everyone as they went to breakfast? Couldn't happen. Even if he did, the cell door would be open.

Albert got to his feet and pushed his face as far as it would go between the bars. No guards, no inmates, no nothing.

"Where the hell is everybody?" he shouted. His voice echoed off the walls. "This ain't funny!" Panic crept into his voice.

166

Minute after agonizing minute, Albert sat alone. Each second dragged by painfully as he thought of a slow torturous death by starvation. Forgotten by the inside and the outside world. *How could they move an entire block except for me*? For the first time in what felt like a hundred years ago, a tear welled up in Albert Ross' eye.

As he raked his sleeve across his face, he saw it – dangling in air, the white jagged line. He focused and willed it closer. It took almost no concentration at all as the small piece of space floated toward him. It looked bigger now – misshapen, stretched like a womb after birth. As Albert brought it to his face, he saw movement through the mist.

Shrouded in fog, two guards stood alert. They were standing in his cell. He couldn't hear a word, but the actions were loud and clear. One kept waving his arms wildly while the other kept looking around the jail cell waiting for the prisoner to reappear.

Albert's fear was replaced with elation. "They think I escaped!" he shouted.

This was better than TV. He stared as two more guards came into his cell and looked around as if he might be hiding under the sink or in the toilet.

"Keep looking, you jerk-offs," he yelled. "Maybe I'm hiding in the bottle of aspirin."

Albert's smile turned into a sneer. Through the open cage walked the warden along with Dr. Hamensham. The guards surrounded the two men, each one spewing questions as the doctor ignored them. Albert could feel his muscles tighten, his blood boil as the shrink invaded deeper into his small domain.

"Concentrate," Albert whispered to himself.

He backed up until he hit the wall, mentally carrying the space with him. "Focus," he said out loud, and the crack became wider. Albert's heart raced; it seemed that the shrink was looking straight at him. "Just a little wider. You see it, don't you?"

The Dr. was squinting just inches from Albert, a look of confusion on his face. Albert could taste tin foil as his heart

167

pounded. The gray mist turned red, as did everything else in Albert's vision. He could feel his "fun" self taking over. It had been so long.

Albert centered as best he could to keep the hole open. Faster than a cobra, he reached through and grabbed the tweed lapels of the psychiatrist's jacket and yanked. As the two men stumbled into the wall, the doctor slipped, and fell down onto his knees.

Their eyes locked. Albert could feel the fire in his, saw the terror in Hamensham's. The doctor scrambled to his feet, turned around, and froze. Not only were the guards not there, but the cage door was locked. No screaming, yelling, confusion – just silence.

Albert smiled. "You ain't no bikini bitch with a pina colada, but I'm sure we're going to have a great time anyway."

THE PERFECT JURY

Seven men and five women jotted sporadic notes as the law-yer stood before them emphasizing discrepancies in the state-ments from previous witnesses. He thanked the jury in advance for their service and then sat down. The judge began instructing the jury as to the definitions of law and what they could and could not consider. When he finished, the bailiff led the jurors into a windowless room with a long oak table surrounded by twelve chairs. Tacked upon the wall hung a bulletin board with assorted colors of thumbtacks pushed into the cork. In front of each chair, a pen, a small pad of paper, and a Styrofoam cup sat on the table. In the middle of the table were two plastic pitchers of water. The deputy tossed the exhibits onto the table. Assorted photographs, police and medical reports scattered across the polished surface. He told them they would be going to dinner in about an hour. If anyone needed to use the restroom, they would have to knock and wait for the bailiff to give them an escort. The door closed, and they were locked in.

~ ~ ~

"We've got a problem," Derek said.

169

Dr. Derek Sorenson stood 5'2", a wiry 128 pounds, with a patch of thin hair greased back on an otherwise bare pate. A white smock hung loosely off his shoulders.

"According to you, we always have a problem," Eugene Washington walked over and stood next to Sorenson. They both stared into the monitor. "What is it this time?"

Washington was as black as Sorenson was white. He stood six foot even and weighed a muscular 210 pounds. Where Sorenson had strands of hair, Washington preferred the completely bald look. The only commonality the two shared was their genius intelligence.

"They just voted that Juror #3 is the foreperson," Derek said. An echo of worry sparked in his voice.

"So what's the big deal?" Washington asked. The small screen showed Juror #3 taking a seat at the head of the table.

"What's the big deal? What's the big Deal?" Sorenson became more animated. "The big deal is that for the seventy-one trials that they've been together, Juror #8 has always been the foreperson in this kind of case. This isn't good. We'd better call it in."

"Calm down," Washington said. His commanding voice was low and resonant. "Turn up the volume and let's observe them for a few minutes." He went up to the console and pressed the green button.

A hole, no larger than a fly, sat undetected in the corner of the jury room where the ceiling met the wall. Behind the wall a red light flicked on and the camera began recording. The two observers watched intently from their office.

"Before we start going through all this evidence, let's just take a quick vote and see where we all stand. Who knows, if it's unanimous, we can all go home in time for supper." Juror #3's Midwestern twang crackled through the tiny speaker. She tore a piece of paper into scraps and passed them around the table.

"They never did that before," Derek said. A spasm triggered at the corner of his left eye.

"That's three for guilty and nine for not guilty," Juror #3 said.

"Nine to acquit?" Eugene shouted. "Are they crazy? These are almost the exact same facts as State vs. Welton back in '29, and very similar to the case of State vs. Boyle just two years ago. These very people found them both guilty in less than two hours."

"That's it. I'm calling it in." Sorenson's hand shook as he reached for the phone.

"Hold it a minute," Washington said. "Before you do that, pull out the last mind scans. I want to be sure we only erased the trial from their brains and not some of their personality. Before we report in I want to be certain that if we screwed up, we find it before the boss does."

"Good point," Derek said. He swung his chair around the desk and began tapping on the keyboard. The computer screen came to life, listing each juror's name, juror number, and an abbreviated bio. Derek clicked on Juror #3's name. Instantly a 3-D image of her brain appeared. He focused on the higher cortical part of the brain and isolated the area for short-term memory, entered equations, studied the electroencephalogram, went over memory loss techniques, and finally concluded they did everything right, at least everything according to procedure. He repeated the task on four more jurors, found the same results, and decided that was enough.

"Negatory. We're in the clear," Derek said.

He looked up and saw Washington staring fixedly at the monitor. The man's dark skin looked ashen, and his lower jaw bobbed up and down like it was attached with a spring.

"I said we're in the clear," Derek repeated.

Washington looked up as if seeing his partner for the first time. He slowly shook his head. "No, we're not. It's coming unraveled, man."

Sorenson shuddered. That didn't sound like his partner. He walked over and stood next to his co-worker and became hypnotized at the screen. Juror #11 had his head between his hands and looked like he was trying to squeeze it until it popped. "It sounds so familiar, but I just can't remember!" he shouted.

"He can't remember what?" Derek mumbled under his breath.

"McCafferty," Eugene whispered.

Just as quietly, Sorenson answered, "Son of a bitch."

Two trials earlier, just four months ago, this jury acquitted Jeffery McCafferty of second-degree murder. They called it a case of self-defense. They should have had no memory of it at all.

Derek walked over to the red phone with no numbers and lifted the receiver. He waited for an instant, and then spoke. "Jury 1-4-7 – code Z." He waited for instructions then put the phone back in the cradle and walked back to the monitor.

"Do they want to call a mistrial, erase their minds again, and start over?" Washington asked.

"Not yet," Sorenson said. "They want to see if the jury will struggle out a verdict. What's going on?"

"Jurors 1, 2 and 9 aren't doing well. They think they've heard of McCafferty as well. Juror #5 has a splitting headache, and Juror #12 misses her baby girl. What else did they say?"

"They want one of us to give a full report in two hours. They don't care which one of us it is." Sorenson snorted. "Her baby girl is older than she is now."

Washington jerked his eyes from the screen and stared at his partner.

"What? What is it?" Derek asked.

"If your face wasn't so pasty white, I'd kiss you."

"What?" Derek asked again.

Washington leapt around him and started typing at his computer. "Stasis. I want to check out what short term constantly repeated stasis does to the brain. Then I want to cross reference it with repeated short term memory cleansing."

The pair got to work. They sat at their computers and felt

completely in their element. The only sound in the room came from clacking keys. They didn't notice, nor did they care, as the bailiff took the jurors to dinner. With only ten minutes before reporting time, they compared notes.

"How does this sound?" Washington asked. "Even when it's not being used, it still ages. When you record over one spot too many times, it will start to degenerate beyond repair. Soon, patches of old recordings will show through before it's totally eaten away. Basically, this jury passed its peak long ago. I'm amazed they lasted this long. Their brains can't handle it anymore." He paused, waiting for Sorenson's reaction. "Do you think they'll buy it?"

Derek smiled. "Let me print out a couple of charts to back you up."

~ ~ ~

Derek sat alone, nervously munching a sandwich and watching the monitor while waiting for his partner. The elevator door opened, and Eugene walked in the room wearing a grin that stretched to his ears and two fists above his head in a thumbs up. Sorenson closed his eyes and blew out a long sigh. Now he could enjoy his dinner, but realized that the sandwich was almost gone. They watched the screen as the bailiff opened the door to the jury room.

"Good news, folks," the bailiff said. "The defendant just entered a plea of guilty. Your jury duty is over. You just have to report to the jury office, so they can sign you out."

Eugene's heart sank and the smile disappeared. He knew what happened to juries when they could no longer serve. "It's kind of like putting a beloved pet to sleep," he said.

"I wouldn't know," Derek said. "I never had a pet. But that's why they give them numbers. It's supposed to dehumanize them, so we don't get personally attached." Derek licked his fingers clean, and then wiped them on his sleeve.

"I know. But these folks were seasoned veterans long before

we started; and I've been here twenty-four years. They deserve more than being terminated."

Derek punched some keys on his computer and an old newspaper article appeared on the screen. "Terrorist Bomb Kills Deliberating Jury." "They were as good as dead when the PR department printed up that story. What difference does it make if they died thirty years ago or if they die tonight? Can you imagine what would happen if Juror #12 went home and hubby sees his long missing wife, and she hasn't aged since the day she allegedly died?"

"I know, I know," Washington said. "It's just not right, is all. I remember my granddaddy telling me about his jury duty once, back in the days when everybody served two weeks."

"Be careful," Derek whispered. "Remember, the walls have ears. As far as you or anybody else knows, that's still the way it is."

"Yeah, yeah, I know."

"Besides," Derek continued. "I like this way. When was the last time you heard a really moronic verdict? I've seen the selection process once. You'd like it, it's very scientific. The screening is done long before the summonses are mailed out. All jurors are fairly intelligent; everyone is put in a group that should get along, at least on paper. Each group has a certain amount of followers and leaders; and in the long run, we've saved millions in tax dollars. And finally, when was the last time you heard a friend or neighbor complain about doing their civic duty? It doesn't happen anymore. People think it does, but it doesn't. The only time is when we have to replace a panel. Any fun plans for the weekend?"

Eugene smiled, appreciating the change of topic. "Yeah," he said. "Me and Pam are taking Brenda to the Waterslide Park for her birthday. She's going to be nine."

"When are you going to marry that woman?" Derek asked. "You've been together, what, six years? And the kid adores you. You're not going to find any better."

~ ~ ~

Eugene Washington came home from work, showered, changed, got back in his car and drove to Pam's. Brenda was playing in the front yard when he pulled into the driveway. She looked up, smiled and ran to his car.

"Hi Gene. Mom's waiting for you. Did you bring me a present?"

"Not this time," he said as he scooped her into his arms. "It's too close to your birthday." He gave her a peck on the cheek then gently set her down.

"Goody," she said as she ran back to whatever she'd been doing. Gene saw a doll buried up to its neck in the dirt. Or maybe it was just its head resting on the ground. He chuckled as he thought it might be something her mother should know about.

He opened the door and succumbed to the aroma of steak broiling in the oven. *What's the special occasion*, he thought. Friday's were usually meatloaf night.

"Smells divine," he shouted.

"Hey, Honey Bear," the sweet voice came from the kitchen. "I was wondering if you could do me a favor?"

Boy, she didn't waste any time. That would explain the steak, he thought. "Anything," he called back as he plopped down onto the couch.

She came up behind him and began massaging his shoulders and pressed her lips to the top of his head. He let out a sigh that sounded more like a purr.

"Would you mind picking up Brenda from school for the next couple weeks?"

It felt like a blow to the gut and a noose tightening around his neck. The smell of food gagged him as his head throbbed. She didn't need to say another word. On the coffee table before him, on top of the bills and other junk mail lay the summons to report for jury duty.

THE LAST PATCH OF
AMERICAN WILDERNESS

The helicopter landed outside the entrance to the North Woods Dome. Jonathan Brice and Drew Stephenson stepped off and looked through the Plexiglas walls. Friends since childhood, they smiled at each other as they saw real birch and pine for the first time. Lillian Farthington stepped off next and took a deep breath.

"I can almost smell the fresh air coming through the walls," she said.

Charles Cutler, and his wife, Deborah, were the last ones off.

The Nationwide Holiday Weekend Promotion, this week, exclusive to attorneys, had only twelve lawyers sign up. The price forced two to drop out and five others had to cancel due to trials they couldn't reschedule. The remaining five stood outside the transparent gate and watched the helicopter whirl away. Alone on the landing pad, they stood in silence and awe. Next to them stood the great North Woods. It cost each of them a standard month's pay to afford what they were about to experience.

The door whooshed open and a recorded voice spoke

through a hidden speaker. "Welcome to the North Woods Tour. The last natural forest in the United States. Please deposit your token in the slot on the right as you enter."

Each one dropped in their disc and the door behind them slid shut. Cooler, damp air embraced them, replacing the hot dry breeze they left outside.

The voice continued, "Over ten thousand acres of this northern forest have been preserved and hermetically sealed from outside influences with oxygen being filtered up through the ground, thanks to PermaAir Corporation, along with the natural oxygen being produced through the plant life."

"I knew there would have to be a plug," Charles said.

The recording ignored the remark as Deborah tried to do the same.

"The scientists at PermaAir have spent years painstakingly researching, then constructing the North Woods Dome. The temperature is maintained at a constant 78 degrees Fahrenheit during the day and slowly drops to 64 degrees at night. The trail is ten miles in length and will take approximately four hours. You will see the Great Pit that before the disaster was known as Lake Superior. There, the trail will stop for thirty minutes. For your fun and adventure, we have set up for you virtual-performance goggles so you can see the mighty waves crashing upon the shore. You will be able to feel the spray from the water splash on your skin as you'll understand how this great lake got its name. From there, you will follow the trail up to the Great Wall of Canada where your journey will end.

"Follow the arrows to get to the beginning of the trail. Do not step off the trail until the end of your hike. Get your vid-cams ready and enjoy your adventure as you live like the explorers did centuries ago."

"I can't believe I'm finally doing this," Drew said. "I've wanted to do this since I was a kid."

"I can't believe the explorers had electra-walks," Mr. Cutler said.

"Shut up, Charles, and just enjoy it," Deborah cut in. The couple leered at each other.

"All I know is this cost me more than my misrepresentation insurance, so I'm going to get all I can out of it," Lillian said, breaking the tension.

Arrows pointed the direction through the brush. Drew led the way. On the other side, an entirely new world opened up. A world none of them had seen before. Plush vegetation covered the ground. Trees grew haphazardly. Some were so tall they even looked as though they might break through the top of the dome. As far as they could see in the dense woods, a miraculous green filled their eyes.

"Everybody on the trail," said Brice. He acted more like a grade-school kid than one of the top civil litigators in California Territory.

The trail, a long conveyor belt with a handrail on each side, curved into the mysterious wonder stretching into the unknown. At the front was a large red button with a small sign below it: DO NOT BEGIN TRAIL UNTIL EVERYONE IS ABOARD. PLEASE HOLD ON TO THE HANDRAILS AND DO NOT STEP FROM THE TRAIL ONCE IT STARTS MOVING.

The machine started to whir as Jonathan pressed the button. The conveyor belt began moving the lawyers deep into the woods.

"I can't believe I smell real pine," Lillian said.

"It is wonderful." Jonathan stepped over next to her and took a deep breath close to her neck.

Stephenson and the Cutlers looked at each other, rolling their eyes.

"So, where do you live?" Jonathan asked Lillian.

"HarvardLaw. Out east."

"A very prestigious city," said Brice.

She smiled. "We're trying to grow as a city, and we are in the process of acquiring land from HarvardMed. But take a simple business transaction and put it in front of a group of doctors . . ."

"My God! A real bird," Deborah Cutler gasped.

The group turned to her and looked toward the direction that she pointed.

"I see it. Give me the camera," Charles said

"I've done research on this," said Drew, while filming. "I'm pretty sure it's called a blue jay."

"It's beautiful," Mrs. Cutler said.

The trail hummed forward and curved around until the lawyers lost sight of the bird. They were in awe.

"So, where are you from, Mr. Brice?" Lillian restarted the conversation.

"Call me Jonathan. Both me and Drew were born and raised in MinnLaw South. Direct descendants from the original MinnesotaLaw, before the disaster. I decided to head west after the great quake. I set up a practice in a new city, BerkeleyLaw. I figured there'd be better business opportunities out there, and I've always been fascinated with disaster suits. Drew stayed here." Jonathan realized he was rambling.

"I just read an article about BerkeleyLaw in WestLaw Journal, I think. I'm impressed," said Lillian. "And you can call me Lil," she added, turning her attention toward Drew.

Drew blushed and turned away, staring at the scenery.

"What about you two?" Lillian asked the Cutlers.

"We're your next-door neighbors actually, YaleLaw," said Deborah. "We were childhood sweethearts."

"That was a long time ago," Charles said.

Deborah opened her mouth to return the insult, but thought better of it.

The sun's light filtered through the dome, casting long shadows of trees and giant boulders. Jonathan drew up close to Lillian and "accidentally" bumped shoulders.

"I've never seen anything like it," he said.

Lillian inched away until she had control of her space, smiled politely and turned her back to him.

The trail moved the lawyers forward. Each one felt the apprehension of fear from the unknown as they crept in and out of the shadows. Charles interlaced his arm with his wife's, convincing himself that it was more for her peace of mind. Drew found that Lillian had moved close to him, and like a puppy, Jonathan was close behind.

"I hope my cam doesn't run out of memory," Drew said. Fascination of the woods overcame his anxiety of Lillian's nearness. "I'm going to line my walls with these holos when I get home. Maybe make a continuous loop so I can just sit back and watch it over and over without moving a muscle."

"Computer geek," Jonathan whispered to Lillian.

"I think it sounds wonderful," she said. "Could you do that for me?"

"Sure," answered Drew. "Just send me your memory chip."

"Look!" Deb Cutler said. "A rodent!" She released her arm from her husband's grasp and pointed.

Not more than ten feet away, almost close enough to touch, a furry little animal climbed up a tree, quite oblivious to the five pairs of eyes that stared in delight.

"It's a squirrel," Jonathan said as he aimed the vid-cam. "Me and Drew saw one at the zoo once."

"You're quite the look-out," Lillian said to Deborah. "Keep up the good work."

Charles felt disappointed. That's twice he'd been shown up by his wife. Like a periscope, he scanned the woods for any sort of movement. He would announce the next sighting.

The path began to hum, unnoticeably at first, and then slowly rising in pitch. The five looked at each other with shrugged shoulders. The path vibrated under their feet and the whine intensified to a soft screech. The conveyor belt pitched suddenly, jolting the attorneys down to their knees.

"Oh my God," Lillian said. "What happened?"

"Is everyone all right?" asked Jonathan.

They all sat, stunned, looking at each other, and waiting for someone to speak while the trail died to a stop. The forest went silent; no birds chirped, and the calm breeze stopped, quieting the rustling of the leaves.

"Does anybody else smell something burning?" Drew asked.

A crackling sound came from under the trail. A puff of smoke seeped up from the belt. The attorneys scrambled to their feet.

With no more warning than a creaking groan, the path buckled, knocking the lawyers off the trail. Charles flipped over the rail as the others slipped under it and onto the hard dirt ground. Drew looked around and asked if anyone was hurt.

"I'm going to sue," Charles said.

"Oh Charles, shut up," Deborah said.

"This is inexcusable. I could've been seriously hurt. We could've been hurt. I'm thinking class action." He got up, wiping dirt from his hands. "Who's with me on this? We can shut this death trap down."

"Enough!" Drew shouted. "Look around, do you see anybody hurt?"

Everyone stared at his sudden outburst. Deborah smiled.

"How can you think of lawsuits?" Drew continued. "Didn't we all come here to get away from that for awhile?" His face scowled red as spittle flew from his mouth.

Lillian walked over and put her hand on Drew's shoulder. Jonathan stared at his best friend. Since he'd known Drew, he had never seen him lose his temper. Maybe practicing law had taken its toll.

The woods were silent as Charles contemplated debating this young lawyer. Later, when he could get them alone, he was sure that he could sway their minds. Everyone except his wife. The stubborn bitch.

Drew let out a sigh. "I'm sorry. It's just that I wanted to do this for so long, ever since I was a kid. I'm not about to let a little setback ruin it for me."

Slowly, a strange smile transformed his face. He looked at

Jonathan, then at each of his fellow travelers. In a half whisper, he asked, "Who wants to go exploring?"

The four lawyers stared in astonishment as if Drew's mind had snapped. Lillian took a step back and bumped into Jonathan, much to his delight. Charles' jaw hung open and he protectively took his wife's arm and led her a few strides back from this lunatic.

"You can't be serious," Deborah said. "You have no idea what's out there."

Even as she spoke, Drew could see a flame of excitement ignite in her eyes.

"She's right," Lillian said. "It could be dangerous."

"You're talking crazy. We wait right here until help arrives. They obviously know something went wrong, and I'm sure help is already on the way." Charles folded his arms across his chest.

Drew looked pleadingly at his best friend. He knew the two of them together would be able to sway the others, at least the women. Mr. Cutler seemed a hopeless case.

Jonathan felt the pressure from the others' gaze. He glanced at Lillian and saw fear in her eyes.

"They're right, Drew," he said with guilt. "It's just too dangerous."

Drew felt as if a knife pierced his heart. He turned away from the group, sat on the hard ground, and stared into the wilderness. The trees, as far as the eye could see, called out to him as the sun drifted farther into the afternoon sky, high above the dome.

"Don't you people realize that this is a once-in-a-lifetime opportunity? Think of what you could tell people when you got home. C'mon, who really cares about hearing more courtroom stories? This is something books could be recorded about."

"You've been out-voted, Mr. Stephenson. Now why don't you just behave yourself until help arrives?" Mr. Cutler said.

Deborah shot her husband a look of contempt. "I don't know, now that I think about it, it does sound rather intriguing."

"Oh, stop it, Deborah," said Charles. "You're not fooling anybody. You know the only reason you're doing this is to irritate me."

Caught. She couldn't help suppress a smile as she looked into the woods. It did look fascinating, though.

"If you promise not to stray too far from the trail, I guess I'm game," she said to Drew, while looking at her husband.

"Great!" Drew sprang to his feet. "You won't regret it. Anybody else?"

"You're not going anywhere." Charles glared at his wife. "You're going to stay here until help arrives. End of discussion."

"Don't be such an ass, Charles. Either join us or wait here. Personally, I'd prefer it if you'd wait, but unlike you, I know people have the right to make up their own minds."

"How about it?" Drew asked Jonathan and Lillian, ignoring the Cutlers' spat.

Color drained from Lillian's face. Goose bumps dotted her arms.

"No!"

Jonathan put his arm around her, easing her to the ground.

"You don't know what's out there," she said. "When I was a little girl, I heard stories that wild animals used to wander around in woods like this."

"What has gotten into you?" Deborah asked. "You seemed normal just a while ago. One minor mishap and you go to pieces. How do you survive in a courtroom?"

Anger replaced some of the fear as Lillian glared at Mrs. Cutler. "This is nothing like a courtroom," she said with venom. "There, everything is controlled. Tell me, Mrs. Cutler, what do you know about survival? What if Drew trips over a rock and breaks his leg? Do you know how to fuse a bone? Can you treat a concussion? If something does happen, who are you going to call? And how?"

Charles smiled, thoroughly enjoying himself.

"And what if no one ever bothered to take chances?" Deborah said. "Mankind would still be living in caves, sneaking out to eat berries when all the animals slept. It's time to grow up, child, and crawl out of your shell."

Deborah and Lillian locked eyes.

Drew spoke up. "Nothing is going to happen. Besides, we're not going to travel very far. And I'd like to get started before they get here and say we can't. Are you coming?" he looked at Jonathan.

"What about you, Charles?" Deborah asked.

"If you think I'm leaving you alone with that suicidal maniac, you're crazier than he is."

Deborah rolled her eyes.

"I don't think so. I'm not going to leave Lil alone," Jonathan said as he took a seat next to her. "Be careful."

Deborah took a deep breath. The pine smell tickled her senses as she followed Drew away from the trail. Charles pounded after them, cursing under his breath as a branch snagged his silk shirt. Drew's eyes opened wide in childhood wonderment as he set his cam on panoramic.

"We're blazing our own trail," Drew said. A thin layer of fear lightly covered each step that led farther away from the security of the trail and into the shadows that man had not been allowed to enter. With nerves prickling, Drew enjoyed every scratch as a new experience.

"You're getting too far from the trail," Charles said. Irritation formed his words as a branch snapped back, narrowly missing his eye.

Drew ignored him and walked deeper in the foliage. The thick, lush leaves felt heavenly as they brushed against his clothes. This was real nature. No buildings rose above the trees; no bumping into strangers on the freshly manicured paths in sterilized parks. Just total freedom to the end of eyesight, the way God had intended it to be.

Deborah smiled at her husband, shrugging her shoulders

sympathetically but keeping pace with the younger lawyer. Charles seethed as he fell further behind.

"Drew, wait," Deborah said. "Right above you, in the tree." She pointed.

High above, a small bird with a white breast and black head perched upon a branch and stared out over the forest.

"Amazing," Deborah whispered. "So natural."

Drew aimed his vidcam and whispered back, "Just think, I'll have my very own holograph of a real woodpecker. That's what it is, you know. And a holograph that I made myself." Then as an afterthought, "And I can probably make a fortune selling copies."

"Quiet. You're starting to sound like my husband."

"What? He's starting to make some sense?" Charles said, tromping through the brush. "Like it's time to head back?"

"Shhhh. You'll scare it," Drew said. He put the lens on close-up.

"Scare what? That? Looks like we scared the hell out of it. Too scared to fly away no doubt." Charles heaved a sigh. "Goddamn it," he said as he looked down and stuck his finger through a hole in his trouser leg.

Deborah let out a long breath. "I hate to admit when he's right, Drew, but I think we should start heading back, too."

"Just a little farther," Drew said.

"It's been an adventure, Drew," Deborah said as she put a gentle hand on his shoulder. "But Lillian and Jon have probably been rescued already, and I'm sure that if we're not back soon, they'll probably send out search parties."

"Yeah." Emptiness rang in Drew's voice as he stared longingly into the wilderness.

"And we'll probably be stuck footing the bill," added Charles.

Deborah started back; Drew reluctantly followed while Charles grumbled, wondering if it was worth mending his slacks.

"Are you coming, or are you going to stand there and whine?" Deborah called.

Something snapped as blood rushed to Charles' head. He'd put up with his wife's insolence longer than he should have. She'd been taunting and challenging the minute they got on the plane. He kept holding back, trying to be decent, thinking she would notice and try to match his attitude. But no, she'd been jabbing her finger in his chest, begging for a fight. It was he who had controlled himself throughout this whole God-forsaken trip. If only she'd have had enough common sense, they would have gone on a wonderfully planned trip to the Poconos. YaleLaw had acquired the land and built a perfectly fine Members Only Club Resort. But no, Deborah Cutler had to do something intriguing, something they could do only once in their life; something that would bring excitement back into their marriage. If the marriage ended now, it was her fault.

"Goddamn it!" he screamed as his toe jammed into a rock.

In a fit of temper, he stomped and kicked at the rock, loosening the ground. Drew and Deborah ran back, wondering why on earth Charles was causing such a commotion.

Deborah saw him first and screamed, "No, Charles. Don't!"

It was too late as Charles hurled a fistful of stones at the unsuspecting bird.

The moment those small rocks left his hand, Charles regretted what he'd done. He saw that his aim was still as good as it had been while playing college baseball.

How many times had his temper gotten away from him? And how many times had he promised his wife that it would never happen again?

The three stared in silence, like watching in slow motion as one of the stones sailed straight at the bird. It never turned its head.

With a ka-thunk, a cold chill covered Charles. Harming wildlife was a criminal offense. He could go to jail for this.

The rock bounced off its target. A popping sound charged the air as a few sparks flashed from the wing as it snapped and dangled from the body by a thin wire.

Too shocked to say anything, Drew stood with his mouth wide open. The sudden rage that Deborah felt toward her husband vanished in a heartbeat, confusion taking over. It was Charles who finally broke the stillness.

"Well I'll be damned. It's a fake."

Deborah looked at him, then at Drew. Drew never took his eyes from the bird.

"It's a Goddamn fake," Charles said again as relief washed over his body.

Drew's mind battled with itself, struggling for any sort of explanation.

Why?

With a tug on his sleeve, Drew's eyes focused on Mrs. Cutler's face just inches from his own. Her eyes looked worried and concerned.

"Are you all right? I thought we lost you there for a minute."

Drew looked up at the trees in vain, trying to find any sort of wildlife. "Not a creature was stirring," he whispered under his breath.

"What?" Deborah asked.

"Nothing. Let's find the others and get the hell out of here." Drew stomped back toward the trail. He tried to return to the little boy mode that kept him so enamored, but deep down he knew that, even besides the bird, this was not right. Nothing he could place at the moment, but something, just out of mental reach.

Charles, feeling his happiest since Deborah convinced him to go on this vacation to Hell, took a deep breath and stopped. Standing next to him, Deborah felt a stab of fear as she thought her husband might be having another heart attack. In an instant, Lillian's words haunted her. What could she do? There was no hospital, no doctors. She felt like kicking herself, insisting that they leave their phones at the hotel, making sure there would be no business interruptions.

All within the space of a few seconds, Charles let out his breath and broke out in a huge, rare, smile. Deborah let out her breath in small gasps, torn between grateful that he was all right and wanting to kill him for scaring her.

"What do you smell?" Charles asked.

Deborah and Drew looked at each other, scrunching their noses in the air. Deborah hated when Charles played this game, but she also knew that he was onto something – something he would take his own sweet time telling, only after he proved how brilliant he was. She wanted to punch that smug face.

"I don't smell anything, Charles," Deborah said. "What's your point?"

Drew stood silently, shaking his head.

"And tell me what you see, or don't see, on the ground," Charles said, so full of confidence that he shook.

Deborah looked ready to scream.

Drew spoke softly. "No leaves. No fallen branches. Nothing is out of place." He felt numb.

Deborah's eyes widened as she caught on. "And it doesn't smell like a forest. In fact, it doesn't smell much like anything at all."

Charles' smile faded. He didn't expect his "students" to catch on so quickly, but he did feel vindicated.

"I guess I noticed it, but it didn't register," Deborah said. "The farther away from the trail we went, the smell just faded away."

"And the ground should be littered with leaves and branches," Drew said.

He reached out to a small branch and tried to break it off the tree. He tugged, bowed, and wrenched the stick, but it kept springing back into place. He finally took a leaf and yanked. The green petal unwillingly snapped off its branch. Drew rubbed it between his fingers and tried to rip it in half. The synthetic material wouldn't tear.

Hard ground clomped under Charles' feet as he approached Drew.

"We can close this travesty down." He spoke with enthusiasm. "Everything inside this dome is one gigantic scam."

"Everything inside this dome is one gigantic dream!"

Charles, Deborah, and Drew whipped their heads in unison. Through the trees, a man spoke in a deep loud voice. His skin was the color of ground coffee, and sweat glistened off his bald head. He wore a tan shirt and tan shorts that strained against bulging muscles. Behind him, two men, both white, stood at ease, their faces hiding any emotion. They were both big enough to be street police outside the safety perimeters of YaleLaw.

"I am glad we find you unharmed. My name is Alvin Turner, head groundskeeper to the North Woods." His voice held a slight accent. "It was very foolish of you to walk away from the trail. Very foolish. The woods can be dangerous to those unfamiliar with its mystery."

"Dangerous from what? Mechanical birds?" Charles said.

Turner's smile betrayed no hint of irritation. "You must be Charles Cutler." He walked over and held out his hand.

Charles shook it. One could always tell a lot about a person by their handshake. Turner's handshake was naturally firm, no strain, his skin callused.

"Ahh, and you must be Mrs. Deborah Cutler." Turner bowed his head and lightly took her hand. "Very lovely."

Drew walked over. "And Mr. Drew Stephenson. A pleasure."

Turner stepped back and made no motion to introduce his companions.

"Gentlemen and lady, we fixed the trail very quickly. No need for you to wander away. Very dangerous. If you will please follow me, we will get you back on the trail, and you may complete your tour."

189

"You don't seem to understand," Mr. Cutler said. "You and your bosses are in some very serious trouble here."

"Not now, Charles," Deborah whispered urgently.

One of the men behind the groundskeeper reached into his pants pocket. Drew shuddered and unconsciously took a step behind Charles. Deborah took a quick breath while her husband stood ready to face a challenge. "I'd better warn you . . ."

The man pulled out a small remote control and pressed the button. A buzzing sound filtered down from the tree, and the woodpecker came to life. Its damaged wing shot out sparks as its good wing fluttered. It lifted about a foot off the branch and then nose-dived to the ground. The man walked over, picked it up, and slid it in his pocket along with the remote.

"You were saying, Mr. Cutler?" Turner's smile became grating.

Charles blushed and mumbled, "I was just saying that a lot of people know we are here."

"Ahh, yes, your friends. Mr. Brice and Ms. Farthington have continued on the trail. They will meet you at the pickup point."

Through the trees and brush, Alvin Turner led the way, with his two men bringing up the rear. Drew felt like a prisoner.

"You see," Turner said, "there is nothing more to see that is off the trail. Yes?"

"I dunno. Seeing sparks fly out a bird I thought was pretty interesting," Drew said.

Deborah did a slight double take to make sure she had heard right, that Drew spoke and not her husband.

"Yes, very interesting indeed," Turner said. "Something we shall have to look into."

Charles blushed.

The six walked silently as the scent of forest became strong again as they neared the trail. Drew looked down to see a smattering of leaves on the ground. They looked like properly placed fakes, but then, everything about the forest now seemed artificial.

"Here we are, back on the trail," Turner said, with a wide grin that showed perfect white teeth.

An electra-cart sat between the rails on an unmoving conveyor belt. In front of the cart sat a padded seat with a row of indentations on one of the arms. Behind it, two short benches sat lengthwise, long enough to sit two people each.

Turner pulled out what looked like an antique walkie-talkie from his shirt pocket; one of the early microchip models. He turned his back on the tourists and softly mumbled in an unfamiliar a language. He put it up to his ear, smiled.

"I do so apologize, but I am afraid you will have to finish your tour some other time. The curator would like to speak with you immediately. If you would please kindly take a seat." Turner pointed toward the vehicle.

"I'm sure he would," Charles said. "And I would certainly like to have a chat with him."

"Very good. Then if you please take a seat, we shall go now. And the curator is a she."

Deborah chuckled even though she found Mr. Turner most irritating. But she did love listening to him speak. She liked the way the words rolled out of his mouth and how he pronounced each syllable distinctly. She smiled at him as she took a seat, and he seemed genuinely charmed. Drew took a seat opposite her and avoided looking at anybody. Charles sat dutifully next to his wife.

Turner gave a nod to one of his men, and the man started to walk. The other man, the one with the bird in his pocket, climbed in next to Drew, squeezing him between the driver's seat and a massive thigh. Drew suddenly felt claustrophobic.

Turner pressed one of the indentations and the trail began to move.

"If the trail wasn't moving, how could Lillian and Jonathan be so far ahead of us?" Deborah asked.

"Ahh, a very good question, Mrs. Cutler," Turner smiled. He thoroughly enjoyed talking to guests. "The trail is divided

191

into sections, separated by no more than seams. When you approach a section, a sensor will automatically start the next part of the trail. You will not notice a thing as your foot glides onto the next section. Very convenient for maintenance and also saves money."

Turner pressed another spot on the arm of the chair, and the cart started moving on its own, picking up speed. The trees became a blur as wind lashed at their faces. Drew's heart jumped for a moment as he caught a glimpse of the Great Pit. Unfortunately, as he comprehended what it was, the trail curved and went back into the woods.

The cart slowed silently to a stop. They'd reached the end of the trail. The Great Wall of Canada reached higher than the dome and stretched past their zenith.

Drew stared in awe at the limitless barrier, marveling at its uniqueness, just as he did the forest. But the wall was real.

"If you would be so kind as to follow me, please," Turner said.

The Cutlers got off the machine. Turner asked again before catching Drew's attention from the wall.

"Very industrious, the Canadians," Turner said. "The wall was completed in less than a year after the disaster. Of course, it does nothing to stop radiation from climbing over the top, but it does keep terrorists from fleeing over the border."

"Doesn't this man ever stop smiling?" Charles whispered to his wife.

Turner led them on a solid path of concrete through the trees to a small log cabin.

"Let me guess," Charles said. "Real logs."

Turner's smile grew, catching the sarcasm. He said nothing.

Inside, Jonathan and Lillian looked up from a video screen built into a tree-stump table. Scenic holograms in artificial light decorated the room, each one ready to sell to tourists wanting to take a bit of forest back home.

Lillian jumped, a smile covering her relief. "I've been so worried about you. Was it as thrilling as you'd hoped it would be?" She looked at Drew.

Jonathan trembled with excitement, looking up at his friend. "Did you see the great pit? My God!"

No way would Drew let honesty devastate his best friend. He tensed, ready to pounce on Mr. Cutler and shove a fist down his throat if he opened his mouth. But Charles and Deborah said nothing.

"If you will please come with me," Turner said to Drew and the Cutlers. He turned to the waiting couple. "This should not take long. Because they went off the trail, there are forms to fill out and other such necessities to take care of. They shall be back shortly."

Turner led the three lawyers through the door.

The tiny room started to hum, and the five could feel themselves being lowered underground.

It took over two minutes for the elevator to come to a stop. The three stepped into a giant cavern of a room. Stale, cool air blasted their skin as they looked at the surrounding rock walls. The elevator door slid shut with Turner still inside.

An enormous desk sat in front of a curtain large enough to cover the side of the cavern. On the desk sat a single lamp that cast a dim yellow glow on the woman sitting behind it. Dark circles under dark eyes, which could have been a trick of the light, accentuated her gaunt face. A long thin nose hooked just above thin lips. Her black hair, tightly tied back in a bun, molded to her skull.

"I understand that you've discovered our little secret," she said without getting up. Her voice sounded old and tired.

Charles took the first step forward, but Deborah grabbed his shoulder. "Diplomacy, Charles," she whispered and stepped in front of him.

"Are you in charge?" Deborah asked before her husband could respond.

The woman said nothing, her eyes penetrating. The corners of her mouth wrinkled and her lips cracked into a smile. It looked unnatural.

"Nora Black," she said. "I am the North Woods Curator." Her smile widened, and her teeth were straight and perfect and yellow from the light.

"What happens now?" Deborah asked.

The tension thickened in the following silence. Despite the cool air, Drew broke out in a sweat as he felt the walls start to close in around him.

Ms. Black spoke. "The most equitable solution would be for you to leave, and promise to never say a word. As a gesture of goodwill, we would be willing to refund your vacation money."

"Hush money," Deborah said.

Nora didn't say a word. Her dark eyes carried her message as they pierced into Mrs. Cutler.

"And we're stupid enough to believe that you would trust us never to open our mouths?" Charles asked. His skepticism seethed.

Nora shifted her gaze. "I suppose we'd be willing to hire you on a contingency basis. I believe you would then be bound by attorney/client privilege."

Charles erupted into a tumultuous guffaw that made his face red and eyes water. "It doesn't quite work like that, he said, trying to catch his breath. "But a good try."

She nodded in appreciation.

"Or," his joviality vanished. "We could start a class-action suit and sue this monumental farce down to its circuits."

"That is certainly another option," Nora said calmly. "Or at least you could try. But I guarantee you, it would take years, and you may very possibly lose. With the new laws regulating attorneys' fees, quite frankly, I don't see many lawyers jumping to take your case. Or would you do it yourself as a personal vendetta? Of course, while you're doing that, how would you make an income? You'd also have to deal with the counter-charges."

194

"What counter-charges?" Charles snapped.

"Oh, there's trespass, destruction of property for starters. We've got a staff of lawyers that I'm sure could make a list. And we've also got cameras throughout the woods. Used for maintenance to catch problem spots so we don't have to wander, looking. And Mr. Cutler, we found a problem."

"If this wasn't a personal vendetta before, you've just made it one, Ms. Black," Deborah glared back. "You'll find that I can be just as stubborn as my husband when I've been pushed."

The curator gave a slight shrug of her shoulders. "No offense intended, Mrs. Cutler. I'm just giving a factual response to your husband's scenario."

"The more you talk, the more you make it sound like a challenge," Charles said. "And I do like a good challenge."

Nora raised her eyebrows and let out a long sigh. "You are not understanding me. I am certainly not trying to threaten you. I am just telling you the way I see things. Let's say you sue us, you win big -- a multimillion dollar verdict. Then what? We declare bankruptcy, and after years of litigation, you get nothing but the satisfaction that you destroyed a park that brought joy and an escape to people's lives. Who do you think will be portrayed as the villain?"

She looked at Drew, wanting a response, at least a sign. It didn't matter if he stuck up for her or sided with the Cutlers. She just wanted to know where she stood. It was unnerving.

The Cutlers noticed her stare at Drew and turned their eyes to him, wondering why. When they broke their gaze from the curator, she pushed a button from under the lip of her desk and swiveled the chair so her back faced the lawyers. A quiet hum filtered into the room, and the giant curtain began to rise.

Blue light flooded the chamber as an underground abyss opened before them. Sloping way down stood row after row of pine and fir that looked to be floating on a soft mist. No doubt to anyone, these trees were real. Beyond the small forest lay a vast body of water that stretched far into blackness.

"Mrs. Cutler, gentlemen, the fabled Lake Superior."

The three lawyers pressed up against the clear partition and stared, unable to speak.

The blue water, a glass sheet that lay next to silent trees. Fluorescent light softly cast perfect reflections, undisturbed by ripples or waves. Only a fog on the shore showed any movement as it waltzed from the ground and dissipated into the air.

"But how?" Drew mumbled.

"How what?" Nora asked, with gleaming eyes.

"How everything?" Words started coming back as Drew asked in astonishment. "The lake, the trees, the light? Where's the light coming from? My God, the space . . . How did you make the room?"

I've got him, Nora thought. "The cavern is mostly natural. The earth is littered with underground pockets. But as far as I know, this is the largest. We did a little expanding and fixing up, but most of it was just as you see it, without the trees and lake, of course." She took a deep breath. "To answer your other questions, the lake was drained. Corps of army engineers, my predecessor told me. There was too much radiation to keep it on the surface. It took almost two generations to drain. Since then, we've been treating the water. Soon, probably not in our lifetimes, but hopefully the next, the water will be clean and safe enough to start pumping back into the pit. On computer, we can do it. In reality, we'll see. There's a lot more work to do.

"We've already started replacing the artificial trees with real ones. You can't see it from the way you came in, but on the far side of the dome, the vegetation is real. We had to cross The Strait into AlaskaWest before we found suitable flora. At first, everything we planted died. After a lot of experimenting, failures, and crossbreeding, it took. Now, not only can it live on the surface, but it thrives. One day, it will all be real."

To Charles the speech sounded prepared and well rehearsed.

"The ground lights are our own," the curator continued.

"Our lab developed these lights that give off the same A and B ultraviolet rays that the sun used in this region, before the tragedy. This is truly a miracle of science and nature working together."

"But why?" Deborah asked in a barely audible voice. "Why the deception, the cover-up?"

"Somewhat ironic that the first three to ever break the rules of the park, instead of being fined and dismissed off the property, get to see the future."

"Just one minute," Charles interrupted.

"What you're seeing," Nora quickly cut him off, "is the future. An incredibly expensive future. You ask me how we could deceive? Let me ask you, Mrs. Cutler, you know how much this vacation cost. Would you be willing to pay that just to look out this window? There's not even one hundred acres of trees out there. Without a steady influx of money, this dream will be just that -- a dream. And only five of you came. That's not even breaking even."

"How very touching," Charles said. "There are a number of other avenues that you could have used to raise money, besides deceit and fraud." Despite his words, he was very impressed.

"All the proper channels had been tried, Mr. Cutler. The government gave us next to nothing. Private donations were minimal. A small group of people took it upon themselves to do what they felt was right.

"Now it's all up to you. In a fraction of a second, you three can destroy what took decades upon decades to build. I can't stop you. Or should I say, I won't stop you."

Sitting behind her big desk, Nora Black suddenly looked very small.

"I think it's time for us to leave," said Charles. He glared at the old woman, ready for a confrontation.

"No, wait," Drew said, still staring out the window. He turned toward Charles and looked into his eyes. For the first time, he saw the man for what he really was – a man still grasping for glory while his best years had long passed.

197

"You saw the look on Jonathan and Lillian's faces. They were enchanted with this place. It's the same look that I would've had, had we not stumbled into this mess. I'd be willing to bet that that's how just about everybody looks at the end of the tour. I will not destroy that." Drew looked out the window. "Or that."

"I agree," Deborah said. "I think there could have been a better way to handle this, but I can't change what's already been done. I'll go along with Drew."

"Thank you," Nora said, sounding genuinely grateful.

"Et tu, Deborah?" Charles said. He looked at Drew in disappointment. They would have made a great team. He felt nothing but contempt for the old woman acting so high and mighty, sitting behind her desk. He imagined seeing her in a court of law, cowering in the witness chair as he bolted question after question, tearing apart her self-complacent facade.

As he opened his mouth to speak, Deborah called out his name. Charles' heart stopped for a moment as he looked at his wife. Something in her eyes, a spark he'd forgotten ever existed, shimmered behind a tear. He'd thought those eyes had died a long time ago. It had been so long since he had felt anything but disdain for her. But looking at those eyes brought back memories of what they once had, and maybe with a lot of work, might have again.

"I'll go along."

Deborah mouthed the words "Thank you."

Ms. Black took a deep breath. One could almost see the strength flow back into her body. Drew clapped Charles on the back and grabbed his hand, not letting go.

Charles couldn't remember another time when he'd bowed to peer pressure, and he hated himself for doing it now. But he'd always been a man of his word. For better or ill, he would stick to it. And somewhere deep within, something told him that this was right.

"Then I believe our business here is concluded," the curator said. "To relieve Mr. Brice and Ms. Farthington of any further suspicions, I suggest that we send your refunds right into your stock accounts."

She reached under her desk, pressed a button, and the soft hum of a motor came from the elevator doors.

"Just like that, you let us walk out of here and trust we will never say a word," Charles said.

"There is little else I can do. Have a pleasant journey home."

"Did you notice something a little ominous about the way she said that?" Deborah looked at Charles.

"What do you say when five lawyers get blown up in a helicopter?" Charles said.

Drew started to laugh. "A good start."

"Not enough lawyers in the helicopter," Deborah added.

"Old jokes never seem to lose their punch," said Drew.

The laughter felt good and seemed to brighten the room, but Nora sensed their nervousness. They were still not sure she could be believed or trusted.

"I'm sorry," the curator said, her face serious. "A new pilot and helicopter were not included in this year's annual budget."

"My God, she's got a sense of humor," Charles whispered to his wife.

"Mr. Stephenson, I'd like to talk to you for an extra minute, if I could," Ms. Black said.

The Cutlers looked quizzically at Drew, then suspiciously at the old woman. Her face gave away nothing, and Drew shrugged his shoulders as he stepped off the lift. The doors closed behind him and he became suddenly filled with apprehension. She looked at him, and smiled. He began to shiver.

~ ~ ~

Deep underground, Alvin Turner and Nora Black discussed the near future.

"Have someone at the airport," Ms. Black said. "As soon as they're separated from their colleagues, have the Cutlers escorted back. We'll have to do a memory erase and implant as quickly as possible."

~ ~ ~

Up in the air, Jonathan and Lillian couldn't stop talking about the trail and the Great Pit, especially after they put on the goggles. Smiling, Deborah Cutler listened as the two rambled on. Surprisingly quiet, even Charles seemed in a decent mood. Jonathan surmised that whatever went on behind that door must have been magic. Even Drew's boyish charm returned. Jonathan assumed that the three would not face any criminal charges for leaving the trail.

Drew stared out the window, lost in his own thoughts. He refused to answer questions about his private conversation with Ms. Black. He wouldn't miss practicing law, of that he was certain. The spark was never really there. He had only done what he'd been raised to do.

So much to learn and so little time. She was getting old. He watched as the giant dome shrunk down to a bubble and disappear over the horizon. One word kept playing over and over in his head. The four lawyers looked questioningly at him as he let slip the word of his future, "Curator."

SENiOR MOMENTS

NOTHING BUT AIR

*H*e's *finally dying,* **Stewart Price's spirit thought as it hov**-ered above Matthew Sporn. After seventy-three years of waiting, it was almost over. The elaborate plans and preparations were coming to a head. The labyrinth was ready. It had been a long seventy-three years, but in a few more hours, more likely minutes, Stewart would get his revenge.

As spirits go, Stewart started out strong, but as time went by, he became weak, very weak. He reasoned it was from all the hard work he had done, the strain he put himself under. Other souls told him to transcend to the next plane, become part of the world's forces before it was too late.

What do they know? Stewart thought. *How could there be a 'too late'? Souls were eternal. Maybe I'm not as strong as some others, but I can certainly take the spirit of a newly dead. Especially if the spirit is from the body of a ninety-seven year old man.*

~ ~ ~

The year was 1924. Stewart and Matthew both loved Emily Pinder, a beautiful woman with long, brown hair that had she not worn it up in a bun, would have reached down to her waist.

Her green eyes sparkled like emeralds, and as Stewart told his friends, her smile could melt butter.

"There's only one way to settle it, Sporn," Stewart said. "We fight for her."

"Winner gets to ask for her hand in marriage," Matthew answered.

"And the loser leaves town. Doesn't even get to say goodbye to her," said Stewart.

Matthew nodded his head in agreement, clenched his fists and took a classic boxer's pose.

"Not here, not now," Stewart shook his head in disgust. "It's broad daylight, you idiot. People will see us."

Sporn dropped his fists and shrugged. "So?"

"If word got back to Emily that we were fighting over her, she wouldn't marry either one of us."

"Oh yeah," Matthew said with a lopsided grin.

"Tell you what," Stewart said. "Meet me in the park tonight, at midnight. Loser has to be out of town by sunrise."

Matthew pulled the watch out of his pocket to check the time, nodded, and walked off. Price stared after him shaking his head in amazement. "Midnight," he called out.

Matthew was a big man, much bigger than Stewart, and Stewart knew he shouldn't take him too lightly. But Matthew was well known as a gentle man. No one had ever seen him lose his temper, let alone get angry. But one lucky punch could end Stewart's dream of marrying the wonderful Emily.

Although smaller, Stewart was quicker and more agile. Plus, he had a temper and one other advantage – he had been in the army, and had gotten in many fights, with men bigger and stronger than himself. Not only did he learn how to fight them, he won quite a few. Like he was ready to defend his country back in the Great War, he was now ready to defend his honor and the woman he loved.

~ ~ ~

The full moon cast a bluish glow over the park. Matthew sat on one of the cement benches that lined the path as Stewart approached. Neither man said a word as Matthew stood up and took a stance like Jack Dempsey. Stewart walked behind the bench leaving footprints in the grass, already wet with dew. Matthew let his guard down and followed closely behind.

With no gentlemanly warning, Stewart spun around connecting his fist in the big man's stomach. Unprepared, Matthew doubled over as the air left his lungs. Stewart followed with an uppercut to the chin. The gentle giant's head snapped back leaving his entire body open for attack. Stewart smiled as he paused for a moment to admire his handiwork. Again, he cocked his fist and drove it into his opponent's gut. There was pain again, all right, but this time it was Stewart's fist that seemed to collapse. It felt as if he had punched a brick wall.

As he delicately held his limp hand, Stewart looked up and saw Matthew glaring down at him. The look of surprise and pain had fled, replaced by the look of contempt.

Out of the corner of his eye, Stewart saw a blur racing toward his face. He ducked just in time as a powerful roundhouse right flew over his head. Instinctively, he countered with another uppercut, this time with his left hand. Matthew saw it coming and easily sidestepped the blow, twisting his body for another roundhouse swing.

Connecting with nothing but air, Stewart's momentum carried him past his threshold of balance. His shoes, already slippery from the grass, came out from under him. It was like watching in slow motion as he saw the ham-hock fist approach. His only defense was to scrunch his eyes shut and hope for the best.

There was a moment of blinding red static as knuckles coupled with his jaw. For just an instant, another sharp pain jolted the back of his head – then nothing.

As the spirit of Stewart Price floated out from his body, he put together what had happened. He had slipped just when Matthew's punch connected. As his body fell, the force of the blow smashed his head into the cement bench. A puddle of blood from behind Stewart's head grew into a pool. Curiosity replaced rage as Matthew stared over the body. Stewart's spirit looked down and saw the murdering coward run away.

~ ~ ~

That was seventy-three years ago, and Stewart remembered it as plainly as if it were yesterday. From the start, Stewart worked hard on his plan for revenge and it seemed to take its toll. At first, when a departed friend would see him, the soul remarked how well Stewart looked. But later, as more friends and relatives passed on, they commented how tired and old he looked. Each one came back one last time, before their transcendence, to try and convince him to come along.

"That was another life," one friend told him. "It's time to move on."

His mother begged, "Look at you, you're almost transparent. Please let it go and come with me."

Even Emily had died, his beloved Emily. She sobbed when she saw what had become of him. "It was an accident," she cried. "Please don't do this to yourself, or to Matthew. Believe me, he paid for it in his heart."

One by one they came until there was no one left and Stewart was left alone. He listened to none, except Emily. As he thought of her words, his hate for Matthew intensified. Of course she didn't want him to destroy Matthew's soul. They had married, had children. Matthew was even a great-grandfather now. *That should have been me.*

They were all against him, he thought. Nobody appreciated how much work dealing with the metaphysical could be, how much time and effort it took to build the perfect retribution.

After years of study and experiment, he went to work. It took decades to learn, to cast all the spells he needed to make it invisible to the other spirits, and more spells to keep them from venturing into his corner of space.

Finally completed, an exhausted Stewart looked down in wonderment at what he had created – his labyrinth of time. A maze with no exit.

A soul, one soul, the soul of Matthew Sporn, would wander for eternity, trapped, never able to transcend to the next plane.

The plan, like the maze, was equally perfect. When Matthew's spirit left the body, Stewart, still hovering above, would be the first one he'd see. Stewart rehearsed his spiel, welcoming him to the afterlife. Sorry about this and that, but that was a long time ago and I'm here to help and guide you now. Matthew always was a trusting soul and his feelings of guilt could only help. Stewart was sure Matthew would follow. Once he got Matthew inside the maze he would seal up the entrance, keeping Matthew's soul locked up forever. Only then would Stewart be ready to transcend.

All at once it started to happen. Stewart, feeling so tired, was hardly able to contain his glee as he saw Matthew's soul begin to waver from its body.

~ ~ ~

As Matthew's soul arose from its corpse, out of the corner of his eye he saw a poof, a tiny wisp of smoke dissipate in the air. For an instant it triggered something, something familiar, but it vanished before he could register what it was.

Matthew looked down at his body lying peacefully on the bed. It reminded him how much he looked like his dad. His father was a philosopher and Matthew felt comforted as he recalled something his dad had once told him as a child when his own grandfather had died.

"As long as there is someone on earth who remembers, a person's soul will live. Only when there is no one left will the soul that has not gone on, cease to exist."

THE VERDICT'S IN

Russell McGintz sat in his favorite chair, made sure his bracelet was on, and flipped on the TV. The black strap clung tight to his wrist; a faint red glow illuminated from its top as the program began.

~ ~ ~

"Edmund Kane, please rise for the reading of the verdict."

Eddie and his attorney stood up from the table. The lawyer put his hand on Eddie's shoulder and gave it a reassuring squeeze as they watched the bailiff carry the envelope to the judge, who handed it to the clerk. That envelope carried the fate of Eddie Kane's future. Sweat formed on Eddie's forehead as the clerk began to read.

"Forty-two thousand six hundred twelve, guilty. Twelve thousand seven hundred and ten, not guilty. One thousand and eight disqualified for not watching the entire trial, and eleven more disqualified because they were related to the defendant."

"Edmund Kane, you have been found guilty of murder in the first degree. You will be held in custody until Court resumes at nine o'clock tomorrow morning when sentencing arguments will be heard."

The Judge took his eyes off Eddie and looked straight into the camera and gave his grandfatherly smile that took him to number one in the ratings. "And I want to thank all of you 'jurors' who took part in our trial and remind you that at nine o'clock tomorrow morning you will be able to vote on the sentence of the defendant, Edmund Kane, just as soon as closing arguments are completed. And, as always, in order for your vote to be counted, you must be tuned in for both attorneys' arguments. Remember, that's 1-900-S-E-N-T-E-N-C. Thank you for tuning in and I hope to hear from all of you eligible jurors tomorrow.

"Oh, and before we cut away, I just want to send a very special Happy Birthday wish to Russell McGintz, celebrating his 65th birthday today." A camera zoomed in on a photo of Russ. "Not only has Mr. McGintz voted in the last 14 straight trials, but he has voted with the majority every time. We at 'Television Jury' wish you the happiest birthday, and just want to let you know that if it weren't for you, and people like you, this show wouldn't be the huge success that it is. We thank you."

Judge Donnell looked above the camera and saw the credits rolling by on the monitor. The clerk was in the corner doing the voice-over. "If you were an eligible juror in the Edmund Kane trial, and you want a say in what happens to his life, tune in tomorrow morning, and after sentencing arguments, call 1-900-Sentence, and cast your vote. That's 1-900-S-E-N-T-E-N-C. One dollar per call. One call per juror.

"And, if you would like to become a juror, just send $9.95 for the monitor bracelet to the address shown at the bottom of your screen."

The cameras faded out on Eddie as the deputy cuffed his hands behind him.

"We're clear. That's a wrap," the director shouted. "Good show, people."

After he said the magic words, Judge Donnell pulled a flask from beneath his robe and took a long, hearty, swig.

~ ~ ~

A nothing, hole-in-the-wall bar, Banter's had eight tables, never any waiting. The atmosphere was perpetual night. The only window, a picture window, broke years ago and had been boarded up ever since.

Russ walked into the bar and met his two drinking buddies. Everyone in the bar started singing Happy Birthday when he stepped in. He turned a bright shade of red as he took a seat.

"Hey Judge, you're late," Adam Hintz said.

Russ waived it off. "Stop calling me Judge. I don't look anything like him."

"Don't you think he looks just like that Judge on TV?" Adam asked his partner. "I thought that Judge was showing his own puss for a second."

"A little bit," Reed said into his glass.

"Do we have to go through this every time?" Russ asked. "Other than the receding hairline, there ain't nothin'. Besides, I used to work for a living. I'd loved to have had a job where I could sit on my duff all day."

"The advertising life was pretty easy," Adam said. "Traveling around, sittin' at a desk, yapping on the phone, making sales. You have no right to complain."

"I could sell sand to an Arab," Russ mumbled with a smile as he reminisced.

"I'm going to vote for electrocution," said Reed.

"Aw, he wasn't such a bad guy. I think lethal injection," said Russell, his mind back to the present.

"Don't matter to me. Dead is dead," Adam threw in.

For over two years these three gentlemen met five nights a week, and every sentencing morning, at Banter's Pub to discuss their favorite TV show.

"How many of those pansy-asses you think gonna vote to spare his life?" Adam asked.

"Not 'nough," chuckled Reed.

~ ~ ~

"Ladies and gentlemen of the jury," the defense attorney said to the camera. "Today, my client pleads with you for his life. I know some of you are just sitting by the phone waiting for me to hurry up and finish so you can condemn Mr. Kane to death. For those few of you I have nothing to say. I am speaking to the rest of you -- the decent, hard working, God fearing, humane folks. What Mr. Kane did was wrong. You know that and I know that, but, Mr. Kane has trouble distinguishing between right and wrong . . ."

"What are you talking about," Eddie sprang up. "I'm innocent."

"Would you shut up," the lawyer whispered loud enough for everyone to hear. "I'm trying to save your worthless ass."

Judge Donnell smiled and winked at his clerk. He knew the ratings would go up after this one.

"Edmund Kane is not a bad man," his lawyer continued. "But a very sick man. A man that can be helped with proper medical treatment . . ."

"Forty-nine thousand seven hundred eight, to one thousand three hundred and six," the clerk read. "Mr. Edmund Kane, you have been sentenced by a jury of your peers to die."

The clerk then spun a little wooden box that sat before him, slid open the tiny door, and pulled out a small slip of paper. "Lethal injection." He pulled out another, "Firing squad." Then a third piece, "Guillotine. Those are your three choices. We'll be collecting votes for the next half hour."

~ ~ ~

Russ McGintz and Reed Flagg called in for the injection. Adam voted for "Off with his head." When they got back to their table they ordered a pitcher of beer for brunch.

At the end of the half-hour, after descriptions of upcoming trials, the Court Clerk came back on the screen and handed

211

Judge Donnell a slip of paper.

The judge read, "Edmund Kane, you have been sentenced to die by lethal injection. May God have mercy on your soul."

Eddie remained emotionless, determined not to give anybody the satisfaction of watching him break down. After the director got bored waiting for a reaction, he had the camera get a close-up of Judge Donnell. Giving his now infamous smile, the Judge again thanked the jury and reminded them to tune in again at noon to start the trial of a notorious child molester.

At eleven-thirty, just before afternoon beers, Reed got up and apologized to his companions. "Sorry guys," he slurred. "It's my granddaughter's birthday today. My son threatened to put me in a home if I miss another family get-together. Damn, I hate to miss this trial, too. Sounds like a good one."

Russ waved him off; belching in his glass while Adam got up to get another pitcher.

By the end of opening arguments, Russ and Adam had already decided the child molester was guilty. They celebrated their decision in the pub until the bartender flashed the lights to indicate closing. As Adam and Russ stood up, the bartender came over and asked if they wanted a cab. Adam wiped his nose with his sleeve and said he'd walk the five blocks home, he needed the fresh air. Russ also said he'd walk but he secretly clutched the car keys in his pocket.

The cold air stung Russ as he staggered to his car. The night was silent as his steps echoed in the darkness. He felt relief as he looked down the street and saw no traffic. A sigh escaped his lips when he was finally able to stick the key into the lock so he could open the door. He hadn't noticed the door was already unlocked.

"I'm jus' fine as long as I'm sitting," he convinced himself.

Russell rolled down the window and let the cold air wash over him. He turned on the ignition and slowly backed over the curb and onto the street. As the streetlights danced around the car, Russ thought how funny it was that he needed both lanes to

212

drive in.

A tree jumped in front of the car and as Russell swerved to miss it he heard the sound that sends chills down the spine of any driver, the sickening sound of crunching metal. It was on the passenger side of the front bumper. The brakes screeched as nausea filled Russell's stomach. Frost made his breath glow like neon in the blackness as the chill of night sobered him.

Up on the boulevard, a mound under a white sweater lay motionless in the dark. Russell's stomach knotted as it tried to rise up his throat. A young woman, not more than twenty, lay crumpled on the ground. Her eyes stared straight ahead as black streams of blood ran from her nose and ears.

Russ looked around. He was alone.

~ ~ ~

The trash men clanging the garbage cans woke the old man from a restless sleep the next morning. Perspiration soaked his pillow. He tried to remember if last night had really happened or if it was just a terrible nightmare.

A cloudy mist covered the events as warm water from the shower splashed his wrinkled body. Feeling more like himself, a steaming cup of coffee in his hand, he sat down in his favorite chair, put on the bracelet, and waited for the end of the trial so he could call in his guilty verdict.

As the testimony droned on there was a pounding on the door. Irritated, he got up to see what the interruption wanted. If he was away from the television too long he'd be disqualified to vote. No salesman was going to ruin his record.

"Mr. Russell McGintz?"

Russ stood frozen in the doorway as the two police officers stared at him.

"Are you Russell McGintz?" the one officer asked again, this time with a little less patience.

"Yes," he answered weakly.

"Mr. McGintz, will you come with us please?"

"Nasty dent," the cop pointed to Russ' car as they walked to the cruiser.

As the officers led the frail old man into the precinct station the desk sergeant said, "Yep, that's the guy all right."

"Looks like a close enough match for me," one of the cops said.

"See ya on the tube," the sergeant called after Russ.

"What's he mean?" Russell asked. His skin turned two shades whiter. Not Television Jury, he thought. I won't stand a chance.

The officers put Russell in a small interview room and left him alone. Just a table and three chairs decorated the otherwise bare space. There was a mirrored window on one of the dull gray walls. On the other side of the mirror, two men stared at the frightened old man, watching his hands shake as he sat waiting.

~ ~ ~

"What do you think?" one of them said. "Can we do it?"

"It'll take some doing, but yeah, it can work," the other one answered.

"A million?"

"Heh, look at the guy. I bet we can do it for half that."

~ ~ ~

Russell thought his heart was going to burst, it beat so fast. He thought maybe he should just spill his guts as soon as the first person walked into the room. On all the TV shows, they always say talk to a lawyer first. What did it matter? He didn't know any attorneys. They were all shysters anyway.

The door opened and a man who looked vaguely familiar stepped in. Russ was ready to break down, sign a confession, anything this man wanted. Anything but go on Television Jury. That was the same as a death sentence.

"Mr. Russell McGintz? I'm Gerald Hanover, executive producer of Television Jury," the man said holding out his hand.

His black hair, slicked back, looked almost plastic, and Russ could tell his suit was not an off-the-rack. It was a matching coat and pants. Hanover even had a red handkerchief sticking halfway out of his breast pocket. This was a man of class.

In his mind, Russ broke down, dropping to his knees, begging for forgiveness. In reality he felt too scared to move. He just stared until the man took his hand away.

"It seems we've got us little problem here, Mr. McGintz," Gerald said. "Seems that a hit-and-run driver killed a young woman last night. Two independent witnesses say they can identify the driver. Sounds just right for our show, doesn't it?"

Russ tasted the bile rise from his stomach.

"The problem is, and this is where you can help us." Russell's knuckles were ready to pop out of his skin he held the chair so tight. "The murderer is our own beloved Judge Donnell."

Russell fell out of his chair.

"That's how I felt too," Gerald said. "Two people swear they saw the Judge get out of his car, look at the body, and speed off. The bastard was so drunk last night, when we talked to him this morning, he didn't even remember going out, doesn't remember a thing. The drunk bastard. Hell, with those witnesses and budget cuts, we're not even going to waste money with an investigation. We pay for that y'know."

"I don't understand," Russell mumbled as he got back in his chair. "What does that have to do with me?"

"Glad you asked," Hanover said. "Judge Donnell, drunken sot that he is, carries that show. Lose him, lose the show. Kapeesh?"

Russ shook his head, totally bewildered.

"Numbers, Russ. And numbers mean dollars. No numbers, no dollars. No dollars, no Television Jury. That's a lot of sponsors shopping for another TV show. A lot of good people would be out of a job."

"I still don't see what any of this has to do with me."

"Let me cut to the chase here, Russ. Can I call you Russ?"

215

Russell never moved. "Good. Here's the deal, Russ. When they plastered your picture on the tube the other day, me and some of the staff couldn't believe the resemblance between you and the good Judge. Thought you might be brothers, checked it out, no go. Anyway, and I'll be blunt here, Russ, we need a scapegoat."

"A what?" Russ mumbled.

"A patsy, a dupe. C'mon, work with me here Russ. Here's the bottom line. We can convince a couple of rube witnesses that it was you, not Donnell they saw. You put on a little make-up, go on the show, get convicted for killing the woman. Don't look at me like that Russ, here's the part I know you'll like. We fake the execution and pay you a tax free $500,000. We give you a new face, a new identity and whisk you away to anywhere in the country you want to go. Of course it has to be someplace that doesn't carry our show in syndication. Retire in luxury, Russ. Whadda ya think?"

Russell's heart raced as he tried to comprehend what he just heard. What it boiled down to was he was going to get away with murder. Not just get away with murder, but get paid for it; get paid more than he had ever dreamed.

"Half a mil, Russ, but I need an answer."

His entire life, Russ felt he never got an even break, always had to work for everything he got. It was about time that something went right in his life. "I'll do it."

Gerald Hanover broke out in a wide smile. "You're a wise man Russell McGintz. I'll tell my people and we'll get the ball rolling. And in the meantime," Hanover winked. "You can't breathe a word of this to anyone. If one of those press vultures gets a hold of this, we'll all be in front of a jury. Kapeesh?"

Russell noticed how straight and white the man's teeth were, and what a firm handshake. This was one of the most impressive people Russell had ever met.

~ ~ ~

"Old man McGintz", Russell said to himself. He liked that

216

nickname the other prisoners gave him. It made him sound like a somebody. They said it in a way that sounded like respect. He sat in his cell ready to go on TV. Gerald Hanover had visited him every day for the past week and made making sure the guards treated him like a king. Russ had his own chair from home, specially prepared meals and even beer. He had never been so pampered, even as a baby.

The defense attorney warned Russell that during the trial he better start looking sad for the jury and audience or a conviction would be certain with that arrogant attitude. Russell felt mildly surprised that his lawyer wasn't even in on the secret. He was dying to tell him that not only was he going to be convicted, but sentenced to die by lethal injection, it had already been planned out. They're fixing the vote count, just like an election. Of course it wouldn't be lethal, just enough to knock him out for about an hour. But Mr. Hanover warned him, warned him every day, not a word to anybody. Nobody could say that Russell McGintz couldn't keep a secret. He was keeping a dilly that even Mr. Hanover didn't know about, and never would.

~ ~ ~

"Russell McGintz, you have been sentenced to die by lethal injection," Judge Donnell said. "May God have mercy on your soul."

The press commented that this was one of the bravest men that had ever been convicted. In fact, his smug behavior brought in one of the largest ratings in five years. He was labeled as a man who showed no remorse, a man who actually seemed to enjoy himself during the trial.

~ ~ ~

Adam and Reed could hardly believe what they had watched. But hey, guilty was guilty and they couldn't play favorites. They both voted guilty. For free drinks they offered to dredge up the past and talk about how they never really trusted old Russ. "Just something' 'bout him, somethin' sinister. Nope, never trusted him."

~ ~ ~

The guards strapped Russ to the gurney in the soundproofed room, and then left him alone with the doctor as the TV techs readied the cameras from outside the glass booth.

As the man nicknamed Dr. KILLdare checked the needle, Russ asked, "Are you in on it too?"

The doctor gave him a quizzical look. "I'm in on everything."

"Good," Russ said. "I've been dying to talk to somebody about this. So, how long will I be out? One hour, two?"

Again, the doctor gave him a strange look. "Don't worry, you'll hardly feel a thing."

"Yeah, but how long before I wake up?"

"Maybe you should have tried the insanity defense," the doctor said.

A cold chill ran up Russell's back and spread throughout his body. He looked to Mr. Hanover standing on the other side of the booth and motioned for him to come in. Standing next to him was a smiling Judge Donnell. Gerald winked back at Russ and gave him the thumbs-up.

The truth came crashing in. There would be no $500,000, no happy retirement. The only thing Hanover didn't lie about was they needed a patsy and, boy, did they find one. Even though he really was guilty, this wasn't right.

Again, feeling frantic Russ motioned for Hanover. Another unfair blow in my life, Russell thought. But maybe, just maybe there was a way out.

Hanover shrugged his shoulders and the judge spoke. "Go see what he wants. I don't want him to die of a heart attack just before the execution."

"Almost there, Russ," Hanover said with a smile as he walked into the room. "Just a few more minutes and you'll be whisked off to parts unknown, a half million dollars richer."

Russell fought to keep the contempt out of his voice. He finally saw Gerald Hanover for the man he really was – a scum-feeding parasite that would sell his own mother for a buck. "Ya know, Mr. Hanover," Russ said innocently. "I've had a lot of time lately to do some thinking. Television Jury has always been my favorite show, and I was thinking about ratings."

Gerald Hanover turned his head away from Russ and rolled his eyes. Judge Donnell winked back.

"Ya know what would really boost the ratings," Russ continued. "If for the first time in history, Television Jury made a mistake. A mistake that they catch just in time."

"Sounds like you're getting cold feet, Russ. We made a deal here."

"Just hear me out," Russ said. Time was quickly running out. "You said there were two witnesses that saw Judge Donnell. Have 'em come forward, you know, save the day type of thing."

Gerald burst out laughing. "You're nuts. People love Donnell. He's a big reason they watch."

If there was ever a time that he needed the skills he had as a young man in the ad sales biz, it was now. Russ started talking and thinking faster. "But look at who's watching. People like me. Senior citizens with one foot already in the grave. Think of the future. You need to attract a younger audience."

A spark caught in the executive producer's eyes. For the first time he looked at Russ with interest. "Go on."

"Think of the audience you'd get for the beloved Judge Donnell on trial. Think of the pre-trial publicity you manufacture. The whole country would tune in."

Russ saw the dollar signs light up in Hanover's eyes. He was hooked.

"To be quite honest, Mr. Hanover, I'm not a greedy man. What am I gonna do with a half a million dollars? I've always led a simple life, it's all I know. I'd be happy to go back to my life just the way it was." Russell held his breath. . .

~ ~ ~

Judge Patrick Mead took his seat behind the bench. He was a man in his mid-thirties, wavy brown hair with a distinguished touch of gray at the temples. He had a Roman nose, a chiseled chin, and a smile that showed perfect teeth. The three men watched him on the TV from their table at Banter's.

"We knew you was innocent," Adam said. "And that's how we voted, right, Reed?"

Russell no longer wore the bracelet. He, Reed and Adam sat and watched as the new Judge welcomed five new stations to the 'Television Jury' family.

"And what perfect timing for you to join us," Judge Mead said, his smile was almost infectious. "Now make sure your bracelets are fastened and you've got plenty of snacks ready. Okay, let's start with the trial; The State vs. Samuel Donnell."

MIDNIGHT STROLL

Fog washed into the park like a tidal wave, which might be one of the reasons why I decided to take a walk. Bulbs of golden light seemed to float along the lined path through the thick air. Even up close it was hard to see the black poles that posted them in place. In fact, it was difficult to see more than three lights down as they disappeared into the mist.

Maybe it wasn't very bright of me to take a walk, what with all of the bodies that had been found in the park. But all of the bodies found had been young men, mostly hoodlums, all homeless. I was no spring chicken. In fact, I had just celebrated my seventy-second birthday. Well, celebrate isn't exactly correct. More aptly put, I turned seventy-two last Tuesday. At the assisted living home where I reside, they don't believe in fanfare for aging. It seems that most of the people there only exist, waiting for death. Not all of us, but then I'm considered one of the kids. I've still got some years left in me.

Also, there is my cane. The handle is made of lead and it's in the shape of an eagle's head. The beak curves down into a sharp hook. I'm no street-tough, but I still work out, and if threatened I'm sure that I could still swing a pretty mean stick.

I suppose that I should mention a third reason for getting out of my apartment. There has been a rash of deaths inside my building. The staff tried to tell us that it's just been a coincidence that six residents in the last month have passed. People there are old. It happens in clusters sometime. Not only did I know four of the six, but those four were in good health, and like myself, were the exceptions to the rule. They enjoyed their lives and wanted to hold off the grim reaper for as long as possible.

Then of course there was the ringer. The other night I just happened to open my door as they were rolling away victim number six. He was one that I didn't know. There wasn't any sheet covering the body, but he was in one of those heavy plastic body bags. To make it even worse, one of the orderlies who pushed the cart was yapping about how the last time he saw anything gutted like that was his last deer-hunting trip. He saw me and quickly shut his mouth, turning a shade of beet red.

Because of the obvious cover-up, I thought it might be an inside job, and I wanted to spend as little time inside as possible. These people were found in their rooms for God's sake. Where on earth can a person feel safe if not in their own home?

The damp, night air felt good against my skin, although I'd probably pay for it in the morning with my arthritis. But my legs needed the workout.

"Hey old man, pretty gutsy for you to be out on your own."

I froze. Too late to get off the path. I had been spotted, and I never heard a thing. I just had my hearing checked a couple of months ago, and the doctor said it was still good. I guess there are different definitions for good.

I slyly slid my hand down the cane. I figured if I spun around swinging, I could catch him off guard. I pivoted and made my move, swinging at what I hoped would be crotch level.

Two things caused my attempt to utterly fail. First, when I made my turn, my foot stepped off the path onto the damp grass. I slipped, and down I went. When I looked up, totally at the young man's mercy, I noticed that even had I not lost my balance, he was at least three feet away from where my cane would have whooshed through air.

Long, black, straight hair, parted in the middle, hung loosely over his shoulders. Even in the darkness I could make out his deep tan complexion. I guessed him to be Lakota Sioux, but I couldn't be sure. He tried to hold back his laughter as his black eyes looked down upon me. I'm sure that I must have looked to be quite a comical sight, and had my ankle not hurt so much, and this young man not about to kill me, I might have laughed with him.

I hoped that my face showed defiance, but I fear my mask was invisible, and I looked as scared as I felt.

He took a couple of steps closer, and I braced myself for a possible kick in the ribs. Instead, still smiling, he held out his hand.

"Let me help you up, Fred Astaire."

In spite of myself I had to smile. Still leery, my fear began to dissipate. I didn't know if I was more impressed with him because a boy his age, he couldn't have been more than seventeen, actually knew who Fred Astaire was, or that maybe he thought I looked like the dancer. I've been told before that we shared a slight resemblance.

I took his offered hand and he pulled me up. I'm 180 pounds, and he used no exertion at all. I think the only muscles he used were in his arm. The reality crashed down that if this young man had meant to do me harm, there would be nothing I could have done to stop him. On the other hand, if he were just being helpful, what a great bodyguard he'd be. I'd have no fear walking with him at my side. Besides, he seemed intelligent, and the company might be pleasing.

Pain from my ankle shot up my leg as I put weight on my foot. Had the young man not had a hand on my arm I would have gone down again.

"Whoa. Take it easy old man." He let go of me and reached

down, picking up my cane. He examined it as he handed it to me. "Nice."

"Thank you." So much for a leisurely walk in the park.

"You shouldn't be out here, an old guy like you. Especially alone during the night. Hell, old people probably shouldn't be out here at all anymore. Don't you know people are getting killed?"

I could feel my face burning red with anger. "Old people have just as much right to walk around here as anybody else." He interrupted me before I could continue my tirade.

"It's not a question of rights, it's a question of safety. Look at you, pretending you're Barry Bonds. Hell, if I wanted, I coulda capped you and gotten clean away."

"But tell me," I added. "How old are all the bodies they keep finding in the park? All kids, right?"

"Besides yourself, who the hell else over eighteen is stupid enough to be walking around here at night?" he shot back. "At least anyone who has someplace else to go?"

My anger faded as the reality sunk in. He was right. I was no match for anybody if they wanted to do me in. I held out my hand. "Francis Worthington," I said.

He gave me a quizzical look. "Francis?" He thought about it for a moment then shrugged his shoulders. "Bear," he said and took my hand.

"Bear?" I mocked his tone.

"No big deal, it's just what people call me," he said.

I've always thought street names were insidious. "And what does your mother call you?" I asked.

He stood silent for a moment. "She used to call me a lot of things. Her favorites were Stupid Shit and Worthless. But I haven't seen her for quite a while."

The pain from my ankle traveled to my heart. I'm not the type of person to pry, and I figured I'd leave it to him if he wanted to talk. I also decided that I'd reach out to him, and do him a great favor.

"Well, Mr. Bear, to prove your mother wrong, how would

you like to earn twenty dollars?"

"I never turn down money," he answered.

"I'll give you twenty dollars if you'll see me safely to my door."

"Sounds fair," he said.

We walked back toward my home. Well, Bear walked, I hobbled. Traveling through this cloud would normally make me feel esoterically whole, but this evening I began to feel more like an escaped felon, constantly eyeing for anybody who might be around. Ever vigilant, Bear kept alert. Every so often he would grab my cane to keep it from tapping too loudly on the cement path. We would chat quietly, nothing more innocuous than the weather, when he'd shush me. Once I thought I saw something move through the shadows, but I couldn't be certain. Finally we reached the end of the path, and through the mist I saw the outline of my building.

I stepped onto the street and Bear stopped.

"You should be safe from here on out. Now you said something about twenty bucks?"

"I believe I said to my door," I answered. I sensed trepidation from him. He seemed reluctant to step outside the park. "Is there a problem?" I asked.

A smile crept across his face. "This is my home," he said. "It seems like I trigger a bad omen every time I leave. The last time I set foot outside, they found Hound the next morning. He was my best friend."

A new voice spoke. "Take him home, we'll be okay."

I thought my heart would burst. Another young man, smaller than Bear, but built equally powerful, stepped from the fog.

"Hector, meet Francis. Francis, Hector." Bear smiled as he watched my recovery. "Too much bad shit going on down here. We have to watch each other's back."

"Do I look like a murderer to you?" I asked. I was insulted but also flattered.

"Like you said, all the bodies have been young guys. Who knows, you might be some Charles Bronson wannabe playing Death Wish 18," Hector said.

I was glad Bear was the one who saw me first. I found Hector to be annoying.

"Tell Jazz to save a bottle," Bear said. "But hey, I'll actually be able to buy one tonight." He smiled and winked at me.

Like dark on black, Hector disappeared in the night.

"Shall we go?" I asked. He motioned for me to lead the way.

As we stepped off the curb, finally my curiosity got to me. "So tell me," I asked. "You seem like a very bright young man. How did you end up on the streets?"

I thought he was going to ignore the question. He was quiet until we reached the other side of the street, and when he spoke his voice became tense.

"I came home from school one day. I think I was in seventh grade. Anyway, I opened the apartment door, and the place was empty. Not just my mom wasn't there – her boyfriend, furniture, everything, was gone. No note, no nothing. Even my room was empty. Clothes and everything – gone. I stayed there for three days waiting. Then the manager came in with another couple, showing the place. She started screaming at me when she saw me, and I took off. For some reason that could only make sense to a kid, I decided that it was all my fault and I didn't deserve a place to live."

"What became of her? Your mother?" I whispered.

"Like I said, I haven't heard from her for a while."

"But you seem so intelligent." We could both hear heartache as my voice choked.

"Credit that to boredom," Bear said. "Just for something to do, I went to school every day. Got involved in as much shit as I could so I could stay as late as I could. Spent a lot of nights sneaking into the library and living out of there. Not much to do in there at night but read." Bear let out a small chuckle. "Every

226

night I pulled out the daily paper that the librarian had thrown in the trash. First thing I'd do was search the obituary section for my mother's name. I thought that if I wished hard enough, I'd find it. Never did, though."

"What about food and clothing?" I asked.

He shrugged his shoulders. "I did what I had to do."

Neither of us spoke again until we walked through the small courtyard that reached the door to my building. "Kinda funny," Bear said. "About a month after my ma took off, I saw some of my clothes at the Salvation Army."

"Did you get them back?" I asked while fumbling for my key.

"We'll have to do this again sometime, Francis. But I really should be getting back, and I think we had a deal."

He didn't call me old man, or Mr. Worthington, but Francis. And it wasn't sarcastic or condescending. I couldn't begin to describe the warm feeling that spread throughout me, like we were friends, or at least peers.

"And what pressing engagements might you have at the park at one o'clock in the morning? It's so pleasant out, how would you like to keep an old man company for a little while? I'll throw in an extra twenty?"

"Trying to buy friendship, Francis?"

The question caught me off guard, and I thought back to how many times, especially the last dozen years or so, it seemed like I had to buy everything, including friendship. I sat on an iron bench that had been placed next to the door. Bear sat down next to me, but not close enough that we'd be invading each other's space.

I stared into the fog, sensing that it must have thinned a little bit. I thought about what I wanted to ask this fascinating young man next, but my thoughts were interrupted.

"So what's your story, Francis?" Bear asked.

"What do you mean?"

"You seem to be sophisticated, upper class. You throw

227

around twenty dollar bills like they have no value and you're living in this dump. I figured a man like you would be at one of those places that have outings planned every weekend, and twenty-four hour nurses on every floor."

I was about to say something in protest but he cut me off.

"Something happened to you, Francis. You still want to come off as the big man, but financially you can't cut it anymore."

It felt like he sucked the wind out of me while he danced in my brain, plucking at my thoughts. My mind went from his life to mine.

"How right you are," I said with a sigh. "What I didn't lose gambling, I spent on alcohol." Staring into the mist, I gazed back to my past. "I had a wonderful wife once, Barbara. She stayed with me much longer than I deserved. She tried so hard to help." A tear leaked from my eye and rolled down my cheek. "The lowest moment in my life was when I went into our safety deposit box and took the jewelry that had been given to her from her grandmother. And I pawned it. That was the final straw for her, and she finally left.

"When you get to the bottom, there's only one place to go. I quit the booze and started my life again. After about a year of sobriety I got a letter from our lawyer. Barbara had been killed in a car accident." Like a little child, I used my sleeve to wipe away another tear. "We were still technically married so I got the insurance. I have no idea why, or even how she kept up the payments, but she did. Double indemnity for accidental death. It would keep me comfortable as long as I didn't get extravagant. Five years ago I had a minor stroke and no insurance. That took care of the money and totally independent living."

I looked at Bear and he was staring straight ahead as if in a trance. I couldn't be positive that he'd heard a word I had said.

"I guess we've all got a lot to atone for, don't we?" he said.

Before I could respond, he asked, "Did you ever read 'The Mists of Avalon' by Marion Zimmer Bradley?" he still stared straight ahead.

"Years ago," I answered.

"There's a huge boulder in the park, by the basketball court. On nights like this I imagine that there's a secret opening in the rock that will lead to Merlin's cave."

I pondered his words and my heart lightened. What a perfect time to change the subject. I added, "'The Crystal Cave' by Mary Stewart is another great one if you're into the Arthur and Merlin saga."

Bear turned his face away from the park and stared at me. His eyes smiled as much as his mouth.

In the distance the sound of a siren echoed off the buildings. It grew louder and shriller as it neared, and was soon accompanied by others. Over the last year or so, this occurrence was becoming all too common for a neighborhood that promised its residence a safe haven.

"Nowhere to hide anymore," I said. "Crime and violence can find you anywhere."

"Too many people," Bear answered. "You find a place to hide, and find out that it's already occupied. Then there's a fight for the hiding place. And too much damned poverty."

"Exactly!" I said.

The sirens were at the point of deafening and I stood up. The pain in my ankle still ached, but it had subsided a little and I could put a more weight on it than I had previously. Bear followed suit and stretched his back as he got up from the bench.

"If you like tea, I steep a pretty mean cup of Earl Grey. You're welcome to come up and join me. In fact, I'd like the company."

Bear stopped in mid-stretch and stared at me like he was weighing my offer. After an unbearable silence, I asked, "Well?"

"What? You're not going to offer me another twenty dollars?"

Bear followed me into the apartment. I tested the weight on my ankle and it felt good enough that I left my cane by the door. I had kept the lights on before I left, and I told him to make himself comfortable while I headed straight into the kitchen.

"I didn't figure you for the TV type," I heard over the splashing of tap water into the kettle.

I have a 12 inch screen television that I use to watch the six o'clock news and nothing else, except maybe the election returns, and I told him so.

As the water heated, I walked into the living room and noticed Bear sitting on my side of the sofa staring at the picture.

"Is this Barbara?" he asked, sensing that I had come into the room. "She was a beautiful woman."

"That was taken on our tenth anniversary."

I sat uncomfortably on the opposite side of the couch, and watched as he picked up the photo album next to the picture. They were all the pictures of Barbara I could gather.

He started at our wedding and slowly thumbed through each page.

Unlike the sirens we heard outside, the whistle coming from the kitchen sounded friendly. Being a night person, I had done this a number of times before, and I knew that the kettle wasn't loud enough to wake my neighbors. As I went off to make the tea, I told Bear that he could turn on the TV if he so desired. He replied that he liked the quiet.

I came back in balancing a cup in each hand. Bear was only halfway through the album and smiling.

I handed him a cup and he put the book down.

"Sugar?" I asked.

"This is fine," he said.

I took my place on the couch setting the saucer and cup on my lap, still trying to get comfortable.

"Not bad," he said and saluted me with his cup.

"Too hot for me. I need mine to cool down for a minute or so," I said. I changed the subject. "While I was in the kitchen I couldn't help thinking about what you said about how we've both got a lot to atone for. I find that very interesting, and very

230

astute. How would you go about atoning?"

He contemplated his answer while taking another sip of tea. "I just try to be a good person and try to make the world a better place to live."

I tested mine and it was still hot enough to burn the roof of my mouth. "You certainly don't fit the mold of a homeless person," I said.

"That actually works to my advantage. People expect to see a drunken Indian. When they see that I'm not the stereotype, I think it makes a stronger impression."

"I can see how that would," I said, and tasted my own cup. Perfect.

"And what about you, Francis? What do you do to atone?"

I couldn't get over how much I enjoyed being called Francis. I tried to think back, and I don't think I've been called Francis since before Barbara left. "I try to do things for people. Do them favors when I can."

"That's me exactly," Bear said. "Take you for instance. I can see into you Francis. You blame yourself for Barbara's death. You've been carrying around your guilt for years until some days it's almost unbearable. Then I come into your life. You don't have many friends, do you?"

I thought about what he was saying. I had convinced myself that I had made peace with it years ago, but the more I considered his words, maybe he was right. "And there is you, Bear," I said. "A little boy abandoned, wondering why. Did she leave because you were a bad son? All those years blaming yourself for something you had no control over. Then you met me. I'd bet your friends in the park are only friends out of necessity. There's no real feeling there."

"Then I met you," Bear said. He put down his cup and rolled up a leg of his jeans. Sticking out of his boot, a carved bone hilt fit perfectly into his hand. He pulled it out and a silver blade that was at least six inches long glimmered in the light. "I'm going to help you Francis. I'm going to unite you with your lovely bride. I

231

guarantee that she'll not blame you for her death."

There was no hate, no menace in his voice. It sounded more like an act of love.

"So many people in this building are plagued with guilt, and I'm only one man. But I must say, Francis, out of all the others, you're my favorite."

I sat too petrified to move as he got up and walked over to me. So shocked, I couldn't even bring up the nerve to beg for my life.

"I have to open your body to release your soul."

With no more words, and not the slightest hesitation, he plunged the knife into my chest. Oh, how it burned.

I looked up at him and saw how he clutched his own chest, like he had been the one stabbed. The cup of tea I handed him was starting to take effect. I so much wanted to tell him how he no longer would need to feel guilty. I felt so bad that unlike the others, I wouldn't be able to carry him back to the park. Everyone deserves to be left at the place they call home.

I watched as a trickle of blood seeped out of Bear's mouth as he dropped to his knees in front of me.

Through my own blood that was gurgling up my throat I managed to say, "Let's carry on this conversation when we get to the other side."

A MISTAKE

Wood splinters flew into the room as the front door caved in, its beautifully carved oak design marred by pounding feet. John and Doris Nichols looked up from the TV and stared at each other in a horror that interrupted their quiet evening. The elderly couple watched helplessly as six police officers stormed into the house. All had their guns drawn.

"Police!" one of them shouted as they spread out.

Some rushed into other rooms, two others headed toward the frail couple.

"On the floor! Now!"

Scrapper Nichols, the couple's cocker spaniel, dropped the bone he'd been chewing on and bared his teeth. Barking and growling ferociously, the dog tried to protect his masters and his territory. He snapped at one of the officer's feet until the man lifted his boot and kicked. Scrapper let out a yelp as the boot caught him under the jaw. He skidded across the hardwood floor, careened off of the dining table leg, and slammed into the wall. A crystal bowl fell from the table and shattered, scattering broken glass across the floor.

"No!" Doris screamed. She was already on her knees as a heavy hand shoved her the rest of the way down.

Scrapper got up limping and dragged himself to safety behind the couch, then resumed his barking.

"Shut that dog up or I will!" a cop yelled.

"Please," Doris cried as her husband was thrown to the floor, his eye narrowly missing the edge of Scrapper's bone.

John and Doris were on their stomachs, hands cuffed behind them. All around they heard the sound of drawers being opened, furniture being moved, and things being broken – all to the music of a deodorant commercial coming from the TV.

Darkness enveloped John as Doris' quilt was thrown over his head. Her mother had made it when Doris turned twelve. He felt his heart break and his rage boil inside as he heard his wife of fifty-one years softly crying just inches away. So close and nothing he could do. If they would loosen his wrist so he could put his arm around her, anything to comfort her. But all he could do was lie there.

What kind of man will she think I am? He was glad that his head was covered so she couldn't see the tear rolling down his cheek.

"Please don't hurt my husband. He's got a heart condition."

I'm all right, sweetheart."

"Shut up, both of you!"

The policeman's voice still sounded commanding, but now they heard a noticeable difference, an uncertainty.

Through the confusion, John heard more footsteps enter the house. Around the barking dog, he heard muffled voices. The shouting had stopped. Now there was a lot of whispering and swearing under breath.

"There's nothing here, Sarge. The only drugs we found is prescription stuff."

"Let me see that warrant again." After a long pause, "Shit."

John felt someone kneel down beside him. The man gently lifted the quilt from his head. Light flooded into his eyes as he squinted to see his wife. An officer was removing a blanket that had been placed over her head.

The man with stripes on his sleeves squatted down, his knees crackling. "Sir, I think we made a terrible mistake here."

He unlocked the cuffs and John crawled over to Doris. They embraced, clinging to each other, her head buried into his shoulder, soft gray hair pressing into his cheek. The intruders were silent as Scrapper continued to bark, and the TV show 'Cops' started its theme.

After an awkward silence the Sergeant spoke. "I'm so very sorry. We've made a dreadful mistake. I hope that someday you'll be able to forgive us. Is there anything we can do for you?"

Doris raised her head and in a shaky voice said that she could use a cup of tea. "There's some on the stove.

"Gibbs, get this nice lady some tea."

The man stopped picking up pieces of broken glass. "Can't sir, we dumped it to inspect the tea bags."

The sergeant's voice exploded. "Then make her some more, dammit!"

Another officer approached the couple, holding out a piece of paper.

"We were supposed to be raiding a crack house," he said. "As you can see on the search warrant, there's a little smudge just above the one making it look like a seven. So instead of raiding 3911, we accidentally misread it as your address, 3917. Of course we'll pay for all damages."

"Does this look like a crack house?" John spat. "Do we look like drug dealers to you?"

~ ~ ~

Scrapper stretched himself out at the foot of the couch chewing on his favorite bone. Above him, Doris snuggled against John as they watched TV.

"I think I'd like to settle out of court," she said. "God knows we might be long dead before this goes to trial."

"It's the principle of the thing," John protested. "They could've killed us. They almost did kill Scrapper."

As the dog heard his name, he looked up and started wagging his little stump of a tail.

"It's enough that we'll be able to live comfortably the rest of our lives. We won't have to worry about Medicare and Social Security anymore," she added.

"Let me think about it," he grumbled. "In the meantime, what's for supper?"

Together, they walked down to the basement and opened the full length freezer.

"We've got some fish, or there's some veal," Doris said. "Or," she bent down and pulled out a hidden drawer on the side, "if you want ribs, we've still got some left from that nasty boy who tried to break in a couple of months ago. Or if you want roast, we got that nice young Jehovah's Witnesses that stopped by last week."

"That reminds me," John said. "Maybe it's not such a good idea to let Scrapper bring his toys upstairs. What if one of those cops recognized what kind of bone he was chewing on?"

SNOW CRABS

Greg Loran stared into the sky and shuddered. The clouds were thick, that was to be expected, but he'd never seen them that color before. A dark olive green with swirling streaks of dirt brown and black stretched to the horizon. They moved as if being pushed by a great wind, like a giant tornado on the other side. But from where Greg stood, inside his screen door, he couldn't feel even a breeze, just a cold chill that seemed to reach inside his bones as the snow silently fell.

He could barely see to the corner where a car slid sideways through the intersection until stopping at the light pole. At seven o'clock in the morning Greg could usually hear the traffic coming from where 35W joined the Crosstown just two blocks away. Today – nothing. The snow muffled all sound, if there had been any to be heard.

Greg stepped back and closed the door. "Is this what my life has come to?"

Maggie Loran looked up from the coffeepot, still holding a scoop of extra rich ground above the filter. She didn't say a word, just stopped and looked at her husband.

"Stalling before I get dressed, hoping my boss will call and tell me to go back to bed, the office has shut down for the day?"

As he spoke Maggie continued to make the coffee.

"It's not such a bad life," she said. "You raised two good kids, put them both through college, avoided going into major debt. No, I'd say you have nothing to complain about. Besides, in two more years you'll probably go crazy, wishing you could go back to the office."

Greg smiled. "Never. I'm going to enjoy retirement. I might miss a few of the people, but I'll never miss the work."

"Well, you'd better find a hobby or two because I like my life just as it is. One thing I don't need is some bored old man hounding me around the house all day. You start driving me crazy and your life is over, mister."

Greg came up behind his wife and wrapped his arms around her waist. She leaned back into him as he nuzzled her neck. He could still smell the baby powder she'd sprinkled on from last night. After thirty-eight years of marriage she could still turn him to putty.

Maggie twisted in his arms, her face just inches from his. She propped her arms on top of his shoulders. Her breath smelled like mint as she pressed her lips against his. Greg pried her mouth open with his tongue then both of them jumped as the telephone rang.

"Keep your fingers crossed." Greg released her and jogged into the living room to answer the phone.

Maggie walked in with two cups of coffee just as Greg put the receiver back in its cradle.

"Well?" she asked.

Greg let out a slow smile. "Screw the coffee, let's go to bed."

Maggie set down the cups and let Greg take her hand. "It's not the coffee that's going to get screwed."

~ ~ ~

Bright red numbers flashed, illuminating an otherwise dark

238

room. Greg stared at the clock then softly lifted his wife's arm off his side. She muttered something in her sleep and rolled over. The clock flashed 12:00 but Greg wasn't sure if it was noon or the middle of the night. It certainly looked dark enough for midnight, but his body alarm told him he hadn't been asleep that long. It slowly sunk in that it was neither. The clock always blinked 12:00 after the electricity came back on after a power failure.

Greg swung his legs over the side of the bed. "We lost power again."

Maggie pulled the blanket up and scrunched it under her chin. "What?"

"It's back on though." He quietly pulled on his trousers.

"That's good," she mumbled. The blanket now covered the lower half of her face.

Greg opened the night table for his watch. He felt around the handkerchiefs and assorted junk but couldn't find it. Deeper in the drawer he pawed upon cool steel. A shudder went through him, not because the gun was there, but because of what Maggie would do if she found it. Quietly closing the drawer he got up and crept out of the bedroom.

The coffee sitting on the living room table tasted cold and bitter. Greg looked around but couldn't find his watch. Outside, the snow had stopped but the clouds still looked thick and muddy. The snow had to be at least a foot and a half deep, and he could see no activity at all in the neighborhood. The clock in the VCR flashed 12:00. He walked back into the bedroom to finish getting dressed. Behind him the clock quit flashing, showing only a blank screen.

Maggie lay curled in a ball under the blanket, only the top of her head poked through. Greg stopped and stared at his wife. How tempting it would be to crawl back into bed and wrap himself around her. After contemplating, he finished buttoning his shirt and decided to shovel and get it done with. It would be a pleasant surprise for when Maggie got up. Maybe she'd make him a nice hot lunch, or dinner, depending on the time.

The back door grudgingly gave way as it shoved the snow aside. Cold air snapped at Greg's face. At least there was no breeze, which meant no wind-chill. He looked at the uninviting ground and closed the door. The snow came up to his knees. Trudging through the buried path to the garage, his boots crunched and crackled with each step. It sounded as if the flakes were screaming as his feet came down.

Each shovel full of snow felt heavier and heavier. Greg's lower back started to burn and the muscles in his arms knotted a little tighter with each throw. He rested a minute, surveying the block. Not another person had dared venture out yet. The car he saw earlier rested abandoned at the corner, half buried in the snow. Minneapolis seemed to be shut down. A sea of white drifted down the neighborhood. Across the street, Mrs. Titus stood at her window waving frantically. Greg waved back, but instead of accepting acknowledgement she continued tossing her arms like a person drowning. After waving a second time he turned his back on her.

Not knowing the time began to grate on his otherwise calm nerves. Was it lunchtime? Dinner? As thick as the clouds were, it was too light to be night. Plus, Greg was sure he hadn't slept very long after he and Maggie reconsummated their marriage.

With only half the sidewalk done, Greg lifted another shovel full of snow, his breath wheezing. "That's it," he said to himself. *The driveway will have to wait.* He was curious why the neighborhood kids weren't out trying to make some money. *They'll be out soon*, he thought to himself.

Walking back to the garage, he noticed how the snow clung to his boots, odd for being a dry snow. The lace to one of his boots dragged on the ground. He took off his gloves and bent down on one knee. Searing pain shot through his hands as snow gravitated toward his exposed skin. Greg screamed as he shot to his feet. It felt as if flaming needles were being thrust into his palms, fingers and wrists. On each hand, white as snowflakes and no larger than thumbtacks, creatures were crawling, weaving between his fingers, trying to get under the sleeves of his jacket. Tiny pincers nipped at the skin, tearing it away as they went. He shook his hands vigorously but only a couple fell away.

Leaving the shovel and gloves where they lay, Greg screamed as he raced back to the house. His hands felt on fire as droplets of blood bubbled to the surface. He threw the door open and jumped inside. The creatures leaped off his hands and as he looked down the snow seemed to come apart on his boots. Snowflakes scurried to get back outside before he closed the door.

"Power's out," Maggie called from the other room.

Greg held up his hands and watched in stunned silence as rivulets of blood dripped down his sleeves.

"I tried calling the Power Company, but the phone's dead too. Are you hungry?"

The pain slowly receded as welts the size of peas rose on his hands. Carefully he slid off his jacket.

Maggie walked toward the back door. "Did you hear . . .?" Her jaw dropped. "My God! What happened?"

Before Greg could open his mouth Maggie was gone. He heard her in the kitchen turning on the faucet. Before he had his jacket hung up she was back, wrapping his hands in a wet, warm towel.

"Now tell me what happened," Maggie said. "We have to get you to a doctor. You can tell me in the car." She grabbed her coat off the hook.

Greg stood in a daze and watched as Maggie buttoned her coat. It wasn't until she turned the doorknob that his emotions snapped back. He pushed her away from the door and twisted the deadbolt. "You can't go out there!" he shouted.

She looked at him like he was crazy. "I'm sure if we can make it to the main streets, they'd be plowed by now."

Greg stood in front of the door, blocking her way. "They're out there!"

"Who's out there?" she asked. "Is it that Jacobs boy? Did he and his punk friends do this? That's it. We're calling the police."

241

She paused for a moment. "As soon as the phone works again." Anger replaced concern.

Greg shook his head. "No, no, no. I don't know what they are."

The pain became a dull throb as Maggie rewrapped his hands. They sat on the sofa, looking out the window. Greg tried to explain about the tiny white snow creatures. Looking at his wife's face, he knew she wanted to believe him. Hell, if she came in and told the same story to him, he'd probably think she went nuts.

As if confirmation had been planned, a Ford Explorer plodded down the street. Every few feet it ground to a halt, backed up then inched forward a little more. They watched as it got to the point where it rocked back and forth, going nowhere. Greg jumped up and pounded on the window as the Explorer door opened.

Across the way, Mrs. Titus could be seen banging on her window, also. Maggie watched calmly as the man outside trudged to the back of his car. A small gust of wind blew a tuft of snow in the man's face. He shook his head then froze for an instant. A faint scream made its way past the weather-stripping and through the window. Maggie dug her fingers into Greg's arm but didn't utter a sound. The man dropped to his knees and the snow around him whipped into a frenzy. They watched the snow turn red as it swept over and then bury the man until only a smooth white sheet surrounded the car and all was peaceful again.

Greg stared out the window his hands still pressed against the glass. He couldn't bring himself to look at his wife. He'd lose control. Her fingers still clutched his arm but he could hardly feel them. He could hear little gasps escaping her lips. If he didn't do something quick she would snap and he would follow.

"Have you seen my watch?" The question came out of nowhere.

Maggie's eyes opened to a rush of tears. She buried her head in his shoulder and wept.

Greg tried to break the tension. "It's only a watch."

After a long moment, Maggie lifted her head. Tear stains streaked down her cheeks, but her eyes were clear. "I took our watches to the jewelry store yesterday to replace the batteries. They told me it would be about ten to fifteen minutes. I told them I had a couple errands to run and I'd be right back." She looked out the window at the empty Ford and fought a new burst of tears. "I forgot to go back." She got up and ran into the bedroom slamming the door behind her.

Greg looked at the closed door then stared back out the window. Blowing snow skirted across the Ford. Finally he got up and went to the bedroom door. Respecting her privacy he knocked with a toweled hand. Not a peep came from the other side. He was about to turn away when the door slowly opened. Maggie had an afghan wrapped around her shoulders. They looked at each other awkwardly waiting for the other to speak

"Mags?"

"We're trapped," she said. Her voice shook as if she had trouble getting the words to form.

"It'll be okay." He didn't believe it himself but he tried to make it convincing. Looking into Maggie's eyes, he knew she didn't believe it either.

"Maybe the phone will come back on and we can call for help." She left the bedroom door open as she turned away.

"We'd better call the kids, too." Greg walked into the living room and picked up the receiver. Not even static. He felt grateful that one lived in Tampa and the other just got a job in Phoenix.

He saw the coffee cups still sitting on the table. The mugs were cold and he noticed that the air around him felt a bit chilly. The thermostat was set at 72 degrees but the temperature in the room said 64. He listened for the hum of the motor coming through the vents. Nothing.

"Oh, shit," he said out loud. The gas furnace needed electricity for the pilot light to stay lit. No electricity, no heat. "What next?"

Swearing under his breath, Greg walked into the kitchen and turned on the faucet. He set it so the water dribbled out, to keep the pipes from freezing. He repeated the steps in the bathroom before emptying out the closet of blankets and sheets.

A car horn broke the quiet. Maggie beat him to the window. *God, she looks tired all of a sudden*, Greg thought. Outside, a small Honda had somehow made its way to the Ford by following its tracks. Two people sat inside the car. The guy laid on the horn again as the girl sitting next to him gave a disgruntled look. Across the street a large hand printed sign in Mrs. Titus' window said 'DO NOT GET OUT OF YOUR CAR'. The couple never looked in that direction.

The driver's door swung open and while the guy got out, the girl slid over to the wheel. Greg and Maggie both started hitting the window. Greg kept pointing to across the street. The man stopped in front of the hood and looked up. He looked at Greg then turned his head toward the sign. Mrs. Titus stood at her window desperately waving her arms. The guy gave both houses a strange look, shrugged his shoulders and started to push while the girl threw the car in reverse. The Honda began to move backward when the man stopped pushing and slapped at his ankle. Snow churned into a cloud climbing the man's legs. He screamed and jumped on the hood of the car. Arms flailed and legs kicked trying to get the creatures off. The girl blasted the horn maybe in hopes of scaring them away or maybe because she didn't know what else to do. White spots crawled up the man's jacket, dots of red opened on his face. He grabbed his head and rolled off the hood toward the driver's door.

Mercifully, Greg and Maggie couldn't see what happened on that side of the car. Mrs. Titus' face told the story. Silent screams from inside the car fogged the windows. The front wheels spun furiously, going nowhere. Finally, the horn stopped.

"We have to get her out of there," Maggie said.

"How?" Greg snapped. "It looks like they're eating through clothes now."

Maggie looked as if she'd been slapped. Slowly the hurt turned to anger. "I don't know, I don't know," she yelled. "But we have to do something!"

Greg took a deep breath, ready to shout back but caught himself. "I'm sorry. I'm not mad at you. I'm angry, I'm frustrated, and scared to death. I've never felt so helpless."

Maggie closed her eyes to shut off a new flow of tears. "I know," she said.

They held each other without speaking.

Outside the Honda's engine revved again and went nowhere.

"She's gonna run out of gas a lot quicker that way" Greg said.

Maggie got up and ran out of the room. Another bout with tears, Greg thought, and decided to leave her in peace. Instead, he got up and went to the thermostat. Down to 62 degrees. He walked into the bedroom for a sweater and when he came out, Maggie was back in the living room taping a sign on the window.

"What's that?" he asked.

"Telling her to conserve gas and wait for help."

"Help," Greg muttered under his breath.

~ ~ ~

Nighttime found Greg and Maggie huddled together under a blanket on the couch. Candles in the living room cast flickering shadows on the wall. Across the street dancing orange light came from the Titus home, and next to her, the Hawkinson's. On the other side of Hawkinson's, the Paretti house was dark. Outside, as night approached, a soft white glow pulsated from under the snow. Thousands of tiny lights randomly clicking on and off gave the illusion of beauty.

"There must be millions," Maggie said. Her voiced sounded flat as if all emotion had been drained.

Greg sat mesmerized. He wondered how far they had

245

spread. The neighborhood? The state? The entire northern half of the country? Instead of the city, they could just as easily have been alone in the middle of nowhere.

Out in the street the Honda engine sputtered to a stop. Like white noise, they hadn't been aware of it until it wasn't there. Hopeful thoughts that the girl might be asleep echoed like a mantra in his mind. Next to him he heard the soft steady breathing of his wife. She looked a lot older than she did that morning.

Maybe if he wished hard enough he could make himself fall asleep. Then, in the morning he could wake up and this nightmare would be over, a quickly fading memory drifting into oblivion of the subconscious mind. "Sleep," he kept repeating to himself until his body finally obeyed.

~ ~ ~

"It's freezing in here," Maggie said.

On the other end of the couch, Greg opened his eyes. "What time is it?" he asked, trying to rub away the sleep. He automatically looked at his wrist, then half-laughed, half-groaned. Maggie had to smile.

Light filtered into the room. Although clouds still blanketed the sky, it was obvious the sun hid behind them. Candles around the room had burned down to the nub. Careless, Greg thought. At the moment they had plenty, but who knew how long this might last?

With an afghan draped over his shoulders, he got up and went to the thermostat. "The needle's at fifty. That's as far down as it goes, so who knows what it's really . . ."

"Oh my dear Lord," Maggie said.

She stared out the window as a film of tears coated her eyes. Greg looked outside. The passenger door to the Honda hung open. Tracks from the car came half way up to their house then stopped as if something plucked her straight up, or pulled her straight down. Greg tried to swallow but couldn't.

"I was about to say how hungry I was," Greg said. "But

now I don't think I could keep anything down."

"We need something to keep up our strength." She walked into the kitchen and poured each of them a bowl of cold cereal, ran the faucet until it got as hot as it was going to get, then let it stream through the coffee and filter into a cup. Bacon and eggs sat useless in the refrigerator.

When she carried the coffee and cereal back to the living room, Greg was again in front of the thermostat.

"How are they?" She nodded toward his hands.

The towels had come off during his sleep. Scabs covered both fists, his knuckles were swollen and red. He flexed them open and closed a couple of times.

"A little stiff. And they itch like crazy."

"That's good. It means they're healing."

She handed him the coffee and set the bowl on the table. Maggie smiled as his face puckered at the taste of the lukewarm brew.

"The way the temperature is dropping in here, at least we don't have to worry about food spoiling. Pretty soon it will be cooler in here than in the fridge," Greg said.

"I'm going to go down to the basement and bring up more blankets," Maggie said. "And I think there's another box of candles down there."

She left, leaving Greg alone with his thoughts. Everything looked so peaceful outside. The only clues of anything wrong were the two abandoned cars in the middle of the street, and the footprints that stopped in the middle of nothing. *Maybe those things are all dead*, he thought. *Like some viruses, maybe they only lived for twenty-four hours.* "And maybe pigs can fly."

A scream shot up from the basement.

"Maggie!" Greg raced toward the stairs.

In the laundry room, Maggie had her ankle in a death grip. A trickle of blood seeped between her fingers. Greg stood in the doorway with his jaw hanging open.

"They're down here," she cried. Her breath came out in a

silver cloud as her words mixed with the cold air.

He looked around and saw a crack in the foundation next to the window. He couldn't be sure, but there might have been a flash of movement. For the first time he noticed so many flaws in the basement. Crumbling mortar, loose bricks, at least three more cracks in the walls, he wondered if the house should still be standing.

Bent over, Maggie limped toward her husband. Together they went upstairs and Greg helped his wife to the couch. He had to pry her fingers off her leg to look at the wound. Dangling on a loose flap of skin, an albino claw, with streaks of blood, clamped tight.

"Get it off me!"

Greg pried the tiny claw open with his fingers. Slowly it unhinged until it snapped and shattered, crumbling to the floor. The wound still bled; a good chunk of muscle had been torn away. Maggie sat and shivered as Greg wrapped her ankle.

"They're growing," he said to himself. He wasn't aware Maggie overheard him until she asked what he meant.

"The ones that attacked me yesterday were no bigger than that one's claw."

"Wedge a towel under the crack of the basement door," she said.

~ ~ ~

Time lingered. Greg sat in his winter jacket, staring out the window while Maggie, bundled in blankets, tried to sleep. Light slowly faded along with the day. Greg went about setting up the candles. Tonight he'd remember to blow them out before going to sleep. He peeked in at his wife and all he could see was a mound on top of the bed. He felt mildly jealous that she could fall asleep under such circumstances while he was wired as if he'd just downed an entire pot of espresso.

Breath became visible inside the house as the temperature dropped. Outside, the snow radiated a ghostly, pale light. Inside,

Greg heard them clicking behind the walls; hundreds of them, if not thousands. He raced frantically from room to room searching for spaces between the floorboards, holes or even hairline cracks in the walls. Light from the candle made it almost impossible because it cast dancing shadows over everything. He knew he should wake up Maggie to help look for weak spots. When she got up, she'd probably be angry that he hadn't. But the less time she had to deal with this nightmare, the better.

Movement caught his peripheral vision. Greg whirled around, almost blowing out the candle. At first he saw nothing. He had to wait for the flame to settle before his eyes adjusted. He felt the color drain from his face as he looked on the floor. A luminescent white circle, about the size of a quarter, slowly crawled toward him. It had thread-like tendrils sprouting underneath from the front and back. They writhed like little feelers crawling along the floor. Toward the front of the circle, a tiny appendage extended out, and attached to that was the claw. Like radar, it swiveled in an arc, sensing, while continuously clicking open and shut. It had no eyes that Greg could see, yet it slithered straight in his direction. As it neared, he brought his heavy boot down on the creature. He felt exhilarated and a little self-satisfied at the crunch under his foot. Then he saw them.

"Oh oh," he whispered to himself.

Through the slats in the heat vent, three more crab creatures dropped to the floor. Just like the first, they glided their way toward him, clacking their claws like snapping fingers. "I can stomp on you all night," he said. Although he wondered how long he could keep it up. He pictured a giant puddle of white goo covering the living room floor.

The boot came down again, smashing the one in the lead. The other two stopped, their tendrils swishing across the hardwood floor. They sensed the vibration, or maybe saw what happened to their comrade. Whatever, Greg didn't care why they stopped, just that they did. Even if they tried to retreat, they'd never make it back to the vent. He took a step toward them expecting to meet them head on. What they did sent chills down his back and set his scalp to shiver. One broke left while the other circled right and they came at him from both sides while more crawled up the heating duct.

My God, they can think!

Like a child's dance, he stomped to the left then stomped to the right, crushing both creatures. Six others waited by the wall as if planning an attack. Their soft pulsating glow was almost hypnotic while their incessant clicking hammered on his mind.

A quick sharp scream came from the startled Maggie standing by the bedroom door. The candle she held dropped to the floor less than an inch from one of the crabs. The flame sputtered but did not die. It flickered then flashed as it ignited one of the tendrils. Like a short fuse, a spark crawled up toward the crab. The claw shook violently as if shaking a fist in defiance. When the flame reached its body, it made a high pitched whine then exploded, popping like a kernel of corn and shooting a fistful of sparks halfway up to the ceiling.

Greg and Maggie stared at the white fragments littering their hardwood floor. The creatures also stopped, their claws stilled for the moment. Constant clicking from inside the walls kept the room from silence. Slowly, Maggie bent over and picked up the candle, a small puddle of wax remained on the floor.

STOMP.

"Lambasted three of 'em at once," Greg said. A crazy man's grin spread across his face.

More creatures scattered away from his boot. Maggie glared.

"Don't do that!" she screamed. One hand clutched her chest, the other shook so badly she looked as if she might drop the candle again. "You startled me half to death."

Clack, clack, clack, the noise intensified. The snow crabs formed a line between the couple. Some broke off toward Maggie, others slid across the floor at Greg.

"My God, they're organized," Maggie whispered.

He brought his boot down and crushed two more.

"Behind you!" Maggie screamed.

Greg whirled around as a glowing white disk fell from the curtain and landed on his head. It tangled itself in his thinning gray hair then hooked its claw into his scalp. With a yelp, Greg grabbed at his skull. He yanked the thing off and heard a soft pop. The shell, still partly imbedded in the skin, stung like hell as he gently tried to pluck it from his head. As if sensing his pain and distress, more and more crabs swarmed toward their prey.

Maggie grabbed a magazine off the table, rolled it, and held it over the candle's flame. The paper smoldered then ignited. Stooped over and holding the makeshift torch to the ground, she sped to her husband. A miniature Fourth of July erupted on the floor. Sparks shot out in all directions. Popping and whizzing noises crackled in the air sending pieces of white flying like confetti.

The creatures ran from the heat. Inside the walls, the clack, clack, clack went on like an incessant drone. Blood seeped down Greg's face as he and Maggie stood and stared as more entered from the kitchen and bathroom.

With an unheard signal, a fluorescent sheet of white charged across the floor in a wave.

Greg and Maggie screamed as the sheet of crabs skittered toward them. As if of one mind, the couple turned and ran toward the bedroom, slamming the door behind them. A snapping claw slid under the door. Maggie crammed the burning paper through the opening between the bottom of the door and the floor. It sounded like popcorn popping on the other side. Greg quickly wedged his terrycloth robe in the space when Maggie withdrew the flame.

Clacking came from inside the room. Next to the dresser, right above the yellow carpet, the vent was filled with white. Like water, the snow crabs dripped through the slats onto the floor. The couple stared from the door, to the vent. Greg ran to the wall and started stomping. Maggie ran over and started them burning.

251

Sparks caught on the rayon carpet. It was a mixed blessing. The creatures tried to rush back to the vent, avoiding the heat. Tiny explosions sent embers throughout the room as they didn't make it. Greg pushed the dresser, blocking their entrance while Maggie beat at the flames, holding the magazine above her head.

It took almost half an hour to clear the room of the snow crabs and put out all the tiny fires. The light had faded as the two sat on the bed, bundled up in blankets. One candle cast dim light around the room as the continuous snapping and clacking throbbed behind the walls.

"As a last ditch effort we can burn the house down and make a run for it," Greg said.

"And where are we going to run to?"

"I was just thinking out loud, okay? I haven't heard any ideas from you."

"God I hate when you do that," she said. "If you can't say anything constructive, just shut the hell up."

"You shut . . ." He stopped. "I'm hungry."

Greg leaned over to his side of the bed and opened the drawer on the bedside table. "Tums or Tic Tacs?"

She rolled over and picked up the Tums. "They've got calcium." She smirked.

Her smile froze then quickly melted. Even with little light she saw the outline. "I thought I told you to get rid of that."

Greg looked in the drawer. "I forgot all about it," he lied.

"I told you I did not want to be in the same house as that gun."

Greg carefully lifted the .45 caliber. Maggie grabbed it out of his hand.

"Be careful, it's loaded."

"How could you?" she screamed. "You lied to me!"

Greg watched the silver vapor from her lips dissipate in the air. He let out a long sigh and watched his own breath escape. "I just couldn't stand the idea of being defenseless in case someone ever broke in. After Russell was robbed, he convinced me that I needed one."

"How nice," Maggie said. "That your brother's concern is more important than mine."

"I'm sorry."

Maggie stared at the gun and turned it over in her hands. "Who knows, maybe it will come in handy."

Greg looked at her with condescending eyes. "Somehow, I don't think we'll be able to shoot ourselves out of this one."

He looked in her eyes and froze. A new chill covered his body as he understood. "No," he said. "No. It won't come to that. We'll get out of this."

"As a last resort," she said.

Greg felt his heart melt. Silently they divided the Tic Tacs and Tums.

Nothing came from under the door, nothing crawled from behind the dresser, but the incessant clacking seemed to intensify behind the walls.

"You look tired," Maggie said. "Why don't you try and get some sleep. I'll take first watch."

As soon as she said those words, Greg felt exhausted. He laid back and watched as Maggie started taking socks and underwear from his drawer and wadding them up, tying them in tight little balls. She placed them carefully next to the burning candle. "Our arsenal."

~ ~ ~

Gray light filtered in the room when Greg opened his eyes to continuous applause. Maggie's smiling face lay inches next to his. Her eyes were closed, her lashes fluttered just faintly, enjoying a dream. He wanted to be inside her head, to be with her happy thoughts. To be anywhere else would be a wonderful alternative.

He raised his head off the pillow and choked. The walls looked alive. Chips of paint and plaster fell away like shedding skin. Thousands of claws emerged as if the walls were giving birth.

Tears burned his eyes as he kept whispering why. *Is it time now for the last resort?*

He found the gun resting on the night table. The black steel shone like a beacon in the room. Calm washed over Greg as he walked to the table. He put extra weight on each step, a self-satisfying crunch under his feet. The gun felt good in his hand. He clicked off the safety and watched a snow crab as it came over the lip of the bed, and took aim as the tendrils slithered across the sheets toward his wife, its snapping claw waving in the air.

Behind him a chunk of plaster dropped from the wall, and glowing white creatures flowed through the hole, dropping to the floor. Greg slowly moved his arm, pointing the gun away from the crab and stopped when the barrel was only an inch from his wife's forehead.

Maggie opened her eyes. Greg watched as the clouds of sleep faded from her pupils which opened wide in alarm.

"What the hell are you doing?" she screamed.

"The last resort," Greg whispered.

"You're crazy!" Maggie rolled away from the gun, on top of the snow crab. She yelled and grabbed her thigh.

The claw had gripped her leg slicing through the denim jeans and into her flesh.

"I love you," Greg said. "We'll see each other on the other side."

He aimed the gun again as the walls around them crumbled. Snow crabs poured in from all sides.

"Please, Greg. Don't." Maggie's voice shook.

The gun wavered in his trembling hands. He tried to look into her eyes, but his head uncontrollably turned away.

"I'm a Goddamn coward!" The gun dropped to the floor and quickly disappeared under a mass of white.

Maggie let out one long sigh until she noticed an avalanche of white cascading toward her. In one fluid movement she rolled to her feet and jumped onto the bed.

Greg looked at her, tears streaming down his face. "I'm so

sorry," he whispered.

He couldn't tell if she heard above the clacking until she leaned over on the bed, buried her head in his shoulder and hugged him tight.

Slowly she separated from his embrace and looked at the sea of snow crabs hovering around the bed. They were still pouring in from the walls, and looking at the ceiling, Maggie noticed spider web cracks in the paint that were growing before her eyes.

"I've got an idea," she said.

Greg showed no reaction at all. Shock. Then his eyes widened, as they slowly seemed to comprehend.

"I doubt it will work, and even if it does, we'll still die, it will just be a much more pleasant way to go."

"I'm all for pleasant," Greg said. He tried to make it sound light-hearted.

"How many layers of clothes are you wearing?" she asked before telling her plan.

They both stood up on the bed and Greg wrapped himself loosely in the blanket while Maggie did the same with the bedspread. She reached in her pocket and pulled out a book of matches. She took a deep breath, said a quick prayer, and struck the match.

The snapping of claws took on a new urgency as Greg's blanket ignited. The small flame quickly spread, but Greg waited until he could see that Maggie's bedspread had also caught. Both aflame they jumped off the bed, crunching dozen's of crabs as they landed. They fought the urge to run. Running causes accidents, and one accident, whether a trip, or snagging the flaming sheet on a piece of furniture, would be fatal.

The bedroom door slowly gave way, pushing a layer of white out of the way. Snow crabs covered everything, giving the hallway and living room a pulsating white glow. Waving the burning towels around them, Greg and Maggie slowly worked their way to the back door. A frenzy of movement on the floor

255

parted a path before them. Firecracker explosions popped all around, panicked snow crabs pushing to give the couple a wider berth.

Outside, the cold breeze slapped at their faces and hands. Fire had already consumed over half of the bedspread and blanket. The threatening wind looked to spoil the rest of their plans by blowing out the flames and whipping the sheets uselessly in the air.

The path to the garage remained virtually unchanged. No new snow, or snow crabs filled it in, the shovel and gloves still lay in the path. The flames were reduced to glowing orange embers, singeing the material, but causing no other threat.

"Run!" Maggie screamed as the path began to close in around them.

Crunching footsteps were drowned out by the thunderous applause of claws. They made it to the back door of the garage when an overwhelming fear wrapped itself around Greg. Snow crabs were already converging and crawling up his boots, snapping and digging into the thick rubber and leather. If the door was locked, how many seconds would he have to dig out his keys? Not enough, he surmised.

The handle turned and the door opened. Greg and Maggie jumped inside, slamming it behind them. They stomped their boots, shaking off the crabs, then instantly crushed them. Slowly and carefully they looked around. They were alone.

Still panting, Maggie said, "Thank God. They must have sensed there was nothing alive in here.

"Don't ever tell me about wasting money again when I insisted we insulate the garage," Greg said.

"I promise." Maggie smiled. Let's get in the car and crank that heat."

They both got in the passenger door. Greg scooted over to behind the wheel. The Olds Cutlass groaned but finally turned over. Without waiting for the engine to warm up, Maggie flipped the heat onto high. Cold air blew from the vents. Maggie snuggled up to her husband. Greg tenderly rubbed off the black ash that had singed a portion of her hair. Neither said a word as the garage filled up with exhaust. Like two lovers they sat, staring out the windshield as if overlooking a beautiful sunset.

"How about some music?" Greg asked.

Maggie reached over and turned on the radio.

" . . . Do not go outside," a professional voice said. "Repeat. The Army and National Guard and are working together around the clock with your local police to eradicate these creatures. If you are safe in your home, do not leave. Crews should be in your neighborhood no later than tomorrow afternoon. If you see a truck, by no means step outside. Wave to them from your window and they will come and get you."

Greg and Maggie looked at each other as the announcer gave instructions on self-preservation. Besides fire, there were household chemicals that became lethal the instant it touched the creature.

Maggie swore under her breath. "We've got loads of that under the sink."

"I don't think I want to go back and get it," Greg said.

"If you're stranded in your car, honk your horn every two minutes. We are listening for your signal. If you hear us, keep honking until we find you. If you are still able to drive, there are safety havens at the following locations."

The voice listed various addresses throughout Minneapolis and St. Paul. The closest to Greg and Maggie was two miles away at Fort Snelling.

"What do you think?" Greg asked.

"I don't want to die," Maggie said. "If there's a chance, I'm all for it."

"My sentiments exactly."

He pressed the button on the remote and the garage door slowly opened. A white carpet scurried in as exhaust fog filtered out. Greg dropped the car in reverse and floored the gas. Tires squealed, rocketing the car into the alley. A white cloud exploded

257

as the Olds impacted the snow. Ice, compacted snow, and crab slime made the tires spin and the car began to lose its momentum. At least it made it clear to the other side of the alley, almost hitting the garage behind them.

Greg put the car in drive and turned the wheel a hard left, never taking his foot off the gas. The car swiveled its back end before straightening out.

"If we can just make it to the street, I think we've got a chance," Greg said.

The moment of exhilaration had left. If they were to die now, it would no longer be the nice peaceful embrace in each other's arms. She tried to block the thought from her mind.

The Cutlass slowed down then stopped, its tires still spinning ferociously, still three houses away from the street. Greg threw the car in reverse. It lurched and started inching backward. He put it in drive again, and gunned the engine. The car jumped forward, and inch by trudging inch, it crept forward.

"C'mon Sweetheart," Greg whispered. "You can do it."

Waves of white rolled toward the car. Greg put all of his weight on the gas pedal, trying to push a little harder.

"Go Baby. You can do it for daddy."

Maggie ignored the gushy talk. She was more concerned at the way the snow crabs seemed to wash up to the car, like an attack.

The Cutlass hit the mouth of the alley. "Yes!" Greg shouted. He yanked the wheel as hard as he could to the right, trying to swing the car onto the street.

Halfway into the turn, the car stopped. Greg screamed and Maggie groaned. He slammed the car in reverse. They could hear the tires spin above the applause of the snow crabs, but the car didn't budge. He tried rocking it back-and-forth, but nothing.

"Dammit!" Greg slammed the palm of his hand against the steering wheel.

"How much gas have we got?" Maggie asked.

"Just under half a tank. That should be good for a few

hours."

"As long as we keep the heat at full blast they won't come in."

They followed the instructions from the radio, blasting their horn every few minutes.

"Do you really think this does any good?" Greg asked, after releasing the horn. "Or do you think it just gives people a false sense of hope?"

Maggie shrugged her shoulders. "Why lie about it? It's not like anybody has anything to gain by it."

"Shhhh. Did you hear anything?" Greg asked.

Beyond the constant claw snapping, Maggie strained her ears. Greg honked the horn again. Faintly, off in the distance, they thought that they might have heard an answer. Greg laid on the horn once more. They waited in silence for what felt like the longest five seconds of their lives when they heard the distinct sound of another horn. They whooped and hollered like teenagers as Greg kept blasting the horn.

They felt the rumble before they saw anything. An army jeep, converted to almost a tank on wheels, turned the corner. Rigged with what looked like a conduit with holes, wrapped around the vehicle as fire shot from its sides. Blue flames soared across both sides of the street well into the boulevards. A miniature Fourth of July erupted as snow crabs tried to scatter, disintegrating into sparks before they touched ground.

"Are you able to drive?" a voice came from a loudspeaker.

"Yes!" shouted the couple, nodding their heads vigorously.

"Please remain calm."

The jeep inched up to the grill of the Cutlass, and stopped. Greg and Maggie could almost feel the heat that radiated from the vehicle in front of them. They could just make out an outline of the figure sitting behind the dark tinted glass. Maggie waved energetically as tears flowed freely down her cheeks.

The jeep backed up and turned around. "Follow me please."

Greg and Maggie looked at each other. Snow no longer obstructed their car. The tires locked onto pavement; Greg finished his turn and followed their rescuer.

The jeep crawled along, stopping every two blocks blaring its horn and waiting, listening for a response. Abandoned cars brought back the nightmare scene in front of their house.

"We must be one of the lucky ones," Maggie whispered. "God help us all."

They turned a corner nearing the safe haven perimeter of Fort Snelling. Soldiers, totally covered in white uniforms, not unlike space suits, held guns with muzzles as wide as bazookas. Waves of heat flowed from the barrels.

~ ~ ~

A mass of orderly activity hustled about as the Oldsmobile pulled up behind the jeep in the safe zone, right outside the makeshift hospital. Not a flake of snow could be seen anywhere, and when they were given the okay to step out of their car, the air felt like a hot summer day.

As the soldier stepped out of the jeep, Maggie raced over and wrapped her arms around him. The man smiled while returning the hug and winked at Greg. A green truck stood parked at the head of the block. Pipe was hitched around it, the same as the jeep, like a hula-hoop. A caravan of green busses with red crosses painted on the side followed another jeep in. On top of each bus, large solar panels reflected wide beams of intense light. Men and women, all wearing white coats, boarded the busses followed by soldiers. People on stretchers were the first to be unloaded. Next, soldiers escorted the ones who could walk, but just barely. People like Greg and Maggie were the last ones off, the ones who were still strong enough to walk under their own power. They were all led into the hospital.

"Just like war," Greg said.

"It is war," answered Maggie.

A small woman in a white lab coat came up to them, escorted by a policeman. She flashed a penlight into their eyes and checked their pulse.

"Shock and malnutrition. Get 'em inside and give 'em a good meal." She told the officer and then looked at the couple. "You'll be fine," she said, and gave them a blink of a smile. As quickly as she appeared, she was off again, walking with a quick gait toward the bus.

Maggie burst out laughing. She couldn't stop. The harder she tried, the more she laughed. Greg began laughing uncontrollably, too.

"I don't know why I'm laughing," Maggie said between gasps. "But I can't stop."

That doubled Greg over.

The officer led the couple up the hospital steps as onlookers stopped and stared, wondering what on earth could be so hilarious in this tragedy. Whatever the reason, it became infectious. As people turned away, they looked to each other, but they were smiling.

~ ~ ~

A ghost town now replaced the once friendly, busy neighborhood. Burnt out shells of once beautiful houses stood vacant. The human skeletons had been taken away for identification, then burial. Harmless snow swept over the surface trying to cover the ugly aftermath. Deep beneath the brown and charred grass and hidden safely deep in the cool ground, millions of eggs lay protected. Waiting.

ABOUT THE AUTHOR

David Fingerman has worked in the Hennepin County Court System for over twenty years. He now writes full time and lives with his wife in Minneapolis.